GLASS

Nan —

I'm so excited to be able to share this with you! I love you very much!

Love,

Kate ♡

GLASS

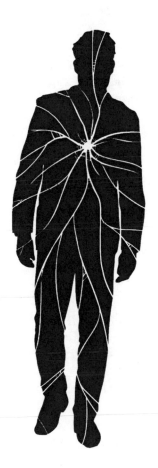

KATE KORT

Brick Mantel Books
Bloomington, Indiana

Published by Brick Mantel Books, USA

Brick Mantel
BOOKS

www.BrickMantelBooks.com
info@BrickMantelBooks.com

An imprint of Pen & Publish, Inc.
www.PenandPublish.com
Bloomington, Indiana
(314) 827-6567

Print ISBN: 978-1-941799-08-6
eBook ISBN: 978-1-941799-09-3

Library of Congress Control Number: 2015951445

Cover Design: Brent Smith

for tim. checkmate.

Acknowledgments

Thank you to so many readers who graciously helped me get *Glass* to its current state (especially Ben, who read more versions than anyone). Thank you to Mr. N8 Willard for starting me on this path, and Dr. Joe Benevento for patiently advising me. I owe so much to the Monday Night Writers' Group in Kansas City, especially Tim Anderson and Denny Young. Thank you to my talented editor, Carrie Walker, and to Jennifer Geist, for giving this book a chance. Jennifer is a wonderful publisher, editor, and all-around queller of fears, and has made this experience the best I could have asked for. I'm also incredibly grateful to Brent Smith for designing a killer cover.

Table of Contents

Prologue
August 1988

Menashe drew his hand back quickly. Several drops of bright blood oozed from his finger.

"Damn it," he muttered as he walked into the kitchen, wiping the blood onto a paper towel.

He didn't have a bandage so he just wrapped the paper towel tightly around the cut as he moved back into the first room of his museum. After searching the table where he'd cut himself, he pulled a hidden shard of glass from behind a large bowl and threw it into the trash can just inside his office. Looking around, he saw the rest of the museum was perfectly clean. Menashe looked down at his watch.

He left the room and continued through the apartment, getting everything ready in time for John's arrival. He carefully placed glass vases, bowls, figurines, and statues throughout the four rooms of his museum, wishing he'd had time to pick up his newest acquisitions on Detroit Avenue. They would have to wait until tomorrow. Stepping back, Menashe took in the untouched beauty of the rooms. He felt a tightness in his throat and turned away.

He was walking back to the kitchen when he heard the brakes of the city bus screech at the end of the block. *I hope those damn kids are out of the street*, he winced. Even the intense annoyance he felt toward the children who lived on West Tenth didn't prevent him from worrying for their safety, certain it was only a matter of time before one of them was abducted or shot or run over.

Menashe cracked his knuckles and made sure all the blinds were shut. He looked down at his dingy jeans and t-shirt and briefly considered changing, but decided against it. John wouldn't care.

Menashe smiled to himself, remembering what John had said about not wanting to risk driving his own car into such a bad part of town after dark. It was only a Chrysler, and he'd had it since they were in college together.

There was a soft knock on the front door. He opened it, letting a gust of the humid air rush past him into the apartment. He was also greeted by the pulsing sounds of The Velvet Dog, the nightclub that occupied the rest of the building. Shouts and waves of laughter echoed throughout the darkened streets as a few motorcycles pulled up to the club.

Menashe closed the door behind his new client. John and Menashe were the same age, though Menashe knew his friend looked much younger. John was athletic and youthfully handsome. Menashe remembered how the girls at school would flirt with him, even after he got engaged. He was dressed casually and a navy Cleveland Indians cap covered his shoulder-length brown hair. Despite the heat he also brought a thick long-sleeved shirt, as per Menashe's instructions.

"Hey, John."

"Hey," he replied, offering a weak smile. "There were some smashed bottles in the street, so I parked over there." He gestured toward the train tracks. "You think that's okay?"

"It's fine. Really, nobody wants your car."

"Yeah, okay." John smiled easily now. "You're right."

"You want something to drink?"

"No, thanks."

He led John down the hallway so all four rooms were visible.

"Now, I know you've been here before, but you want to take a closer look around?"

John peered past Menashe into the first room and nodded. He walked around the shining pieces and breathed in sharply.

"Ash, this really is something," he said. "It's just so different now, coming in as a client."

"I know this looks like a lot, but we won't go any faster than you want to."

Menashe knew it was strange, almost celestial, being surrounded by so much clear glass. There was nothing in the rooms but light—raw light streaming down from bare bulbs affixed to the ceiling. It reflected and refracted in all directions, punching holes in the walls with its white beams. That night, the first room held entirely vases: some were simple and smooth, others were etched with ornate sheaf-and-diamond patterns or textured with swirls and waves. Most were standard size, about a foot tall, but Menashe always kept his eye out for unusual pieces. The shimmering vases rested on dented stainless steel tables and shelving Menashe had been able to acquire from a food-service manufacturer at a steep discount. They caught the light brilliantly themselves, causing Menashe to squint. In so much transparency there was nowhere to hide.

John once again drew in his breath. "And you really want me to do this?"

Menashe nodded. "Don't worry about it."

They walked back into the hall. John stopped and frowned.

"You okay?" he asked, indicating Menashe's crudely bandaged finger.

"Yeah. It's nothing." He looked away. "You want to sit down?" John shook his head. "We could always go back to my office and talk more," Menashe continued, indicating the room behind him at the end of the hall. "I mean, if you're not ready—"

"No, no. I don't have any problem. I just—I don't know. It just seems kind of wrong, you know?"

"Yeah," Menashe agreed, slightly amused. It was strange to see John nervous, but that only strengthened his confidence in their plan. "I think you'll change your mind, though."

"And you don't think it'll be weird?" John asked. "That we're friends, I mean."

After nearly twenty years in Cleveland, John retained only the faintest hint of his former Houston drawl. Menashe still noticed it, though. It reminded him of how long they'd been friends, and how far they both had come to be there.

"No, I really don't. I think you're in a better position than anyone else who comes in here because I already know what won't work for you." Menashe smiled. "And it took you this long to get your stubborn ass down here, so I think we should give it a try."

"Okay," John finally said.

"Okay?"

"Yeah," he nodded.

"All right," Menashe replied, putting his hand on John's shoulder and leading him back toward the first room. "Let's get started."

Chapter 1
Student Deferment
August 1988

"Dr. Johnston?" Menashe called hesitantly through the slight opening in the doorway. "Should I come back another time?"

"Who is it? Carducci's friend? Come in, come in!" Johnston barked without turning his eyes away from the television screen. "Can you believe this idiot Voinovich? He's got a lot of nerve, threatening these layoffs."

Menashe was not much of a political enthusiast, so he decided to remain silent until Dr. Johnston was done seething. For some reason Menashe had expected him to be frailer, and more refined. The news flashed to sports, so Johnston turned off the television and settled back in his wheelchair, fanning himself with an old magazine.

"You can sit down, you know," he remarked, glancing at Menashe. Menashe obediently moved out of the doorway and took a seat on Johnston's worn, brown couch.

"Thanks. It's nice to meet you, Dr. Johnston."

"It's Terry. And you're Matthias?"

"Menashe."

Johnston squinted at him, as if he hadn't heard him right.

"Min-ASH-uh," he said again slowly. "Menashe Everett. But I go by Ash."

"That's right," Johnston replied, snapping his fingers. "Weird name, should've remembered."

"No problem," he said. His restless eyes roamed the room. The place was packed with junk and he sensed a haze in the air. He blinked a few times.

There wasn't much art on display, but Menashe saw the elderly doctor had brought out one particular piece to showcase: on the coffee table between them sat the largest vase he'd ever seen. Its thin, delicate base opened up into a wide sphere that took up much of the table. An intricately molded lid, topped with a figure of an elephant, covered the impressive piece. It would certainly be a good addition to his museum, even though few people would ever see it.

Menashe sighed. He wished he'd been able to put together that normal life he and Jamie had always talked about, with the good job in some fancy gallery. Flexible hours. A place where eccentricity was expected. He pushed the thought away as Johnston turned to him.

"So, you've known Mel a long time, right?"

Menashe nodded. "Dr. Carducci was my advisor when I was an undergrad."

"Can't be that long," Johnston snorted. "You're still a young man."

"Thanks," Menashe replied, smiling uncertainly.

"Though you do look like you've seen some action," he said brightly.

Menashe laughed and dug his fingernails into his already sweaty palms. *What the hell does that mean?*

"Actually, I haven't really dated much since my divorce."

Johnston's gruff persona dissolved as he descended into laughter. He then began coughing hoarsely and motioned for Menashe to hand him his inhaler. Menashe picked it up off the end table and gave it to him, his face flushing. The old man took a long puff and sat back, tears sparkling in his eyes.

"No, son," he began, stifling the last bit of stubborn laughter. "You have the look of a young man who's seen action in the service. Vietnam?"

"Oh, no, I wasn't over there. I got student deferment."

"Ah," Johnston acknowledged.

He thinks I'm a coward.

"You know, I think it does a man a lot of good to spend a few years in the service. Helps him remember what made this country great."

Johnston leaned back in his chair with a look on his face that was so peaceful and nostalgic Menashe found it hard to believe he was thinking about war.

Maybe it's the hair, Menashe thought, self-consciously touching his head. His dark brown hair was thick and disheveled, but in spite of his youth was steadily going gray.

Menashe's eyes again moved around the room, but the clutter overwhelmed him. It was almost too much for his eyes to take in, a peculiarity he remembered from visiting his grandmother when he was very young. That claustrophobic feeling quickened his heartbeat. He pulled at his shirt collar and tried to focus his attention on something in the room—the gold diamond pattern in the carpet. It was a trick he'd learned as a kid to avoid panic attacks.

"You all right, son?" Johnston asked.

Menashe nodded, fumbling in his shirt pocket. "You mind if I smoke?" he asked, already pulling a cigarette out of its package.

Johnston frowned. "I'd rather you didn't," he replied. "But if you want to step outside for a minute, I'll wait. You seem upset about something."

"Oh, no," Menashe laughed. "Just can't go too long without one. But I'll be fine; it'll be good for me to hold off." He slid the package back into his pocket.

"You ever tried to quit?"

"Yeah, three times. Never lasts."

The old man grunted but Menashe wasn't sure what he meant by it. Maybe he'd made a mistake. He could still leave. The place made him nervous, as did most things that reminded him of the past. *Just bring in a grungy pink chair and I'm in Safta's shitty place.*

Like Johnston's, his grandmother's small house had been musty and completely filled with disintegrating relics, but she hadn't seemed to notice any of it. She just sat peacefully in that faded pink armchair, asking the same questions over and over. "How old are you now? You in school? What're you studying?" Then, when Menashe remained silent, she would look up at her son, confused. "Your boy can speak, can't he, Lewie? You should teach him some manners."

"Ma, he's only seven," his father would say patiently. But the years went by and Menashe never seemed to find his voice. *It was that house.* It was the house that was so small yet composed of seemingly limitless dim hallways which twisted and snaked, exposing sad, unoccupied rooms that made his stomach pitch and his voice catch. It was the dank smell of mothballs, old books, frozen dinners, and something else he couldn't quite pinpoint that weighed upon his throat. The years went by, but as Menashe got older his nervousness only worsened. "He's only fourteen," Lewis would say, but quietly now, with less assurance in his voice.

Menashe glanced at Dr. Johnston's framed photographs clustered together on the wall, trying to make out the people's faces. *Probably all dead.* He briefly caught a whiff of mothballs and thought he heard Dr. Johnston's voice, but from a small, faraway place.

"I'm sorry?" Menashe asked.

"Your museum, son. I was asking you about it."

"Oh, right," he said quickly, trying to retrieve some memory of the past five minutes and secretly wishing his father was there to bail him out. "I'm really sorry. I don't know where my mind was." *He's only thirty-seven.*

"So what's it like?"

"Well, it's quite small," Menashe replied vaguely. "And very clean. Only glass," he said, indicating the vase. "Just a nice, simple place, really. I know a lot of people would probably find the museum boring, but . . . I don't know. To me there's something really beautiful about it."

Johnston sat back thoughtfully, his chin resting between his thumb and forefinger.

"I like you, Everett," he announced. "You know, when most people hear you've spent your life as an art historian and've got advanced degrees out the ass, they either try to act like the Queen of England around you or they assume you're too much of a pretentious windbag to waste their time. But you," he leaned forward, narrowing his eyes. "You are different."

Menashe was inclined to agree with him. He had his own advanced degree in art criticism that at times allowed him to speak about various pieces and movements with a certain authority, but he couldn't do that with Johnston. Anxiety had choked off his attempts at extroversion, as it sometimes did, and he was grateful that the old man found it charming.

"And I find," Johnston was saying, "as I get older, I feel the need to simplify. Though you'd never know it from the looks of this place," he added. "But you've got to start somewhere, and I think by next year I'll have unloaded all these pieces I don't want anymore, and I can start sorting through all this other nonsense." Johnston looked around the room, waving his hand disdainfully. "My goal is to clear everything out of this damned house except for my chair and the TV."

Menashe smiled at this, feeling a little better.

As evening set in, he walked out of Dr. Johnston's house, staggering under the weight of the glass vase. Menashe was not a particularly large man; he was tall with a medium build and occasionally had trouble transporting larger pieces. He maneuvered the large glass vase into the padded carrier of his Datsun pickup. He was embarrassed for Johnston to see his decrepit old truck, its dull orange paint gouged out by rust and weathering, but it didn't seem to matter to the old man. He was watching the sky as the low-set sun glowed gray from behind the darkening clouds.

"Gonna rain," Johnston stated without turning his eyes away. "You got a tarp?"

"Yeah," Menashe said. He closed up his truck and walked back up the cracked concrete path to the front doorway where Johnston had wheeled himself. "Should I come back another time for the rest?" he asked.

"No need to wait. I'll be here if you just want to go back and forth. If you don't mind the weather."

"Sure." He smiled at the doctor. "Thank you so much, Dr. Johnston," he said, shaking his hand.

"Nonsense. Like I said, you're helping me out. It was a pleasure."

Menashe stepped off the porch and walked to his truck, small drops of cool, fresh rain spitting at him as he went.

Chapter 2
John's Vietnam
August 1988

Menashe looked up from his paperwork as John Cook stumbled into his office from the third room of the museum, breathing heavily. His light-brown hair was pulled back into a ponytail and beads of sweat glistened on his forehead.

John sat down across from Menashe and brushed the accumulation of fine, white powder off his shoulders.

"How do you feel?" Menashe asked, setting aside his work and sliding his yellow legal pad in front of him.

John leaned back, took the hand towel off Menashe's desk and used it to wipe the sweat off his face.

"I feel all right," he said, with a certain degree of surprise. "Better."

"Do you want to talk today?" John hesitated. "We can wait if you're not ready."

"No, it'd probably be good," he replied, and Menashe noticed a particular brightness in his eyes. "It's so weird," he added. "I really do feel better. Lighter."

"What did you think about?"

"I really tried to think of Dak To. I mean, there was the ambush and everything that happened with Donnie, you know?" Menashe nodded. "I just kept forcing it all to the front of my mind and, I know it's not gone or anything, but it's like I can finally think about it without feeling like shit."

"That's great, John, really," Menashe remarked, pouring him a glass of water from the pitcher on his desk. He was surprised. He had only been seeing John as a client for a few weeks.

"Yeah," John agreed, clearly still on a high and slightly breathless from his session. He took a long drink. "I know I've just got to focus on what's happening now—really pay attention to my family."

"How are they dealing with it?" Menashe asked, thumbing through John's file.

"I know they've been worried. Well, Abby at least. The kids are too young to really understand."

Menashe looked up. "What makes her worry?"

John paused. "It's hard to explain," he said, frowning as he shifted in his chair. "She can just see that I've been unhappy. And I can't really hide it much from her. Like when I wake up from a nightmare and I see she's already awake, then I know I was talking or yelling or something in my sleep." John cracked his knuckles. "There are lots of things like that—like I still can't go to places with fireworks or anything. Remember," he laughed, "when we went to that Fourth of July double-header with my brother, and after the first game I told you guys I had to leave because I thought I had the stomach flu?"

Menashe nodded.

"It was the fireworks display. Although I did throw up," he added.

"Why didn't you tell us the truth?"

"Oh, come on, Ash—a grown man afraid of fireworks? How do you explain that? And that's not the worst of it. I can't even use a ceiling fan because the sound of the blades spinning around reminds me of the helicopters." His golden-brown eyes darkened. "Pretty weak, huh?"

"Not at all," Menashe answered. "Everything you went through, it doesn't just go away. And you're not alone in the problems you're describing. It's textbook Post-Traumatic Stress Disorder."

John gave him a dissatisfied look that let Menashe know he'd heard this before, from all the other therapists he'd grown to distrust.

"You make it sound easy. Like I could find the answer in the teacher's edition and 'poof,' I'm cured."

"Sorry. I didn't mean it was easy. I meant it's common. Too common."

John leaned back. "Got that right."

Menashe turned to a page of notes from the week before. "Now, I know you don't drink," he began, "but what about when you came back from the war? You never tried to make those thoughts go away?"

"No, not like that. I mean, isn't it a sickness—drinking to make things go away?"

"I guess it can be," Menashe acknowledged.

"No, that's nothing I wanted to get into. I saw some of the guys I knew over there really ruin their lives when they got home, but I think most of us have adjusted okay. And I've got my family to think of."

"Right," he nodded, absently scratching the scab off his finger and causing it to bleed again.

"I guess I shouldn't be that worried about all of this," John sighed. "I mean, it's really nothing new. Everyone gets fucked up by war, in one way or another. That's how it's always going to be. But it's over and I've just got to separate myself from it—let some cocky young kid take my place."

Menashe raised his eyebrows as he wrote but said nothing.

"Did you know," John remarked suddenly, "I never shot with my eyes open?"

"What?"

"I never shot a gun with my eyes open. It became automatic for me, closing my eyes right before I pulled the trigger."

"Why?"

"Why do you think?" John grabbed the towel again to wipe his face. "It made my CO crazy. He said I'd never be a good soldier till I could get past seeing people die. But I knew that'd never happen." He paused thoughtfully. "I never wanted to be there in the first place," he murmured. "I never wanted to be there. I mean, you know I'd hoped for deferment, too, but . . ." He shook his head. "My dad was just so set on me going. Thought the army would give me some kind of direction. Anyway," he frowned, "what does it say about you if you can shoot a man and then forget about it?"

"I don't know."

The room was silent for several seconds before John spoke up again. There was an edge to his voice.

"What do we do next?"

"Well," Menashe said, turning back to his files, "how did you like the free association writing?"

John shrugged. "I don't know. I'm not sure I really got anywhere with it, but . . . it was okay, I guess."

"Sounds like a breakthrough to me," Menashe smiled, scribbling a few notes. "Will you try it again? It really does take practice."

"Sure," John said.

"Okay." He crossed out a few words. "Looks like we're done for today."

"There was something I wanted to ask you," John said, rising to his feet. "Can I refer someone to you?"

"Of course. That's the only way this works."

John nodded. "I've got a friend who's in really bad shape—Austin. You don't know him. We were in Nam together."

Menashe handed John a few business cards. "Just give him one of these. There's not a lot of information on it, just my name and number, but have him call and we'll set something up."

John took the cards hesitantly.

"I'm not sure if he'll come in right away. Or at all. Lately it's been hard just getting him out of his apartment, you know?" Menashe nodded. "Knowing Austin, he'll probably throw your card in some drawer until he's in even worse shape," John laughed sadly. "But I'll give it a try."

Chapter 3
Eighteen Hours
May 1978

It was nearly six when Menashe finally arrived at Wesley's preschool.

Shit. Jamie's probably been here an hour.

He'd had to stay late at work and the rush hour traffic was far worse than he was used to. The tires of his maroon Vega squealed as he steered into a parking spot. He got out, feeling his hands shake as he closed the car door. Menashe's wife and son had carpooled with the family of one of Wesley's classmates, and she probably thought he'd lost track of time. He jogged inside, checking his watch. *These things never start on time*, he assured himself as he followed the construction paper signs leading him to the kids' year-end, patriotic concert. He couldn't hear any music.

When he came to the large common room used for the event, Menashe saw all the kids were up front. He spotted Wesley, standing happily in line while his teacher called out names and awarded diplomas to those who were moving on to kindergarten and certificates to those who, like Wesley, would remain in preschool for another year. A rush of pride overcame Menashe as he watched his son wait for his certificate. It was a bittersweet glimpse into a future of graduations from high school, college, and maybe, Menashe fantasized, graduate school. He smiled and found a seat next to his wife, not quite ready to think about Wesley growing up and leaving him.

"You're really late," Jamie whispered, still watching the ceremony.

"Yeah, sorry. It was a bitch trying to get here."

"You got stuck in traffic?" she asked. "I thought it'd only take you half an hour."

"I had to stay late. Is this all they've done so far?"

She nodded.

Menashe finally relaxed his muscles and leaned back in his chair, but his palms were still sweating. He'd hoped they would stop once he sat down. He wiped them on his khakis and looked back up to the front of the room, trying to focus all his attention on Wesley. He could hardly see through the now blurry lenses of his eyes. The more he tried to calm himself down, the faster his heart and mind raced. He had come straight from work. He hadn't had a drink in over eighteen hours.

"How long does this thing go?" Menashe asked his wife, trying to conceal the desperation in his voice.

She looked over at him, staring into his dark, sullen eyes in a way that always made him uncomfortable.

"Maybe an hour or so," she said, shrugging. "I don't know. Are you all right?"

"Yeah, it's just—does it feel really hot in here to you?" he asked, loosening his tie and rolling up his sleeves.

"No."

Jamie turned back to the program.

Menashe rubbed his forehead, and his hand came back glistening with sweat. He should have stopped off somewhere. He leaned over to tell Jamie, to say he had made a mistake, forgotten something, and he had to leave for twenty minutes but he'd see the second part of the show. He took her hand, as if he could explain to her that eighteen hours was a long time and he needed to start the clock over again, when she squeezed it back, smiling in the direction of their son. Then the music started. This Land Is Your Land.

Menashe closed his eyes and tried to push past what he knew was selfishness. He tried to think about what was happening now: the concert, the ceremony, his son. *I'm leaving in ten minutes.* God Bless America. The Star Spangled Banner. Yankee Doodle.

Menashe smiled, temporarily distracted. He had become a United States citizen less than a decade before, after leaving Toronto to attend school in Cleveland. Frustrated with the limitations of his student visa, he had decided to begin the process of U.S. citizenship early in his first year of college—and finished just in time to qualify for the draft.

"Look, Ash," Jamie whispered. "Look at him. He knows all the words."

Menashe nodded, trying to focus. At that moment he wasn't sure he could pick Wesley out of a lineup.

"I was thinking," she continued, "maybe we could go out for dinner afterward? This is a pretty big day for Wesley."

"No," Menashe said immediately. His heart pounded wildly. "No, we can't afford it. We should just go home."

He didn't turn to face Jamie, but he could feel her watching him.

"Did you come here right from work?" she asked.

"Yeah, I did," he snapped. "Why?"

"You didn't stop anywhere?"

"No," he practically shouted, causing a few people to turn and frown at him. "I told you I got stuck in traffic."

"Okay."

"I'm sorry," he said in a lower voice. "It's just been a long day."

"It's okay. We don't have to go out."

"This thing, it's almost over, right?"

Jamie looked at him carefully. "Yeah."

Wesley ran over to his parents after the concert was over, throwing his arms around first his father then his mother.

"You were great," Jamie said, picking him up.

Wesley smiled but was clearly more excited by his newly awarded certificate than his role in the year-end concert.

"Look at the stars!" he exclaimed, pointing to the stickers that liberally covered the paper. "I got five blue ones and five green ones. Jeremy only got three blue ones."

"Nice," Menashe said, running his hand over Wesley's hair.

"You ready to go home?" Jamie asked her son, returning him to the floor.

He shook his head.

"Aren't you hungry?" Menashe asked, looking at his watch—an action that, over the past hour and a half, had become as frequent and necessary for him as breathing.

"Can we go to Pebble?" Wesley asked eagerly.

Menashe looked at his wife. "Pebble" was how Wesley referred to his favorite restaurant, Mi Pueblo Taqueria. They had only eaten there two or three times, but Wesley had fallen in love with it. He looked up at his father excitedly, no doubt hoping he would soften and give in as he had so many times before in the face of that expectant look.

"Yeah, let's go," Menashe said.

Wesley shrieked with joy. Jamie smiled quizzically.

"You sure?" she asked.

He nodded. "Definitely," he answered, smiling down at Wesley. "Is that all you've got to wear?"

Wesley nodded. "It was hot waiting for my paper."

"Well, we should probably stop home first and get you a sweatshirt in case it's cold."

"Ash, I'm sure he'll be fine. He's hardly ever cold in restaurants."

"But just in case, we should get it. It really won't take any time. It's on the way and I can just run in and grab it, all right?"

"Okay," Jamie said slowly.

"Great," Menashe replied, taking Wesley's hand.

Wesley made a face and let go of his father's hand when he felt how sweaty it was, but Menashe barely noticed. He followed his family out into the parking lot, drawing in a deep breath as the cooling air met his face.

Chapter 4
The Museum
August 1988

It was early evening and the wind had picked up, blowing leaves and stray bits of trash into small, short-lived tornadoes. Menashe narrowed his eyes, protecting them from the wind, and surveyed his street cautiously. It was a poor part of Cleveland's urban downtown and in desperate need of renovation.

He lived between McAllen Payday Loans and Lowry's Liquors, and there was no doubt in his mind that the placement of those two businesses was anything but accidental. He had seen McAllen suck the life out of his poor neighbors with alluring access to immediate cash at four hundred percent interest. How many times had he watched a visibly tired and defeated workingman slink out of McAllen's and into Lowry's? Menashe tried not to think about it. Instead he thought about the work that lay ahead of him as he stepped into the museum, exhausted after another long day at the bank.

Menashe sighed grimly. Instead of putting that advanced degree to work, at the age of twenty-three he'd found himself settling for an entry-level job in the student loan department at Ohio Savings Bank. Sure, he'd just been a kid with enormous debt and a wife and new baby to think of,

Wesley

but he never left. He'd slowly moved up the assistant ranks from intern to junior loan representative, but the work never mattered to him. Menashe was still essentially an office lackey: he made copies, filed papers, entered data, and occasionally answered calls from students. Most of the students he talked to were already far in debt but felt that, if they could just make it to graduation, they would immediately be recruited for the high-paying job of a lifetime and all their money problems would be over. *Poor fuckers*, Menashe would think. *If they only knew what they had coming.*

While normal working hours were spent at the bank, he then opened the glass museum by appointment between the hours of 8:00 and 11:00 p.m., Monday through Thursday, and 8:00 p.m. to 1:00 a.m. on Friday and Saturday nights. He ran the museum practically parallel to the hours of The Velvet Dog.

Menashe stomped his muddy feet on the rug that lay just inside the door. The space he occupied was the basement level of a building owned by Chase Stephens, the manager of The Velvet Dog nightclub. Chase was a good landlord and rented Menashe the basement level of his building for a very reasonable rate, most likely out of fear that he'd never find another tenant willing to take on the constant noise he dealt with. But that was not a problem for Menashe; he wanted the space just as it came.

From the street, his museum was entirely hidden. Someone approaching the entrance of The Velvet Dog would have to look far to the right to notice the narrow, corrugated iron staircase leading down to the converted residence.

Once inside, it became apparent that the basement had an unusual floor plan. There were two small rooms on the left side of the hallway and two on the right. A brightly wallpapered bathroom was sandwiched between the two rooms on the right side of the entrance, and at the end of the hallway was an office (doubling as Menashe's bedroom) and a kitchen.

Menashe threw his keys at the small table that stood just inside the front door, but he missed and they clattered to the floor. He removed his muddy shoes and walked into the first room on the left. He let his eyes wander, taking in the details. His vision was hazy from fatigue, but still, it was striking. Its crisp simplicity was reminiscent of a city just blanketed in snow: fresh, sparkling, untouched. He moved silently out of the room and briefly looked into the others, making sure they were in order. Although the museum's four rooms were filled all the time, the majority of his pieces were stored in a space he rented farther downtown.

Menashe shuffled into his office and sat at the desk to look over his most recent forms and paperwork. He swiveled over to the filing cabinet and ran his fingers over the file folders, but the form he was looking for wasn't there. He checked all the desk drawers and even lay flat on the floor, scanning the darkness under his bed. *I guess I took it to work*, he thought, annoyed.

In one last attempt to find the form, Menashe re-opened the top drawer of his filing cabinet and searched carefully, scrutinizing each individual piece of paper. When he came to the end of the row, he reached behind the drawer to see if the paper might have gotten caught in the track. When he pulled his hand back, it wasn't a tattered form he'd recovered but rather a small, dusty bottle. It was a trial size bottle of vodka—the kind they give you on an airplane. He murmured in surprise when he saw the small souvenir resting in his unsteady hand.

Chapter 5
The Radio Drawing
December 1978

"I just don't do well with flying, okay?" Menashe firmly explained to the young stewardess. His patience was wearing thin. "I mean, there could be one tiny piece of metal sticking out on a wing or something that your crew guys missed, and that could fuck with the drag and thrust and all that—The smallest problem could send this plane down and you know that." He gave her an authoritative look. "And how do you know our very own pilot isn't helping himself to a few of these?" He shook one of his empty vodka bottles at her. "The man should really have more respect for himself."

"Please, sir," she hissed. "You might upset the other passengers."

"Well, they should be upset! This is very dangerous business—" He peered at her nametag, "Marian." He looked pensive for a moment. "I'd like to speak with the captain, please."

Marian shook her head and glanced around the cabin. The other stewards and stewardesses were already serving meals.

"Sir, that's really not how it works."

Menashe leaned in. "So you don't think he's drinking on the job?" he whispered.

"Of course not!" She turned away from his alcoholic breath. "Now please stop making trouble. I'm letting the others know you are not to be served any more alcohol."

This declaration made his heart pound. He'd already had a half-pint bottle on the cab ride to the airport, but still couldn't handle the thought of being cut off.

"Whoa there, Mare," he laughed nervously. "I admit I was out of line before, but I'll behave, I promise, if you just let me have a couple drinks for the road. Not even here, I'll save them for the hotel. Please? Don't make me buy more at the hotel. You *know* they screw you with those mark-ups."

He sounded like a child who had finally pushed his parents too far and realized he might lose television privileges. Marian looked at him warily, her eyes resting on the healing gashes that covered both his hands, but ruefully passed him three tiny bottles of vodka.

"This is it!" she reminded him in an exasperated whisper. "And don't drink them here."

She walked away as Menashe blew exaggerated kisses at her.

"I love you, Marian! My Maid Marian!" He laughed suddenly. "Like from *Robin Hood*. Man, I must've seen that movie a hundred times. My kid loves that shit . . ." he trailed off slowly, his energy plummeting.

In the next five minutes he was dozing with his head leaning against the window, still clutching the small bottles in his hand.

What had lapsed in Menashe's mind was the fact that he was on his way home. His inebriated mind led him to believe he was going to Las Vegas, courtesy of a radio drawing he had won, when in reality he'd already spent the weekend there and was on the return flight to Cleveland. There would be no hotel, no outrageous mark-ups, and no hedonistic carnival waiting for him at the end of his flight—only the sad and desolate Cleveland-Hopkins International Airport and a long cab ride home.

It was Monday, December 4 when Menashe learned he had won the drawing. A local radio station, 98.5 WNCX FM (Cleveland's Source for Nonstop Classic Rock), had placed small glass fishbowls in restaurants throughout the city, inviting patrons to leave their business cards for the chance to win a weekend for two in Las Vegas. This was not an ideal vacation for either Menashe or Jamie, who were both naturally cautious and quiet people, but nevertheless, Menashe had impulsively dropped his card into the bowl at Hunan Coventry on a warm, sunny day while Jamie took Wesley to the bathroom. It was actually his boss's card that he'd saved in his wallet and changed the name on at the last minute. He had looked it over carefully before letting it mix into the pile of other business cards, as though he were afraid he might forget the information on it—information that defined his life but at the same time had nothing to do with him.

Menashe Everett
~~Kevin Grier~~
Ohio Savings Bank, Student Loan Dept.
~~*Department Supervisor*~~
3300 Warren Road
Cleveland, OH 44111
216.941.3000, Ex. 406

He was positive nothing would come of it. It was more an effort to interact with the world, however slight the gesture was.

As they walked out of the restaurant, Menashe turned to his wife with an unusual smile. She looked at him questioningly, her arm wrapped around his waist and her left hand holding Wesley's right.

"What?" she laughed.

"Happy birthday," he answered, kissing her forehead.

"No, you're up to something."

"I just entered us in that radio drawing."

"For what?"

"A trip to Las Vegas. For two," he added.

"Have you ever won anything?" she asked.

". . . No."

"Neither have I," she said. "I think we're due."

Jamie smiled at him and Menashe laughed.

"Well, they won't announce the winner until December, but I think you're right."

He picked up Wesley and hoisted him onto his shoulders. He started jogging, gripping Wesley's legs with his hands to keep him from falling.

"Hee!" Wesley squealed. "Faster!" And Menashe sprinted down the sidewalk leaving Jamie far behind, laughing at them.

Seven months later, Dan, the morning DJ from WNCX FM called Menashe up at work to tell him he'd won the trip. He actually called Kevin, since it was his telephone number on the business card he'd entered in the drawing.

Kevin had tapped on his window, motioning for Menashe to come inside his office. He'd whispered that it sounded like this guy was trying to sell him something, but then shrugged and handed him the phone.

When Dan began the scripted announcement of his success at being randomly chosen in a drawing, Menashe sat down in Kevin's chair and sighed deeply.

It felt like years since Menashe and his family had been to that Chinese place on Coventry Road. He had, understandably, forgotten all about the drawing.

"Thanks, that's great," Menashe mumbled when Dan gave him the news. "I just—well, I guess I just didn't think it would be me, out of all those people, I mean."

What he wanted to say was he wished it hadn't been him. He would never have put his card into that fucking fishbowl if he had known it would be thrown back in his face this way.

"Well, somebody's gotta win!" the cheery morning DJ replied. "So, when do you want to pick up the tickets?"

He looked back at Kevin who had turned away to sort through phone messages.

"Could you just mail them to me, Dan?"

Menashe went to Las Vegas with the unconvincing idea that it would be good for him. He landed at McCarran, sore from the flight. He took a cab downtown into pitch blackness ignited by seizure-inducing lights that shimmered and sparked like flashbulbs. Everything was doused in red, green, and gold, with giant fake trees on every corner. Menashe had forgotten about Christmas.

He gripped his bag tighter. He never checked anything. He carried his tattered duffel bag, which held a few sets of clothes and not much else. He wasn't accustomed to staying in hotels, and assumed his would provide most of the travel basics. And if he were to run out of clothes or spill something on himself, he would be out of luck because there was no way in hell he was buying anything in such an overpriced city as Las Vegas. Anything but a drink, that was.

The cab dropped him off at the Hilton on Paradise just after nine p.m. His room was at the end of the hall on the fifth floor. It was a great room with an enormous bed and an equally impressive television set. And there was a smell Menashe found to be the same in all hotel rooms. It always reminded him of Florida. Like flowers and coconuts liquefied into a mass-produced air freshener. He had only been to Florida once, to the ocean with his parents on the first vacation they had ever taken together, and the same smell had been present at the place where they had stayed—some shabby guesthouse in Fernandina Beach that his mother had found charming.

He was tempted to stay the rest of the night in his room and investigate all the cable channels on that mammoth TV, but another part of him, a much stronger and more desperate part, told him it was time to investigate the hotel bar. He slipped a tan corduroy jacket on over his t-shirt and descended the stairs five floors to the lobby. The bar was pretty crowded, but since many people were standing around talking, there were a few empty seats. He slid onto a stool and tried making eye contact with one of the bartenders. He imagined there were far more exciting and posh hotels in downtown Las Vegas, but this place had no problem packing them in. There were plenty of older businessmen who had no doubt just finished some important meeting and were ready to loosen up. Lots of young couples, too, but most of the people in the bar were parts of larger groups. Menashe finally caught the eye of one of the bartenders—a younger guy named Roy.

"Hi, there. What can I get you?"

Roy had a nasally whine to his voice. He wore a black button-down shirt with shiny vertical stripes. He had an earring. Menashe was already tired of him. He thought he was probably one of those guys who worked as a Vegas bartender but was pursuing something else at the same time. *A bartender/actor? Bartender/comedian? Bartender/stripper?* They were all reasonable possibilities.

"Vodka, please."

"Neat?"

"Yeah, that's fine."

Roy set a red paper napkin down on the bar and went to retrieve the vodka. Before he returned, a young woman—about the same age as Menashe—sat down next to him. She took off her coat and draped it over the empty stool next to her. She had her head turned away from him in an effort to signal Roy at the other end of the bar, but what he saw of her was beautiful.

She had long, wavy hair that was so dark brown it was almost black. When it hit her shoulders it split, most of it cascading down her back while the rest fell casually in front of her, spilling over the top of her delicate dress. She was moderately thin and athletic looking, with a pretty tan that made her skin glow. On second thought, Menashe decided it wasn't a tan but rather her skin's natural color. She seemed vaguely foreign and exotic to him, and he wished he dared to gaze more forwardly at her. *Italian, maybe, or Greek*, he speculated.

Roy came back with Menashe's vodka and asked the girl what she'd like. Menashe then turned to look at her. He smiled slightly to himself. She had a dark, glowing complexion and serene, hazel eyes that were accentuated by a slight amount of smoky eye shadow. A few freckles were sprinkled lightly over her face, which to Menashe made her seem even more angelic. *She's perfect.*

He admonished himself, knowing he wasn't thinking clearly—that he didn't even know her—but he still couldn't help repeating the words over and over in his head. And when she spoke, he felt she was someone he could have been friends with. She sounded real.

"Can I have a screwdriver, please?" she asked Roy. Menashe must have made a face or even a sound, because she looked at him squarely. "What?" she asked, smiling good-naturedly.

"I'm sorry?"

"You made a sound."

"I did?"

She laughed and he was forced to smile. She had a soft accent he determined to be Spanish. He looked down, suddenly aware of how sloppy he looked. His faded jacket, his torn Maple Leafs t-shirt, his worn jeans. Travel clothes.

"Oh, you know you did. You were making fun of my drink."

Menashe was embarrassed, but sensed they were playing some kind of a game and didn't want to disrupt its flow.

"I guess I'm kind of a purist when it comes to vodka," he answered as he looked down at the bar, rearranging his napkin.

"So you don't believe in making it taste bearable?"

"Not really," he answered with a smile.

"You know, you would probably faint if you saw what I do to my coffee."

He laughed. It felt good. Even though he had turned his eyes away again, he could feel she was still looking at him.

"I'm Eva," she said after a moment.

He nodded and turned to her, extending his hand. He then wondered if it was too formal a gesture.

"Ash."

"Is that short for Asher?"

He shook his head. "Menashe."

"Hm, I never met a Menashe," Eva replied, taking his hand.

"I suppose it's not too common."

"No," she agreed. "But it's nice. Kind of . . . ancient." She nodded to herself. "A strong name."

They both sat back for a moment, sipping their drinks. Menashe noticed for the first time a tiny Christmas tree that sat on the bar, trimmed with minute strands of tinsel and glass ornaments the size of pebbles. He inadvertently frowned at it.

"So," she began, "are you here celebrating Christmas?"

He looked back at her uncertainly, but Eva kept smiling her natural smile. It seemed she was just used to asking what she wanted, telling what she wanted— basically being herself.

He shook his head. "No."

"You're not doing anything for Christmas, then?" she asked in surprise.

"I never have," he smiled. "I'm not Christian. Not religious at all, really. My parents always were but not me. Not anymore."

He liked this answer to the religion question better than his old one. He found it more honest. He used to just simply answer, "I'm Jewish," but then somewhere down the line realized saying it felt no more significant to him than saying, "I'm six foot one," or "I'm a Gemini." So he cut it out.

"You are lucky," she laughed. "My family is Roman Catholic. Very Roman Catholic."

"Really?" Menashe had finished his drink so he signaled to Roy for a second. "Would you like another?" he asked Eva.

"Oh, no, thank you."

"So what are you doing in Las Vegas?" He realized her bluntness was rubbing off a bit on him, so he tagged his question with, "If you don't mind my asking."

"I am actually here for a wedding. My little brother, Javier's."

"Little brother?" Menashe repeated, surprised.

"Yes, he's nineteen. Hard to believe, really." She paused, looking amused by his reaction. "I'm twenty-two, by the way."

He nodded. He had always been bad at guessing ages.

"I'm twenty-seven," he replied. He glanced at her to read her reaction, but she continued on with her story.

"I mean, I really like his girlfriend, and they are completely in love with each other, I just, I never thought about this kind of thing at nineteen, so it is hard for me to wrap my mind around, you know?"

Menashe nodded. He found it charming that she rarely used contractions when she spoke.

"So the wedding's tomorrow?"

"Yep."

"Why did they choose Vegas?"

She laughed. "Oh, believe me, this is completely their style. And I really think Javier wanted to see our entire conservative family completely uncomfortable in this place—but they all came, and I'm very glad my parents were able to give them their blessing. I—" she stopped suddenly. "I am so sorry; I have been talking too much."

This remark surprised Menashe. He had felt at ease listening to the smooth cadence of her voice and had welcomed the opportunity to gaze overtly into her face as she spoke.

"Oh, no," he assured her, "I've been asking a lot of questions. Please—" he motioned for her to continue.

"Well, there's not really that much else to tell. Javier and Angela will stay here for a few more days to have their honeymoon, and the rest of us will leave on Sunday to go back to LA. I work for a counseling center there," she added. "I just got my MSW a few months ago."

"Wow, congratulations."

"Thanks," she said, smiling. "So how about you? What brings you here?"

"I won a radio station drawing back in Cleveland. I got an all-expenses-paid trip for two here for the weekend. Not bad, really."

"For two?"

"What?"

"You said a trip for two."

"Yes."

"But you came alone?"

"I like having an empty seat next to me on the plane," he said.

She laughed. "You're very funny," she remarked thoughtfully, in a way that let him know she was filing this information away, using it to compare him to past boyfriends, maybe even other guys she'd met in Las Vegas.

But a sense of dread pulled at his brain, clouding his good time. Something wasn't right about this. A part of him felt muddled and on edge, like he had been a witness to a traffic accident and was too shaken to put the events in order. *Why is she talking to me?*

He liked her a lot—so much, in fact, that he faintly considered telling her about his life. The truth. But he never would. Eva was young, smart, optimistic, and genuinely good. And Menashe knew he wasn't going to change. He would only make her unhappy if they somehow did end up together. *I would never end up with her.*

He really didn't know her, but now understood that he didn't want to. The sadness of his life would destroy the optimism he saw in hers.

Menashe let out a disillusioned sigh and hoped it had been inaudible. Just as he was about to make some excuse and leave, Eva spoke, glancing at her watch.

"Oh, I'm sorry, Menashe, but I should go. I have to be up really early."

He liked hearing her say his full name and the warmth in her voice made something inside of him ache.

"I understand. Tomorrow's a pretty big day."

He saw she was looking at him thoughtfully again.

"You know, if you want to—" she began, then stopped. He supposed she had thought better of what she was about to say, but had gone too far to take it back. She took a breath. "I think I'd like to see you again."

He nodded but remained silent.

"Well, here's my room number, and if you have time, maybe we could see each other before Sunday." He nodded again, his eyes fixed on the number. Eva got up to leave, then turned back around to look at him. "Menashe?"

He looked up and saw her bleary image.

"Mm hm?" he answered.

"Have a good night."

"You, too."

She said good night to Roy and walked away, her dress swaying slightly from side to side as she moved. Menashe knew she was smiling. He sighed again heavily, pulling out his cigarettes and motioning Roy back with a wave.

By one-thirty a.m., Menashe was feeling pretty good. Over the few hours after Eva left, Menashe managed to knock out another six vodkas (neat) and two whiskey shots, and learn a lot about Roy, who turned into quite a talker once the bar cleared out. As Menashe had suspected, Roy was a slashie: a bartender/singer. The details of this, however, rolled off Menashe's mind, which was now slick with alcohol, and he started to grow tired of Roy's enthusiastic storytelling.

"Roy, let me just stop you right there," he said, cutting him off as he tried to explain to Menashe that even the most talented singers had to pay their dues in Vegas. "Do you remember that girl who was here before? Eva?"

"Sure."

"Pretty, right?"

"Yeah, I guess."

"Do you think she seemed nice?"

"Sure, she was really sweet. And she remembered my name. I like that."

"Yeah, you see?" Menashe leaned forward in his seat, bumping his nearly empty glass with his elbow. "That's what I'm saying. That is . . . exactly what I'm saying." He buried his face in his hands. "This is unbelievable."

"What's the problem?"

Menashe popped back up, as if startled out of a dream. "Roy," he said impatiently, talking as he sometimes did to Wesley when he didn't understand a simple concept, "do you really see a girl like that with me?"

"You're a good-looking guy," Roy said doubtfully. Menashe shot him a look. "You don't buy the 'opposites attract' thing?"

"Oh, let me explain something to you." Menashe was in teaching mode. He took two empty shot glasses, holding one in each hand. "Let's say you've got your positive and negative particles here," he said, stretching his arms across the bar. "Now, if they come together," he began, glancing to his left and then his right hand, both of which were shaking badly, "the bad force and the good force will be so strong that they won't just come together—they'll collide. And the stronger one, the bad one, will probably be okay, but the good one won't make it."

He brought his hands together with surprising speed, considering his condition, and the two shot glasses shattered into his hands. Neither of the glasses survived, so it wasn't clear whether or not he had proved his point, but Roy's attention had turned to the fact that Menashe was bleeding all over his bar.

"Jesus, what's the matter with you? You're sick, man!" Roy handed him a couple towels. "Use these, all right? You're dripping."

Roy made a face and turned away from the sight of the blood. Menashe gently removed the shards of glass and wrapped his hands carefully in the towels. He wasn't all that surprised or upset by what had happened. He leaned toward Roy.

"I think this might spoil my plans," he smiled, holding up his mummified hands and using them to slide his empty glass toward Roy.

"You're done, Ash," Roy said seriously. "You should go get cleaned up anyway."

Menashe glared at him. "I'm fine."

"You're drunk. Go back upstairs before you injure someone else."

"It's just you and me."

"Yeah. Go back upstairs."

Menashe grumbled as he reached for his wallet and pulled out enough money to pay Roy. He slid off his stool and staggered to the elevator.

It was only after standing up that he realized how incapacitated he was. He could barely walk the twenty steps to the elevator, and the journey made his vision darken and swirl. He wobbled and, sensing that gravity was about to fail him, flung his towel-bound hands out in an attempt to hit the elevator button. He struck air, which made his inevitable fall that much faster. He faintly heard giggling from somewhere and when he looked up, there was a blonde woman standing over him. In his state, this was quite a surreal experience.

"Are you okay?" she asked, still laughing.

It sounded as though she was underwater. She helped him grasp the wall with one hand then took the other and let his arm rest over her shoulders, using her weight to help bring him to his feet. He slowly regained his balance and turned back toward the elevator, wondering if he should make another attempt to open the doors.

"I'm having a little trouble with the elevator," he explained.

"I see that," she said, pushing the up-arrow.

She looked to be in her early thirties, but Menashe wouldn't have bet money on it. A large nametag was pinned to the corner of her sheer black blouse.

"Laura," he read slowly.

"Yeah, I waitress at the restaurant here. I was watching you, you know," she said.

"Oh, really?" He was starting to feel a little better.

"You seem like a pretty fun guy," she smiled.

"Yeah. How do you like working here?"

"The hours are pretty much shit, as you can see," she laughed, idly touching the hem of her short red skirt. "But I do meet lots of interesting people."

"I bet." The elevator arrived and its doors parted before them with a soft ping. "Going up?" he asked with a smile.

"I was actually on my way home. Just wanted to make sure you got the elevator."

"I appreciate it. But who knows what'll happen when I try to get that damn room key into the door," he said, holding up his hands pathetically.

"Could be bad," she replied.

"You have no idea."

Three hours later, they lay in his hotel bed. She was sleeping with her head on his chest as he stared up at the ceiling, wondering what was on all those cable channels at five a.m. He looked around the strange room. He looked down at the strange woman in his bed whose makeup was rubbing off on the sheets. He looked down at his hands. Laura had bandaged them properly with gauze from the hotel first aid kit. Menashe thought he should get up, maybe have a shower and try to clear his head, but before he could resign himself to this action, he fell back asleep with his hands locked behind his head and bleeding slightly through their bandages.

When he awoke again, it was nearly noon and Laura was gone. She had safety-pinned a note to the gauze on his left hand, written on Hilton stationary. "Come see me anytime—9 pm to 2 am. Laura." Menashe stayed in bed and slept on and off until mid afternoon. He turned on the TV and watched a few minutes of pro wrestling, then switched over to the hotel's channel. But even that made him uneasy. He felt drowsy again but fought back the feeling and forced himself out of bed. All with great effort, he removed his bandages, showered, and tried to rewrap the gauze in the same way Laura had, but ultimately got frustrated and gave up. The cuts were really not that bad, so he decided to put Band-Aids over the largest ones and leave the rest to air out.

Menashe did not venture down to the bar that night. He didn't feel like seeing anyone. He would simply find something to eat, watch TV, and relax until he fell asleep, and if he needed a drink, he would have to shell out for the mini bar.

After splurging for the most expensive burger he'd ever seen, Menashe climbed into bed with his shoes still on and four small bottles of whiskey in his hands. He turned on the television and flipped around until he came upon a channel playing exclusively war movies. After *The Dawn Patrol*, he kicked his shoes off, changed into pajama pants, and cleaned out the rest of the mini bar. He watched *The Great Escape* and *Paths of Glory*. He staggered to the bathroom. He clutched the sides of the sink intermittently as he washed his hands in an effort to keep himself from falling. Walking carefully back into the bedroom, he noticed with a pang of misery the collection of empty bottles that littered his floor and bed.

At that moment, a strange feeling came over him. Menashe picked up one of the bottles closest to him. He threw it and it struck the wall, shattering forcefully. *What would Jamie think of me, coming here without her?* He stepped hard on another and listened with satisfaction to the crunch. He shattered two more into the dresser mirror. He knelt and punched at the bottles with his bare fists, smashing them to shards. Power rushed through his body. He laughed. He was beyond caring.

He stood in the middle of the room, swaying slightly and dripping blood from his now twice-injured hands. He looked like an inmate from a mental hospital, with hollow eyes and plaid flannel pajama pants. He picked up an intact bottle and threw it against the wall. It exploded brilliantly and finished with a delicate chiming sound. *I'm so sorry.* He threw the remaining glass bottles, one after another, at the walls of his hotel room and watched with satisfaction as they shattered. Nothing else mattered. At that moment, all he needed was the sound of breaking glass and the burning pain of the shards cutting his skin. *It should have been me.* He finally felt in control. He finally felt relief. With every bottle he smashed, he felt as though he were chipping away at the dark and insidious parts of himself. The phone rang and Menashe was dimly aware of the sound of fists pounding on his door, but he ignored them both. *It should have been me.*

When there was nothing left to throw, Menashe picked up the ringing phone and did his best to give a genuine-sounding apology to the front desk clerk on the other end. He made up some excuse about a sleepwalking accident and assured them that, no, he didn't need anyone to come clean anything up that night. After hanging up the phone, he began walking around the room, unaware he was cutting his feet on splinters of broken glass. *I wish it had been me.* Blood seeped into the dull beige carpet. He started to cry and within a few minutes found himself lying on the floor, breathing heavily and clutching his bleeding hands to his chest. It was in that position that he awoke nine hours later at noon, just in time to get his shit together, buy one more bottle of vodka, and make the 1:59 flight back to Cleveland.

* * *

And so there he was: unconscious and slumped unattractively against his window after drunkenly badgering a poor TWA stewardess for more tiny bottles of alcohol.

He awoke with a start. Drool had dried down the side of his mouth and on the window against which his face was pressed. Flying always made him nervous and landing was the worst part, but luckily he had slept through all but the final touchdown. Menashe gulped down one of the vodka bottles he still clutched in his hand and placed the remaining two carefully in the pocket of his corduroy jacket. He would drink another on the cab ride home from Hopkins and store the last bottle in the drawer of his desk at home. It would be safe there, and he would always be careful not to break it when he opened and shut the drawer.

Chapter 6
Austin's Interview
August 1988

"I'm not sure I should really be here, but John gave me this . . ." Austin began nervously, producing the torn, gray card for Menashe to see.

He was soft-spoken, which contrasted his rugged appearance. He wore a dirty tan t-shirt, tattered jeans, and scuffed work boots. Menashe guessed he and Austin were about the same age, though Austin's thick, short hair was fully gray. He looked like he hadn't shaved in a few days, and the smell of gin had been overpowering when they first shook hands. He held a purple baseball cap advertising some school Menashe had never heard of, and absent-mindedly fidgeted with it as he sat in his chair.

"I know he's been real happy with you, and he said I should probably give it a shot."

"Good." Menashe opened Austin Gendron's file and took out the blank forms. "I'll have to get some information from you, if you don't mind."

He kept the paperwork for each client in plain manila folders, organized neatly in his filing cabinet. Menashe first had the client fill out a personal statement in which he would describe his problem as best he could in the space allotted. Depending on the problem, Menashe would then have him complete screening tests for various disorders such as depression, anxiety, personality disorders, and substance abuse. The tests were old models he had Xeroxed out of his psychology textbooks. Next came a general waiver the client would sign if he still wanted to proceed with the treatment. Menashe honestly wasn't sure if the waiver had any legal standing, but it was an addition that comforted him. Last of all was a form the client would fill out at the start of each session. It asked questions related to mood, state of mind, and general happiness, and he would simply circle a number from one to ten indicating his feelings on that particular day.

Menashe glanced through some of the papers he would have Austin fill out and looked up to see him looking ill. Austin's red-rimmed, watery blue eyes looked thoroughly worn out, and refused to meet his therapist's gaze.

"Are you okay?"

"I just, I ju—"

Austin shuddered as though suffering from an intense fever. He regained his composure, but didn't continue his sentence. He looked at Menashe worriedly.

"Listen, the interview is just so I can get to know you a little better before we begin. All right?"

His dark eyes searched Austin's for understanding, but all he found was that familiar trace of hopelessness.

Chapter 7
Stranger
August 1988

It was nearly nine p.m. the next week when Austin knocked on Menashe's door again. He looked around uneasily. The pounding music from the street was making him sweat. His hands shook as he knocked again.

Who lives below a damn nightclub anyway?

Menashe finally opened the door and Austin entered quickly, relieved to be inside.

"You've got some loud neighbors."

"They never fail me," Menashe answered with a faint smile, shaking his hand. He motioned for him to come back to the office.

Austin sat down, awkwardly folding his tall frame into the small chair as Menashe finished some of his paperwork. He noticed Menashe looked scattered; his hair was in disarray and he was still wearing a work shirt, wrinkled and missing a button. He scratched a scruffy cheek absently as he wrote a few notes on a form. There were several piles, all crumpled and disorganized, on his desk. Austin sighed and took off his faded cap, rubbing his forehead with the back of his hand. As he looked around Menashe's cramped office, his heart suddenly locked in panic. *This is all wrong.* He scanned the room. The filing cabinet, the drab, off-white walls, the piles of papers on the shoddy desk, and the stern, tired man sitting behind it; it all made Austin think of the army recruitment offices. He began to feel claustrophobic. This was a mistake.

"Ready?" Menashe asked softly, rubbing one of his red eyes with a shaky knuckle.

Austin's tormented thoughts turned abruptly to the man who was talking to him. *He's not with us.* The stranger was telling him to get up, wanting him to go somewhere. His heartbeat was now so violent it caused him physical pain and he looked around the room. There was no escape. Menashe looked up.

"Austin?"

His mind jolted him away, back to An Khe. He was walking through a thick, suffocating marsh and stepping over deep puddles sunken into the dirt path. Droplets of water exploded on him from the gigantic green leaves above. Sunlight glinted on metal as a bullet whirred past his head and disappeared into the undergrowth. He heard a faint rustling and whirled around.

"Stay back, man," Austin growled, automatically reaching above his left shoulder in a motion he had done a thousand times, but nothing was there.

He heard a distorted scream and stumbled to his feet, suddenly noticing the blood that polluted the puddles and mixed with the muddy path. When Austin turned to run, he felt someone reaching for him.

"Get the fuck away from me!" Austin shouted, pushing blindly at his attacker.

He once again reached over his shoulder and felt tears welling in his eyes.

"Austin, what's the matter? What's happening?"

He looked up. The green of the jungle had begun to mix and swirl with the blue sky, red blood, and the flashing silver of the bullets. To Austin it looked like frosting, when you tint it different colors and blend it with the mixer. It was beautiful and for a moment he felt calm. He relaxed his muscles and the colors began to fade.

"Austin, look at me," Menashe commanded.

The voice sounded faint and distant, but Austin looked. His vision began to focus and he saw Menashe, the office, and everything else as it had been a moment before.

"It's only me—Ash Everett. You're here in Cleveland with me and you're safe, okay?"

"Okay," he answered hesitantly.

Menashe put his hands on Austin's shoulders. "What do you see?"

"Nothing. I'm fine." Austin shook him off and sat back down. He felt normal again. But it wouldn't last.

"You sure? You don't see anything bad?" he pressed.

"Just your shitty office, man," Austin replied, grinning weakly.

Menashe laughed and went back to his desk. "Well, that's not going anywhere, sorry to tell you."

Austin thought about leaving then. He thought about telling John it just wasn't for him and he'd be fine on his own. But he waited a half hour or so, trying to calm himself down and relax. He talked to Menashe and decided to go ahead with it. Menashe took him into the hallway where he was able to see all four rooms of the museum. They were all more or less the same size, each displaying maybe thirty pieces of glass. The glass shined intensely from the light bulbs above. Menashe assured Austin he kept an economy pack of spares in his office closet and told him not to worry. He looked around nervously.

"How many rooms?" Menashe asked after a moment.

"I guess . . . " he trailed off, "I guess one to start." He looked back uncertainly.

"Sure." Menashe led him into the first room. "Just come down to my office when you're through. Take your time."

Austin nodded and he left, closing the door to the first room behind him. Austin took the hockey gear and helmet Menashe told him to use and put them on, looking around at the mystical beauty of the room. There were vases and bowls, huge statues and small glass shapes that looked as though they would shatter if touched. All the pieces were clear and uniform, sitting on metal tables and shelves. He walked over to the scratched and worn wooden bat leaning casually against a corner. He picked it up and moved into the middle of the room.

He lifted the bat and brought it down with frightening speed, shattering a massive statue. Slivers of glass sprayed outward and the large chunks broke apart at his feet. Austin surveyed the room greedily and was no longer nervous. *Just get out! Let me fucking rest!*

He lost control.

He tore through the room while memories flowed in and out of his head, and he fought to clear his muddled mind. He yelled and cried out as he furiously smashed the glass pieces, and then smashed their shards that had fallen to the floor. The bat made a satisfying, deep explosion against a large bowl, while the fragments chimed daintily as they hit the floor. Shiny particles shot out in all directions like sparks from a fire, covering the room and lodging into the walls. Austin's yells were ragged and coarse against the delicate sounds of the glass. He felt drunk and ridiculous, but he didn't care. He stomped the slivers with his heavy shoes. It reminded him of stomping on icicles as a kid. He realized he wanted more. He wanted to break everything there was.

He threw open the door and charged the next room. *Steve.* Sweat rolled down his neck and arms and into the gloves that gripped his bat. *He was out there alone.* His arms rose high above his head, then came crashing down, obliterating a large figure of a knight riding a horse. *Why the fuck did I get to come home?*

Austin destroyed all four rooms before collapsing in a shivering heap on the floor of the hallway. After about five minutes, he stood up gingerly and surveyed the damage he had caused. The rooms looked as though they had been covered in powdered sugar. He dropped the bat and staggered to Menashe's office, tears still sliding down his cheeks and pulverized glass dusting his clothes. Menashe looked up from his work.

"Why don't you tell me about Vietnam?"

Chapter 8
Double Digits
June 1961

It was early morning on June 14 and Menashe lay in his bed, wide awake. Sunlight streamed through the holes in his blinds and he turned his head away to avoid the beam shining in his eyes. It was Wednesday and he delighted in the knowledge that he wouldn't have to get up for school. The year had ended the previous week, but he had not yet become accustomed to summer vacation.

He heard soft footsteps come up the stairs and pause outside his door. As the knob turned, Menashe closed his eyes and pretended to be asleep. He wasn't sure why he had developed the habit, but whenever anyone entered his room when he was expected to be sleeping, he felt compelled to pretend he was.

"Happy birthday, sweetie," his mom called in a cheerful whisper through the small opening in the doorway.

"Thanks, Ma," he replied in a falsely groggy voice, trying to hide the excitement he felt. He loved his birthdays, not because of the extra attention or even the gifts, but because he couldn't wait to get older. In his own mind, life was just beginning for him. And this birthday was more significant than most: Menashe had reached the milestone of double digits.

"You want to come downstairs for breakfast?" his mom asked, now entering the room. She was already dressed for work in a blue skirt suit and bright-red lipstick. Her sunset-red hair was curled loosely and she was always running her fingers through it while she talked. "I'll make you something special." This invitation drew Menashe out of bed with images of delicious sticky buns, homemade pancakes, and French toast flooding his mind.

As Charlotte prepared thick slices of cinnamon French toast—Menashe's favorite—he sat at the breakfast table with his father, who scanned the business section of the paper.

Lewis smiled at him over the paper. "So what are you going to do today?" He wore his new glasses, the ones with thick square frames that made him look like Buddy Holly.

Menashe hadn't thought about the details of his birthday. They didn't really matter to him; he was ten and that was enough. He knew his older cousin, Shira, would be over to watch him soon. He knew he would have a few friends over for dinner and birthday cake, but that was hours away, after his parents got home from work. And, of course, the weekend held a special trip to the Sculpture Centre.

"I don't know," he began. "Maybe go ride bikes with Alan?"

His dad nodded, still smiling. Charlotte set the giant plate of French toast between them, her glossy red fingernails gently clicking against the table as she released the plate. She went back to the kitchen to retrieve the milk and syrup.

"Thanks, hon; this looks great," Lewis said as his wife sat down next to him.

"Yeah, thanks," Menashe said as he stabbed a slice of toast with his fork and dropped it onto his plate.

"You're welcome. Happy birthday, Menashe," she said, a contented look in her eyes. Lewis folded the paper and placed it on the empty chair at the table.

"You know," he began, turning to face his son, "now that you're getting so grown up, how would you like to come to work with me today?"

Menashe stopped chewing, his face stuffed with syrupy French toast.

"Really?" he managed to ask, though the question was nearly unintelligible. Lewis laughed, nodding.

Menashe was far more excited at the prospect of spending a day at real adult work than most boys his age would have been, but there were many ways in which Menashe differed from most boys his age. He looked over at his mom to gauge her reaction, but he could tell by her smile and the way she put her hand tenderly on his father's arm that it had been her idea.

Lewis and Menashe arrived at the Traveler's Hotel in the stylish Bloor District of downtown Toronto shortly before nine a.m. Lewis had worked as the Assistant Daytime Manager there for the past five years. He always wore a suit to work—that day it was a classic gray polyester-wool blend with a thin black tie and black shoes—and would inspect himself carefully in the mirror before leaving the house, straightening his tie and searching for traces of lint on his coat. Menashe didn't own a suit, so he wore the nicest clothes he did own: a gray Oxford shirt with a shiny blue tie, brown dress pants, and brown leather shoes. This was the outfit he saved for attending synagogue and special events.

The Traveler's Hotel was decorated in elegant white and gold, with swirled marble floors and countertops that beautifully complemented the luxurious, overstuffed leather chairs and couches in the lobby. Giant mirrors hung behind the front desk and over the smooth, clean fireplace, making the hotel look twice its already enormous size. Menashe had been to his dad's workplace only once before, a long time ago with his mom to drop off some important papers he had forgotten.

As they walked through the main entrance, Menashe stopped. His eyes lit up and widened immediately at the sight of the place.

"Looks different, doesn't it?" Lewis laughed. Menashe was still taking it all in, his head tilted up toward the ceiling.

"It's amazing," he breathed. "It's so much bigger."

Lewis nodded. "Yeah, all the renovating has really paid off." He paused. "Here, I want you to meet somebody."

Menashe followed as Lewis led him behind the front desk to a hallway of offices. He stopped in front of a door marked "George Daniels, Manager." Lewis knocked firmly.

"George? You in there?"

"Yeah, come in."

Lewis opened the door to a deceptively large office furnished with the same fine leather and stylish decor found in the lobby.

"I'd like you to meet my son, Menashe," Lewis said, motioning for Menashe to step in front of him. "Menashe, this is Mr. Daniels." He gave him a gentle nudge forward so he could shake Mr. Daniels's hand.

"Nice to meet you," he said shyly. He was always on the brink of panic when it came to meeting new people.

"Oh, the pleasure's all mine, young man," Daniels replied pleasantly. He was a distinguished, sturdy man of about fifty-five, with gigantic hands and wiry gray hairs on his fingers. "Your dad talks about you all the time—we've all been looking forward to meeting you." His smile went from Menashe to Lewis, and then faded as he turned back to his desk.

"Anyway, I'm sorry to lay a problem on you right when you walk in the door," he began, frowning at a stack of paperwork, "but the shipment of table-cloths and chairs for that MP's wedding this weekend never came. The truck was supposed to get here yesterday and we still need time to set the damn thing up." Daniels was grinding the lead of his pencil into his desk with frustration as he spoke and Menashe noticed his other hand was clenched and white.

"Don't worry, I'll take care of it," Lewis replied. "What's the company?"

"Soirée Wedding . . . something or other," he sighed, handing him the papers. "Bastards," he added under his breath.

Lewis chuckled as he and Menashe left the office. He stepped into his own office just long enough to toss the stack of papers onto his desk.

"We'll deal with that in a minute," he explained to Menashe as they walked back to the lobby of the hotel.

Menashe felt he was already falling behind. But he had loved how Mr. Daniels had carried on with hotel business as if he were just another employee; he hadn't even censored his language, as most adults did in his presence.

He watched his dad greet some of the hotel staff, but hung back cautiously, uncertain of what he should do.

"Menashe," Lewis said, smiling. "Come here." Menashe obediently moved a little closer, but his palms had begun to sweat. He wished they could just go back to his dad's office. "Guys, this is my son, Menashe."

"Nice to meet you," he said to no one in particular, avoiding their eyes. Everyone was friendly enough, smiling and reaching out to shake his hand, and they all seemed charmed by his nervousness.

"Okay," Lewis said briskly, running a hand through his thinning hair. And with a single breath he set the day into motion.

"Do you want something to drink?" Lewis asked his son back in his office, holding up a couple of root beer bottles from the common refrigerator down the hall.

"Sure," Menashe said. Lewis popped the cap off against the edge of his desk and handed him the sweating glass bottle.

"So how do you like it so far?" his dad asked, leaning back in his chair.

"I like it," Menashe answered thoughtfully. "You're really busy," he added.

"Yeah," he laughed. "There's a lot to do and I know it seems crazy, but it's really a lot of fun."

Menashe nodded. "Can we see a room?" he asked, curious about the rest of the hotel.

"Sure, just let me see about this shipment, okay?"

"Okay," he answered, secretly delighted he would be allowed to stay and eavesdrop on the conversation. Lewis glanced at the papers Mr. Daniels had given him and picked up the receiver of his telephone, dialing.

"Hi, Lewis Everett here from Traveler's." He paused, listening. "Uh huh, yeah. Listen, we were scheduled to receive a very large and important shipment from you yesterday and it never came." Another pause. "Yeah, let me give you the address." He read the hotel's address to the person on the line and waited, frowning. "No, excuse me, I don't want to leave a message," he declared. "We do a great deal of business with you and if this isn't sorted out immediately, we'll find another supplier." He turned to Menashe, rolling his eyes. "Sometimes you have to get tough with these people," he whispered, covering the receiver with his hand. Menashe smiled. "Yes," he answered, turning his attention back to the call, "I'd love to speak with the manager." He smiled and took a drink of his root beer, his dark eyes shining.

Menashe said little on the car ride back to the house. His dad probably assumed he was worn out from the hectic day, which he was, but he was also deep in thought. He envied his father's confidence. He wanted to someday be the man everyone went to when they needed to solve an important problem. He wanted that effortless intelligence and passion, but he feared it wasn't in his nature. And he knew that, no matter what, it would never come easily.

They pulled into the garage and Lewis cut the engine, then turned to his son.

"Happy birthday, buddy," he said affectionately, smiling a simultaneously tired and happy smile. "Thanks for coming to work with me. I had a good time."

"Me, too."

Menashe managed a smile even though in truth the experience had left him feeling slightly depressed and overwhelmed, as if he were only just realizing the length of the yardstick against which he would constantly measure himself.

Chapter 9
Coming Up for Air
September 1988

Menashe was wrestling with his key, trying to force it into the rusted lock on his apartment door when he heard footsteps behind him. Chase. *What does he want?* He was coming down the iron steps, sweating, and lugging a briefcase as he often did.

"Got to get you a new deadbolt for that door," he said apologetically. "It's really gone to hell."

"There's just a trick to it sometimes," Menashe replied, using his pocket-knife to scrape away some of the rust. He shoved the key inside and successfully opened the door.

"So, what can I do for you?" he asked uneasily.

"Can I come in?" Chase asked. "This'll just take a second."

"Sure." Menashe reluctantly led the way, hoping all evidence of the museum was out of sight.

Chase walked in, fanning himself as he leaned his bag against the wall. He was a big guy, average height but maybe fifty pounds overweight, and was always out of breath. He was wearing one of his usual "club" shirts (a term Menashe had coined in his mind): brightly colored, dressy, collared shirts with a little sheen to them. That day it was vivid green. Menashe liked Chase; he was genuinely kind and helpful, but it always made Menashe nervous to have him in the apartment.

"How's everything going here? Water still running?"

"Yeah. Thanks for taking care of that faucet." He led him back to the kitchen. "Nothing else to report, I think."

"Good." They both sat down at the kitchen table and Menashe got them some water. "I wanted to ask you something," Chase began.

"Oh, yeah?" Menashe glanced toward the closed rooms of his museum.

"I feel kind of bad that we've never gotten to know each other. I mean, you've been renting from me for, what, ten years?" Menashe nodded. "I've generally tried to leave you alone because you seem like a private person, and honestly, sometimes I forget you're down here." He chuckled and sat back in his chair, idly rubbing his neat blonde beard. "Anyway, I wanted to know if you're interested in joining a poker game I started a few months ago. Just a couple of friends, really casual. We meet every other Sunday night upstairs," he motioned to the nightclub. "The club's closed, so we've got the place to ourselves." He smiled warmly but Menashe's head was starting to pound.

"Oh, I don't know, Chase. That's really nice of you," he said, absently scratching some food remnants off the table with his fingernail. "I'm just not very social, you know?"

"Yeah, I've noticed you don't get out much," he laughed. "You should think about it, though; it really is a lot of fun. And lucky for you, you could just walk home after. At first I was worried about the guys driving home, since I basically give them run of the bar, but I just told them if they don't come in a cab I'll cut them off at two drinks." He winked. "That did the trick."

Menashe laughed. "I bet."

"So, what do you think?" Chase pressed. "Want to come next Sunday, see how you like it?"

"Sure," he replied after a moment, feeling calmer and finally meeting Chase's eyes. "It sounds like a good time."

"The best," Chase said excitedly, rising from his chair. "So, nine o'clock, okay?"

Menashe nodded. "I'll be there."

"Great." Chase moved back down the hallway to the door, retrieving his briefcase. "And the place has really been okay for you? No other repairs, you're sure?" Menashe shook his head. "I'm on the deadbolt, so don't worry about that. Just let me know if anything else comes up."

"Okay," Menashe smiled. "Thanks, Chase."

Menashe couldn't remember the last time he'd gone inside The Velvet Dog. He usually just slipped his rent check in Chase's mail slot so there was really no reason to. And he didn't like the idea of going there for a drink. Too close. And definitely too loud for his taste.

He walked in, automatically rubbing the sweat off his palms onto his shorts. With the music off, it seemed like a typical dive bar. It was a good size, dimly lit with cheap, white Christmas lights strung up along the ceiling. Signs advertising various beers and liquors hung over the bar, and the rest of the walls were decorated with mostly black-and-white photos, many of Cleveland, and some of people he didn't recognize. There wasn't much of a smell in the place, which Menashe appreciated, but the floor was sticky and pulled against his shoes with each step. He took a breath. He'd already had a drink before leaving the apartment, just to take the edge off his nerves.

Chase was sitting at a table at the back, with nicely combed hair and wearing a silver and blue striped button-down. He sat with two other men, one maybe forty-five, about Chase's age, and the other somewhat older, around sixty.

"Ash!" Chase called, waving him over as if there were other groups of people he might be confused by. "Good to see you."

Menashe smiled as he made his way to the back and sat down in the chair Chase was indicating.

"We're still waiting on Sam," he continued, "but you can meet the other guys." Chase turned to the man about his own age, who had dark, kind eyes and a sparse horseshoe of hair. He was stocky, with a friendly smile, and wore a PBR t-shirt. "Ash, this is Paul. We actually grew up together not far from here."

"Nice to meet you," Paul said, shaking his hand.

"You, too."

"And this old guy," Chase began affectionately, "is Lenny. Lenny works for one of my vendors here, so we've gotten to know each other pretty well over the years."

Lenny grunted a salutation and Menashe gave him a slight smile in return.

"So," Chase began as he got up, walking to the bar, "what can I get you guys?"

"Vodka, rocks," Lenny said shortly. It seemed he didn't have to think long about it. He shifted in his chair, digging a lighter out of the pocket of his fishing pants.

"Just a beer for me, Chase," Paul replied, shuffling the cards. "Any kind's fine."

"Sure." Chase poured the drinks and looked up. "Ash? Don't be nervous, now."

"Whiskey would be great. Thanks."

Just as Chase was delivering the drinks, the club's door opened again and a young man who looked to be around thirty stumbled in, as if The Velvet Dog wasn't his first stop of the night.

"Chase, seriously, will you fix the goddamn step? It's going to kill somebody."

"I would, but you seem to be the only one who trips over it."

Sam made his way to the back of the room, wiping sweat from his forehead. He pulled off the unbuttoned plaid shirt that covered his gray t-shirt, fanning himself.

"Hey, all," he said, then turned to Menashe. "You're the new guy, right?"

"This is Ash," Chase interjected. "He lives downstairs. Be nice, huh?"

"I'm always nice." Sam smiled broadly and extended his hand. "Sam Oliver. I'm glad you could come."

"Thanks. Me, too." He took a drink of whiskey and glanced toward the others. Paul had started to deal out the cards and Chase had gone to the back room for something. Lenny was sitting back silently, looking slightly amused. *They seem all right*, he thought, relieved. He took another drink.

"Paul, how did the thing go?" Sam asked as he walked up to the bar. He began pouring himself a gin and tonic. "Did Riley do okay?"

"She did," Paul smiled. "My daughter," he explained, turning to Menashe. "She had her first dance recital yesterday. She has a lot of trouble with shyness; I didn't think she'd do it."

"Fantastic," Lenny said quietly.

"That's great," Menashe replied. "How old is she?"

"Ten."

"You have kids?" Sam asked, sitting back down.

Menashe's stomach twisted into a hard knot. He shook his head.

"Married?" Sam persisted. They were all looking at him now.

"Divorced."

"Hey, me, too!" Sam exclaimed merrily. "Listen, we've got to stick together, man. These guys have no idea what it's like out there for us."

Menashe started to feel his vision distort. His breath was coming in shallow intervals and he looked desperately around the bar, silently praying the panic would subside. He rubbed the back of his neck. There. His eyes locked on picture of Cleveland's skyline—a blown-up, framed photograph, done in sepia tone. He studied it for a moment, then took a drink and started to feel better.

"What are you talking about?" Paul was laughing. "You go out with a different girl every week."

"You think that's easy? And I don't know about you, Ash, but my ex hates my fucking guts, so it's not like any of that is a real picnic."

"Whoa, whoa, wait a minute," Chase interrupted, walking back into the room. He passed Lenny a bag of pretzels. "You want to tell him why she hates you? Or were you just going to leave that part out?"

"Ugh, Chase," Sam groaned. "Fine. Okay, I might have been messing around a bit, but it was only because she was such hell to live with. I mean, a real control freak. She didn't even let me eat in bed."

Menashe laughed. "That does sound rough."

"Yeah, Sam's got his own little *Othello* going on," Paul said, rolling his eyes.

After another hour of playing cards, Menashe began to feel like his old self. He was having fun. He'd forgotten what it was like to interact with people without probing them for painful details about their lives. These guys told jokes. They mocked each other relentlessly and were already including him in their jabs. It was like coming up for air.

"So, Lenny, where are you from?" Menashe asked after a few more drinks, curious about the reserved older man.

"New Jersey."

"How did you end up here?"

"Just followed the jobs," he answered in his gravelly, flat tone.

"Lenny worked in restaurant management," Chase added. "Took him all over the world."

"You got to go to Cleveland to make the big bucks, though," Sam winked, his speech starting to slur.

Lenny just shook his head and went back to his drink. Chase shuffled the cards and started dealing, counting to himself as he passed them around.

"You know, Ash," Chase murmured, slowing down as his focus became divided, "after we were talking the other day, I realized you and Paul have something in common."

"Oh, yeah?" He glanced toward Paul with interest. Paul shrugged.

"Yeah, you both went to the same college. John Carroll, right?"

"Wow. Yeah, that's right," Menashe replied.

"No way," Paul smiled. "When did you graduate?"

"Seventy-three. Then I did a grad program at Case Western. You?"

"Earlier than that," he laughed. "What were you studying?"

"Art history and psychology. Perfect for the student loan business," he added wryly. He felt embarrassed to admit that his college ambitions had no connection to his day job.

Paul chuckled. "Hey, I was studying theology. I wanted to be a priest back then." He shook his head. "Things change, man. Nothing wrong with that."

"You did not want to be a priest," Sam teased. "That's fucked up, Paul. You know they can't have sex, right?"

"No, Sam, I don't think I've ever heard that."

"And you were all signed up to do it anyway? Geez . . ." Sam sat back and lit a cigarette, smiling at Paul. Menashe guessed he'd been one of those impishly charming frat boys back in college. The kind who'd wake up in the quad now and then, with no memory of how he got there.

"I would have thought you'd be recruiting guys to be priests," Paul laughed. "You know, get the competition out of your way. God knows you could use an advantage."

Sam, who had been taking a swig of his gin and tonic, suddenly laughed and began choking, coughing violently and waving his hand. This made Paul start laughing, which got Sam going again until neither of them could catch their breaths.

"Okay," Chase smiled. "I think we've all had enough for tonight."

"What time is it?" Lenny asked.

"Nearly one." Chase stood up. "Thanks, you guys, for another memorable evening. Now," he said, waving them off good-naturedly. "Go call yourselves a cab."

"Aw, Chase," Sam croaked, tears sparkling in his eyes, "you know we've been much worse."

"Oh, I know," he said, helping Paul as he attempted to stand.

Sam reluctantly got up and headed toward the door.

"Good night, you guys." He wavered as he stood. "Ash, you're fun," he remarked thoughtfully. "Come back next time."

Menashe laughed and said he would. He and Chase waved good night then sat back at their table. They could still hear Sam's powerful laughter continue to resonate as the three walked down the street.

"Well," Chase sighed, "thanks for coming. I hope you had a good time."

"I did," Menashe smiled. "They are really funny."

"That's one word for it," he laughed.

"So, what's Lenny's story?" he asked, looking toward the door. "He's so serious."

"Yeah," Chase began, his voice lowering slightly. "He's got quite a past. Went to prison for ten years."

"What? What for?"

"Embezzlement."

"Wow—that's crazy. Does he have a family?"

Chase shook his head. "Nope. Never married. Likes to keep to himself. He's a really good guy, though, once you get to know him."

Menashe nodded and stood up slowly, gripping the table. "I think I'd better head off to bed. Thank you, Chase. I'm glad I came."

"See you next time, then. We'll always be here."

Chase smiled, and for some reason Menashe really believed him.

Chapter 10
Murray Signs Up
September 1988

Murray Henderson smiled timidly as Menashe opened the door.

"Hey, Murray."

He stepped cautiously into the apartment. Menashe led him down the hall and into his office.

"Mr. Everett, thank you so much for seeing me again."

"Please, call me Ash."

"Okay," Murray replied, but wasn't really comfortable with the idea. He'd met Menashe the previous week and didn't yet know what to make of him. He seemed sympathetic and genuinely interested in helping him, but there was also something dark about him. He didn't smile much, and Murray suspected he'd been hung-over at their first meeting. Murray looked around. Menashe's place was pretty dingy and so devoid of personal touches it didn't look like anyone lived there at all. But when he'd toured the museum the week before, Murray had felt a rush of emotion that was so vivid and hopeful, he knew he needed to come back.

Menashe looked up from his papers. "Now, I know the first time we met I threw all this paperwork at you, which was pretty overwhelming. But now that you've had time to fill out the forms and think things through a bit, I'd like to tell you a little more about what normally happens here, okay?"

Murray nodded.

"Usually a client will come in a few times—or even only once—just to talk, before having a session. That way I can get to know him better and have a greater understanding of the situation. From there, we decide if he's ready to take a room, and if so, how many. After each session we talk more extensively, and that's where we really make the progress. Does that make sense?"

Murray nodded again. "Yeah."

"Good. And if at any point you become uncomfortable with this process, or you decide you want to try something else, just let me know. It's perfectly okay."

"Okay. Thanks, Mr. Ev—Ash. Sorry." He looked at the floor uncomfortably.

"Okay." Menashe swiveled in his chair and reached for more papers. "In your statement you wrote about having a lot of anger and anxiety, but not really understanding what's behind it." Murray avoided Menashe's eyes, looking down at his khakis. He felt a sick churning in his stomach and knew he was getting in over his head. He took a few deep breaths, trying to calm his system, but the pressure was rising to his throat. He looked desperately around the office.

"Are you okay?" Menashe asked, eying him with concern.

Murray could only shake his head, not trusting himself to speak. He got up and stumbled down the hallway until he found the bathroom. He'd barely collapsed on his knees before his stomach forced everything out. Murray gripped the toilet as he heaved, sputtering and grimacing at the acidic taste in his mouth. After another minute he finally stood, wiping tears from his eyes and catching his reflection in the mirror. *I look like absolute hell.* He'd always been a tall, awkwardly lanky kid, and never felt quite comfortable in his own body. But now, seeing his bloodshot eyes edged with dark circles, and ashen skin shining from the effort of vomiting, he couldn't even stand the sight of himself.

Murray took a few drinks of water from the bathroom faucet before trudging back down the hall to Menashe's office. He found him still at his desk, but with his face buried in his hands, as if he had a bad headache.

"Mr. Everett?"

"Murray, hey," he started, quickly lifting his head and sitting upright. "Are you all right?"

"I think so."

"Something you ate?"

Murray shook his head, sitting back down across from Menashe. "No, I just get that sometimes. It's my nerves, I guess."

"You throw up when you're nervous?"

Murray nodded.

"Okay," Menashe replied, leafing through his paperwork. "You still want to do this?"

"Yes."

"Good. Okay, so I have some more questions for you. Is that all right?"

"Sure."

"Okay. You live with both your parents?"

"Yes."

"Go to school?"

"Case Western. That's where I got your card, at the University Counseling Center."

"From Carrie?"

"Yeah. She said you really helped her brother out—Marshall, I think. She told me she looks out for students who might need something different, like this."

Menashe nodded. "I'm glad she did." He wrote a few more things down. "What are you studying?"

"Political science. I have a job, too, working for a law professor. I want to go to law school," he added quietly.

"Great. It's a good school. Okay, can you tell me a bit about your family?"

"Well, I've got two older brothers who have moved away. Matthew lives in Toledo, and Jake lives in Chicago with his wife. So it's just me and my parents now."

"And what are they like?"

"Great. My mom stayed home with us, growing up, and we've always gotten along well," he said slowly. "My dad is usually pretty busy with work, but he always makes time and everything. I don't know. Everything's pretty normal in that way."

He looked at Menashe uncertainly, hoping he would agree and say that, of course, it all sounded perfectly normal. But the serious and slightly stern look did not leave his face as he took quick notes on his legal pad.

"What was your childhood like?"

"It was all right, I guess. Normal."

"Is that how you think things should be? Normal?"

"I guess."

"I just want you to know, you can say whatever you want to me—even if you don't think it's normal."

"Okay."

Menashe sat back in his chair. Murray waited for him to speak, but he just sat there, watching. Finally, Murray broke the silence.

"There are some things I can't remember," he admitted.

"From when you were growing up?"

"Yeah."

Menashe leaned forward. "Why do you think that is?"

"I . . . I don't know, really," he stammered, absently pulling on his fine, blond hair. He was starting to panic. *I shouldn't do this. Mr. Everett's a stranger.*

"But there are gaps in your memory?"

Murray nodded.

"And you're, what, nineteen?"

"Yeah."

"Hm, that's really interesting," Menashe muttered, more to himself than to Murray. "I mean, it's unusual—I, well, I haven't had a lot of experience with that before. It's most often the result of trauma, though."

"No," Murray protested, "no, it isn't like that. My life has been really typical and plain, and that's why none of this makes sense. I . . . I don't even know what to do anymore, it's getting so bad."

Menashe swiveled around and poured him a glass of water from a dull plastic pitcher that sat on top of his filing cabinet.

"What doesn't make sense?" he asked, handing the glass to Murray.

"Why I have such bad thoughts." He paused cautiously. "I mean, really dark thoughts."

Menashe leaned forward, resting his elbows on the desk. "Can you tell me some of them?" he asked gently.

Murray hesitated, rubbing his left arm, which was beginning to throb. He knew he either had to tell Menashe everything or he had to leave without saying a word. He couldn't decide, and instead just sat silently, looking at him with large, miserable brown eyes. Menashe was getting a strange, distant look in his own eyes, and Murray was worried he was becoming impatient with him. When Menashe spoke it was in an odd, strained tone he hadn't heard before.

"You know you can tell me anything, Wesley," he murmured.

This broke Murray of his silence. "What?" he asked, confused.

"Oh, I . . . I'm sorry, Murray," he apologized, looking flustered, as if he had just been released from a spell. "I haven't had much sleep lately and, you know, I'm not the best with names." He laughed anxiously. "It's just, you look kind of like someone else—someone I used to know. I'm sorry."

"Oh, it's no problem," Murray said, but was glancing at him uneasily.

"Thanks," Menashe replied, taking a large gulp from his coffee mug. "I don't want you to think I'm not listening or that I don't care."

"No," Murray shook his head. "I didn't think that." He paused. "Are you okay?"

"Yeah." He smiled slightly. "Thanks. But let's get back to you, okay?"

"Okay."

"So you were going to tell me about some of the thoughts you have?"

Murray nodded. "Just like——" He stopped, looking at Menashe as if to make sure he could trust him. Menashe nodded for him to continue. "Wanting to hurt people, or hurt myself, or even kill myself. It's like . . . it's like I can't control it."

"Do you ever hurt anyone?"

"Sometimes," he said. "I've tried to hurt myself a few times. I've taken knives from the science labs and cut myself in the bathroom. But, I mean, I got scared and stopped before I did any real damage."

He rolled up his sleeves and showed Menashe four long gashes trailing up the insides of his forearms, covered over by flaky red scabs. Murray's heartbeat quickened as he understood how much he was revealing, and a familiar panicky feeling overcame him. *I shouldn't talk about this. It's not safe.*

"And why do you think you do this?"

"Because I have to."

"You have to?"

"I know it's weird but I . . . I feel better when I do it. I feel relief."

"Relief from what?"

"From thoughts and pain—from myself, I guess." He laughed suddenly. "I'm sorry, this sounds really stupid now that I'm saying it out loud——"

"No," Menashe broke in sternly, "this is important. And it's not stupid, okay?" Murray nodded obediently. Menashe took a breath and his tone softened. "So you feel powerless, like you can't stop what you're doing?"

"Yeah. Like in high school, I'd get into fights a lot, but I don't know why. I don't remember having problems with the guys I knew, it just happened. And I was stupid about it; I'd start fights with big guys who easily beat me." He paused. "God, I know this sounds weird, but when I felt really bad, I'd pick fights just to get hit. I wouldn't hit back. I guess it's like cutting myself—for some reason it felt right, so I'd feel better."

"You feel like you deserve to be hurt?"

"I guess. Sometimes I feel like I deserve to die."

Menashe stopped writing and looked up, but this time Murray didn't stop.

"And I mean, most of the time, when I do something dangerous, I have no idea I'm going to do it until it actually happens. Like when I get angry and I sometimes just explode out of nowhere."

"Okay," Menashe muttered, writing again on his tablet. "Have you ever hurt anyone else?"

"It's gotten so out of control lately," he murmured. "I wish I could stop it, I really do." He paused and took a drink of water. "I'd get the same way with my girlfriend. I'd just explode over nothing and hit her. And afterward, I would hardly remember doing it. It's like something came over me—like it wasn't even me."

"Are you still together?"

"No. She broke up with me a couple months ago."

"How did that go?"

"Not very well. And now, I don't even trust myself to go out with anybody." Murray let out a pained sigh. "It's not anything I wanted to do," he added, hoping Menashe would understand. Menashe nodded and lowered his head, a desperate look in his eyes that Murray didn't recognize.

Chapter 11
Farmtown, USA
June 1971

Menashe walked up the front steps of the Brennans' run-down farmhouse in Fletcher, Ohio, lugging his duffel bag and cursing the small town's lack of proper lighting and street signs under his breath.

"Menashe," Jamie whispered, causing him to look up and notice her for the first time. "Where've you been?"

"Sorry," he said, looking at his watch. "I got a late start."

"It's okay. I was getting a little worried, though."

He walked up to the door and kissed her. "Is your family still up?" he asked uneasily.

"Just Dad and Aunt Tracy." She took Menashe's bag and put it on the stairs. "Are you okay?"

"Yeah, just worn out." He grimaced as he stretched out his arms. "Can we go up to bed?"

"Sure, let's just go say good night first, okay? I know they're excited to see you."

Jamie looked down the hall, and Menashe shook his head. He knew she was exaggerating her family's feelings toward him. He was pretty sure her younger brother, Will, was the only one who actually liked him. An aspiring artist himself, Will loved hearing about Menashe's classes and plans for working at a museum or gallery after graduate school. The two got along well, and he made the visits a little more bearable for Menashe.

"Okay," he responded, eyeing his bag on the stairs. "But not for too long, okay? I'm pretty tired."

"Sure." She led him down the hall to the living room, but before they could reach her family, she grabbed his arm.

"Menashe," she whispered.

"What? What's wrong?"

"Don't mention the war."

Menashe was relieved to hear that Herman, Jamie's older brother, would not be coming to dinner that night. He was outgoing, tactless, and, at twenty-nine years old, seemed to believe he was in charge of his younger siblings. He was also harder on Menashe than any other member of the family and would mercilessly berate him about his city background, ambitions as an artist, and, occasionally, his strong spirituality. It comforted him to know Herman was about three hundred miles away, picking up some kind of farm equipment.

Menashe sat down heavily on the guest room bed, digging through his bag agitatedly. He'd forgotten his collared shirt.

"You need something?" Jamie asked, walking over to him.

"I thought I'd packed nicer clothes," he explained, "but I can't find them now."

"Don't worry," she laughed. "Remember, this is cowboy country."

He shrugged but continued digging through his bag. He knew her family wasn't big on dressing up, but, for whatever reason, he was still trying to make a good impression. He sighed and tossed his razor and hairbrush aside. It didn't matter; they'd find something else wrong with him.

"Really, it's fine," she said. "I'm just wearing what I've got on."

He looked at her closely for the first time and smiled. She was wearing a sky-blue cotton skirt that hit just below the knee and a white t-shirt he knew she liked because it made her look tan. Her blonde hair was pulled back and, because it was short, stuck straight out from the back of her head.

"Sorry," he said, relaxing slightly. "I just wanted this weekend to go well."

"It *is* going well."

"I don't know."

"You're just nervous."

"No, I'm not," he said seriously. "I really—I don't know what to do."

"About what?"

"Our plan . . . for tonight. I'm just thinking maybe we shouldn't tell them. Not yet anyway."

Jamie sat down on the bed next to him. She stayed quiet for a moment, and Menashe watched her carefully, not sure what she was thinking.

"Menashe, this is important to me," she began finally. "And we made the decision; it was all set. It's not like we're getting married tomorrow—we'd tell them we're waiting another two years until after graduation."

He nodded and looked down. "I know. I just wish your family liked me. And don't say they do, because I can tell, all right? I happen to know Will is the only one who even pretends to—"

"He's not pretending," she broke in. "Really. He wants to be just like you."

"It's not about Will, though. It's really your dad—I just feel like things would be easier if I could get on his good side. And I know the money stuff doesn't help."

"What money stuff?"

"I'm pretty much living off of loans. I can't afford a ring right now."

"That doesn't matter."

"It might matter to your family. It'll look like I won't be able to support us or something."

"But we're still in school," she protested, turning toward him. "After graduation, I'll be working full time. And once you finish your master's, you'll get a job in some fancy gallery and we'll be fine."

"Yeah, no pressure or anything."

"What is the matter with you?" she snapped.

"Nothing. Jesus, I was just making a joke."

"Great timing, as always," she scowled, getting to her feet and pacing anxiously.

"Well, what do you want me to do?" he demanded, his face reddening. "You think these visits are easy for me? Every time I think I've got a little piece of good news to give them—the scholarship, or the internship—they turn it around and act like I'm trying to be better than they are."

"No, Menashe, they just don't understand."

"They don't want to understand," he retorted. "They don't want to hear about me or my plans for the future. Every time I talk about my family, and my courses, and my favorite artists, do you know what they're thinking?"

She looked nervous, like she didn't want him to continue.

"They're thinking I'm just a big-shot, city Jew, and their daughter could do a lot better."

She shook her head. "That's just not fair."

"You think I'm wrong?"

"Why does this have to be so hard?" she exclaimed. "Menashe, none of that even matters. We're talking about *our* future. We shouldn't make our decisions based on what my family will think. Do you think I spend much time on my dad's good side? You know both my parents hate that I'm going into commu-nications. According to them, the only reason I should be in college is to study agriculture." She shook her head. "We need to start thinking of each other as family, and do what's right for us."

"Maybe I don't know what's right for us," he muttered.

"What, you don't want to get married?"

"No, I really do," he said, taking her hand and motioning for her to sit next to him again. "But can we wait maybe a few more weeks before we say anything? I'm just not comfortable doing it tonight."

He rubbed his forehead and looked at the floor. He'd give anything not to have to go down there for dinner.

"I guess," Jamie said flatly. "If your mind's made up, I guess that's what we'll do."

"I just need a little more time."

"Should we go help with dinner?" she murmured. He supposed she didn't want to be alone with him anymore.

"Sure," he replied, still staring at the floor.

Downstairs, Jamie's mother, father, and aunt were all gathered in the kitch-en. Her mother was scurrying around, occasionally delegating jobs to Jamie's aunt, but largely trying to get everything done herself. Jamie's father watched on, amused.

"You always leave those biscuits till the last minute," he observed. "Can't rush 'em."

Jamie's mother looked up. "You'd best get out of my kitchen," she replied bluntly.

"Fine," he laughed. "It'll all get done, I suppose."

"Can we help with anything?" Jamie asked.

"No, no, thank you, kids. You know I've got my system." She wiped her brow with the sleeve of her cotton blouse. "Why don't you check and make sure the table's set, and keep your father out of the way."

Jamie and Menashe double-checked the table, setting out a few missing napkins and salad plates. Jamie's father was already in the dining room, opening up the hutch dresser.

"I think it's about time for an appetizer," he remarked, pulling down a bottle of Ten High whiskey, and a shot glass. He poured the liquor right up to the brim and slurped it down with a quick tilt of his hand. He then set the glass down on the hutch and shook his head vigorously.

"Man!" he exclaimed. "That's good." He looked over and saw Menashe watching him. "You ever had a whiskey?" he asked, already pulling down a second shot glass.

"Dad, no," Jamie said quickly.

"I'd give it a try," Menashe replied.

"It takes a little getting used to."

"We have that soda you like," Jamie broke in again. "Let me just get you one of those."

Menashe knew what she was worried about, and it irritated him. She was thinking of John's homecoming, several weeks before. Menashe, admittedly, had gotten a little out of control, but it was a big celebration. And she knew how worried he'd been about his friend fighting in Vietnam. It was a release, and had meant so much more to him than some drunken party. But he couldn't make her understand.

"Now this isn't the fanciest you'll find, but I like it," her dad was saying, pouring him a shot. "It settles the stomach, anyhow."

"Menashe, come on," she said sharply. "Whiskey's too strong."

"Don't worry," he said, watching her father carefully as he filled the glass. "I can handle it."

By the time everyone sat down to dinner, Menashe had downed another two shots of whiskey. Jamie's father placed the bottle in the center of the table. *Maybe I'll finally be able to relax.*

"Oh, Menashe," Jamie said as they started eating, "remind me to introduce John to my friend, Abby. I think they'd really get along."

"Sure," he said absently. He took a bite of stew. "This is really great," he said to Jamie's mother. "Thank you again for having me." He touched Jamie's knee under the table and she took his hand, squeezing it.

"Our pleasure," her mom replied.

"So, James," her dad piped up, "how's school going?"

"It's good," she replied, reaching for a biscuit. "I can't wait for this Narrative Radio class I'm taking in the fall."

He frowned. "What does that mean?"

"We'll get to write and produce stories that will actually air on Cleveland's public radio." Her father's expression hadn't changed and Menashe saw her smile was fading. "It's real reporting," she explained. "It's what I want to do."

"That sounds like a neat class," Menashe said.

"I'm sure it will be a great experience," her mother began wistfully. "Just remember, after you graduate lots of people will be going for those flashy reporting jobs. TV and radio especially. I don't want you getting your hopes up too high."

Jamie took a deep breath as her face reddened.

"I do it all the time," Menashe interjected. "It's really not so bad."

Jamie shot him a look. "I won't get my hopes up," she said evenly, "but this is what I'm doing."

Her mother shrugged in a "suit yourself" kind of way, but her father wasn't finished.

"You should think about your options around here, though," he said. "I know the Wilhelms would give you good work. They were really impressed that summer you helped them out. And you know," he winked, "Trevor was always pretty fond of you."

"Grant," Jamie's aunt said sharply. Jamie's father looked up, bewildered, as if he had no idea what he'd done wrong.

Jamie turned to Menashe, who had helped himself to the whiskey again.

"Wow, a boyfriend," he said slowly, feeling his stomach start to churn. "That's a great deal." He smiled weakly and Jamie took his arm.

"You don't have to do this," she whispered. "Why don't you go to the bathroom, and I'll get us out of the rest of dinner?"

He nodded and stood shakily. He moved carefully out of the dining room and down the hall, where he found the bathroom. He collapsed onto the toilet lid, and sat with his head in his hands, wondering how the hell he could stay there another night. Jamie was great, he knew; she would tell her family to grow up and be nice to him, but that still wouldn't change anything. He just hoped she really didn't care about what they thought—that their opinions wouldn't wear her down.

Menashe returned to the dining room a few minutes later, not exactly composed, but ready to get the night over with. Jamie stood when he entered and turned to her family.

"We're leaving," she said firmly.

"Just one second," Menashe answered, holding up his hand and walking to the table.

He calmly sat back down at his place and reached again for the Ten High bottle. Instead of a shot, though, he poured several ounces into his water glass, which at that point held only a few ice cubes. He took a long drink and then smiled over at Jamie.

"I just want to say," Menashe began, addressing the whole table, "I love Jamie very much."

"Menashe, don't," she pleaded in a low voice.

"I care about her more than anything and there's nothing I wouldn't do for her. You should know that," he said pointedly. "And I think you should also know that we're engaged."

Chapter 12
Austin's Vietnam
September 1988

Menashe watched Austin carefully. He sat rigidly in his chair even though he looked exhausted. He was sweating and Menashe could see sparkling fragments of glass that had found their way into his hair. It reminded Menashe of the freezing fog he used to see back home—shimmering white on gray. Menashe leaned back in his desk chair, rolling a pencil between his fingers absently as he listened to Austin. Even though their session had only been going on for about twenty minutes, his yellow legal pad was crammed with messy notes.

"At first I thought I was doing something good. We all did. They told us the worst fucking things and we believed them all. They said the people there were different—said they didn't even care if they lived or died."

Austin was having trouble catching his breath so Menashe poured him a glass of water.

"We jumped at every noise there was. And even when there wasn't any noise. We learned to shoot like . . . like we needed it." His gaze rested firmly on Menashe. "And that really tore me up." He looked down at his water. "Got anything stronger?"

"No," Menashe answered, reflexively eyeing the drawer that, at any given time, held three bottles of hard liquor.

"Probably just as well," Austin sighed. "After I got back, I got into the habit of drinking myself to sleep. Now, I don't think I could get to sleep at all without it."

"Why? What will happen if you don't?" Menashe leaned forward, watching him with concern.

"It just gets too real. That's the only way I can describe it. I need to take the edge off my thoughts." He frowned hard, as if in pain.

Menashe nodded slowly, taking a few more notes.

"Okay. Can I ask you something very personal?"

Austin nodded but looked at him guardedly. "I guess so."

"Have you ever tried to kill yourself?"

"What? Jesus, why would you ask me that?!"

"Because I need to know your background if I'm going to help you."

"You don't know what you're talking about!" he shouted. "I mean, are you even qualified for any of this?" He waved his arm around the room, glaring at Menashe.

"No," Menashe admitted. His hands began to sweat.

"Then don't try this shit on me!"

"I'm just trying to help. I thought you didn't want another traditional therapist."

Austin leaned back and cracked his knuckles. "Just ask me a fucking question about Vietnam, all right?"

Menashe tapped his pencil. "All right."

"Okay."

They both sat silently for a moment. Menashe could feel sweat beading up on his forehead.

"Do you want to talk about your friends who went to Bi Quan?"

"They weren't my friends."

"Okay." Menashe scribbled something down. "But was that when you realized you didn't like what you were doing in the war?"

Austin nodded but wouldn't make eye contact with him. "Yeah, basically." He pulled at a loose thread on his olive-green t-shirt. His leg jittered against the chair. Menashe sighed. He regretted making Austin retreat like that. Maybe he should have softened the question more, given him hypotheticals. Menashe watched him, wondering how many times he'd thought about it. And how close he'd gotten.

"Can you tell me about how it started?"

"Oh, hell," he sighed, "I guess it started with this guy, Dereck. He was in Bravo Company when they got the mission to Bi Quan. Dereck was the one who turned into Veneman's fucking lapdog," he added, finally looking up.

Menashe nodded, remembering what Austin had told him earlier. Apparently Dereck had served as a company spy, revealing even the smallest of infractions to the vicious officer.

"He was always real tough on the villagers. I think the life out there was really getting to him, and that week one of his buddies was wounded by a mine.

Almost killed. I could see he wanted to get even, but we never really knew who we were fighting against.

"After Bi Quan, most of the guys came back quiet and wouldn't answer any of our questions, but Dereck came back bragging. He told me and a few others how they killed everybody they could find and set the place on fire. I mean, they killed these little kids just standing there with their families." Austin paused. "But I don't think that's even what they saw. I don't know. The goddamn VC, they really got into our heads."

Menashe nodded. He'd known very little about the war until he starting taking on veterans as clients. He'd been twelve years old when that picture of the Buddhist monk came out everywhere. He saw the monk burning himself alive in the middle of some street in Saigon, and that was it for him. From then on, he did his best to avoid the torrent of news reports, footage, and photographs, and he didn't think twice about invoking his right to deferment six years later as an American citizen.

"Please, go on."

Austin's voice began to shake and his eyes started to look vacant, as if he was seeing everything play out in real time.

"So I asked Dereck about the families and the kids. I wanted to know how he explained it to himself. He said the babies could've had grenades hidden on them. He said the mothers might hand them over, pretending there was an emergency or something, and then they'd be blown to hell."

"Did they know what the mission was before they went in?"

"They knew it'd be about revenge. Lieutenant Veneman had asked for permission to brief Bravo the night before, even though he wasn't from the company. This squad leader, a friend of his, had just been killed the day before and Veneman was pretty messed up about it. Man, Dereck was right there with him." Austin shook his head. He turned his cap over and over in his hands.

"It made me so fucking sick the way he'd just spit back all that shit they'd told us in training. Especially Veneman. You should've seen this guy—he was just as scary as anything we saw out in Nam. And he always had his precious cigarettes with him that he'd light up right in the middle of a mission. Yeah, he was a real asshole. Anything you messed up, no matter how small it was, he'd lay into you for it."

"Do you feel guilty about your other missions?" Menashe asked, directing Austin back to his original point.

"I guess. I mean, I know most of us were trying to do the right thing. Most of us were good to the people there. But, I don't know, the platoon that went in could've been mine."

"You're worried you would have done the same thing?"

"Fucking hell, Ash. What I'm saying is I don't know. Those guys weren't all like Dereck. I liked some of them. And I was a guy who'd always follow orders, mostly because I was nineteen years old and didn't know shit about war. Now, if my CO had told me to mow down five hundred people, I like to think I'd have thought about it first, but I just don't know. I didn't know how to feel about anything. I'd see somebody get shot or see their house burn to the ground and I'd just stand there. Numb. I thought that'd go away, but it didn't. Not even after I got home."

"And you can't sleep anymore?" Menashe asked.

Austin shook his head. "I hear things when I try to sleep."

"Like what?"

"Listen," Austin began, rubbing his eyes, "I think I'm done for now."

"Okay."

Menashe put his notes into Austin's file and stored it back in the cabinet. He got up to walk him out, but saw Austin was still sitting there.

"Austin?"

"It's just . . ."

"What?"

"I don't know. It's like my head is never clear."

He nodded and Austin rose from his chair. They walked to the front of the museum and Austin left hesitantly after shaking Menashe's hand. Menashe closed the door and trudged down the hallway into the kitchen.

Chapter 13
No Shrink Necessary
September 1988

Menashe was washing dishes when he heard John's voice at the front of the apartment.

"Menashe? Are you in here?"

"John?" He dried his hands on a paper towel and walked out of the kitchen.

"Hey," John smiled. "Sorry, your door was open."

"It was?" Menashe walked over to the door, checking the latch. "That's weird." He turned back to John. "So what's going on?"

"Sorry to come by like this, I know I'm not scheduled for today or anything, but I wanted to talk to you."

"Sure."

"I was getting a little worried since you haven't been returning my calls lately."

"I know, I'm sorry about that," Menashe shifted uncomfortably. "I've been busy these last couple weeks, taking on Austin, you know."

He nodded.

Seeing John was such a stark contrast to the time he'd now spent with Austin. John was energetic and put-together, with a contented rhythm to his speech and innate self-assurance. Talking about the war had actually helped him. The glass had helped him. Menashe couldn't imagine Austin's eyes were ever so clear and sharp, even in his youth, or that his laugh had been so genuine as his friend's.

Menashe motioned for John to follow him back to the kitchen where they sat at his small, scratched-up table. John tossed his Indians cap on the table and tucked his hair behind his ears.

"So, what's on your mind?"

"Well, for one thing, I was hoping to have you over to our house again soon, maybe for dinner." He paused. "But whenever it's good for you. No rush."

"Thanks, John. That's really nice."

Menashe was expecting this. It had been a while, but that was fine with him. He absently bit at his thumbnail.

"What was the other thing?"

John laughed. "Oh, I'm thinking about quitting my job."

"At the newspaper? I thought you liked it there."

"I do," he replied. "But there's something I want to do more. I have for a while now."

Menashe smiled. "That's very mysterious. Should I guess?"

"No, you're pretty bad at that." John leaned back in his chair. "I want to be a writer."

"But you're an editor," Menashe said. "Isn't that about the same thing?"

"No, I mean I want to write creatively."

"Oh, like how you did in college?"

"Yeah, just not so shitty."

"You know there's not a lot of money in that, right?"

John laughed and gestured toward the museum.

"Remind me what it is you do, again?"

"Hey," Menashe said, standing to get a couple sodas and his cigarettes, "I could be making the big bucks, but I suffer for my art, all right?"

He caught sight of his wall calendar on the side of the fridge and smiled. He wrote himself a quick note to clear out the top pieces. John shook his head.

"Don't we all."

Menashe returned to the table.

"So, what's your plan with writing?"

"Well, I'm really hoping to make a go of it full-time. I know it seems dumb to quit the paper, but I feel like I need the time and I need to clear my head if I'm going to do this right. And I'll tell you something," he said, pointing meaningfully at Menashe. "Being here, sorting out some of these issues, has made me realize I just need to go for it. I'll hate myself if I don't."

"Have you told Abby yet?"

"Only that I've been thinking about it. She seems pretty okay with the idea, though."

"Well, that's great, John. I'm sure it'll work out."

"Thanks."

Menashe lit a cigarette and offered one to John. He shook his head, looking thoughtful.

"Can I ask you something?" he said after a pause.

"Sure."

"You won't get mad?"

"No, I didn't say that."

"Fair enough. Are you seeing anybody?"

"What, like a girlfriend?"

"Not exactly." John smiled and Menashe started to feel queasy because it was a sad, sympathetic smile—the kind he saw frequently after his divorce.

"You mean a shrink."

John nodded. "I just worry about how you're doing sometimes. You can be a tough read."

"I'm doing okay. No shrink necessary."

"Would you tell me if you weren't?"

"I'd be more likely to tell you than anyone else."

"I'm not sure if that's good enough for me," John laughed. "But I guess it has to be."

Menashe smiled, hoping to exhibit some degree of confidence as he spoke. "You really don't have to worry. And I'm starting to get out more," he said brightly. "Chase invited me to join his poker game and it was actually a lot of fun."

"Great. That's a great idea," John replied, but didn't look convinced. "Just know that you can talk to me, okay? You don't have to do everything yourself."

"Okay. Thanks."

"You bet," John answered, standing up. "I'd better get home. My parents will be over soon."

"Are they babysitting?"

"No, just coming over for dinner."

Menashe nodded. "Keep me updated on the writing."

John said he would, smiling as he left, as if the reminder of his new endeavor had lifted his spirits considerably. It seemed like a nice feeling.

Chapter 14
Growing Up
April 1963

Menashe was lying awake, studying the paintings on his bedroom wall. He'd made more of them than he could count at Dr. Kauffman's office, and at some point his mother suggested displaying them in his room. He narrowed his eyes, trying to see them in the dark. The colorful, geometric one—he'd been trying to paint like Klee. And the one with soft blues and whites and golds was his attempt at Turner. He sighed, remembering how hard he'd tried to find something that felt right—something that would take the pressure off his mind.

He lay there until nearly midnight, when the voices of his father and mother drew him out of bed. He'd slipped silently out of his room and sat on the thick carpet, occasionally peeking around the side of the staircase, hidden by the shadows of his upstairs hallway.

"What do you think about Park Shore?" Lewis asked his wife as he scooted closer to their kitchen table and peered at pages of notes he'd made. "With the extra money, we could definitely afford something there."

"But I like where we are."

"We need more space, Charlotte. Not a lot—maybe just an extra bedroom—but something bigger. I mean, what if somebody wanted to visit? We couldn't even fit them here."

The Everetts lived in the middle-class Kensington Market neighborhood of Toronto. Theirs was a red brick, two-story home built in the late 1940s with a fenced-in backyard. It had two bedrooms, two bathrooms, and a small den Lewis had converted into an office. Every room had been wallpapered in a different pattern, and Menashe's room was decorated in blue and gold bears. His parents had picked out that wallpaper when he was a baby and hadn't yet found the time to replace it. He didn't really mind; it was mostly covered by his artwork now, anyway.

"Sure, we could get a new place, but then you'd really have no life," she responded, idly fidgeting with one of her earrings. "I just want to make sure this promotion is what you want."

Menashe held his breath and waited for his father's response.

"I think it's the right move for our family," his dad said after a few moments. "This job will put us in a secure place financially, and it's really what I've been working for all these years. I mean, I know it'll be hard and I'll end up putting in a lot of hours, but it's the next logical step. For all of us, I think."

Charlotte nodded and Menashe sighed from his hiding place. He didn't want a bigger house and he certainly didn't want his dad to be away more.

Just go down there, he thought. *Go tell them you don't want to move. You don't want Dad to take that job.* But he knew he didn't belong in the conversation. Whatever was going to happen, he would hear about it after it was decided—a system he wasn't happy with but one he'd grown accustomed to over the years. It was in this manner that he'd learned in first grade his mother was going back to work, in third grade that his cousin, Jacob, would be spending the summer with them and sharing his room, and in fourth grade that he would be removed from Briarcrest Junior School and placed in the Toronto Hebrew Academy where he wouldn't have to worry about the other kids pushing him, laughing at him, or calling him a kike.

We can't move. By the time his thoughts turned back to his parents, they were already talking about something else.

"I don't think it's a good idea," his mom was saying. "You just said we don't have the room. And what about Menashe?"

"What about him?"

"You know what I'm talking about. Noah's too out of control. He won't even consider getting treatment, no matter what you tell him. And he says anything he wants, even with the kids around."

Menashe frowned. He knew his uncle was a source of tension between his parents, but he never understood it. He had nothing but wonderful memories of Noah.

Lewis laughed. "Charlotte, he's my brother. And he's trying to move his family halfway across the country. If he needs a little help and someplace to stay while he's looking, I'm not going to turn him away." He got up from the old oak table and walked over to the refrigerator. "Do we have any more of that meatloaf?" he asked, opening the door. "Or did we finish it?"

"Lewie, come on," she sighed. "We need to figure this out."

"All right," he said, digging around the refrigerator and pulling out a pan covered in tinfoil. "I think we should let him stay."

"And you don't think it'd be bad for Menashe?"

"Charlotte, you need to give your son a little more credit. He's smart and he can think for himself. What would be bad for him is seeing his parents turn away family who needs us."

Menashe smiled and stood slowly. The house had grown cold overnight, so he quietly went back to his room and retrieved one of the heavy wool blankets off his bed, wrapping it around him. As he tiptoed out the door, he also grabbed the hockey stick his Uncle Noah had given him for his tenth birthday.

"Bottom line is he needs to come out and look for a house while the girls finish out the school year. That's only a couple more months. It'll just be him so he can sleep on the couch. I mean, he's already got to move all the way out here from Lethbridge and start over," Lewis explained. "Can't we do this for him?"

"He could stay with your mother," Charlotte offered weakly, as if she already knew it wasn't possible.

"You know they're not speaking now, Charlotte." Lewis frowned. "See, this is what I'm talking about; he's already being shut out because of this weakness . . . we can't do the same thing."

"I still think it isn't good for Menashe. I'm sorry, but he's so anxious and shy—I'm just worried he's too vulnerable right now."

"There's nothing wrong with Menashe," his dad said in a strained, even tone. "And my brother is not some kind of a maniac, okay? He's got three kids of his own and he's been a great father to them. Charlotte, you haven't given him a chance." Lewis stuck his fork emphatically into the pan of meatloaf, a sharp expression on his face. "Remember the last time he came to visit? Menashe had a great time—wanted to know why Uncle Noah had to live so far away."

"And what about you? A visit is one thing, but if he lives with us you know there will be alcohol in the house. Are you okay with that?"

"Charlotte," Lewis began with calm irritation, "I know it's hard to understand, but you don't have to worry about me. I'm not about to jeopardize nearly an entire decade of work. And you know I wouldn't put Menashe in a situation if I thought it could be dangerous."

"It's not just about danger," Charlotte sighed. "I really don't want Menashe to see Noah drinking all the time. He's impressionable, whether you want to believe it or not, and I'm just not comfortable with that arrangement."

"You're not comfortable with anything that might force Menashe to think for himself," he replied shortly. "And the minute he says something that's on his mind, you turn it into an issue. I mean, one day you say he's got anxiety problems, then you think he's depressed, then it's turned into manic depression or whatever Dr. Kauffman told you. Charlotte, he's not crazy and he's not sick—he's just growing up. And you have to let him."

Menashe sat cross-legged on the soft broadloom carpet that covered the upstairs with his back against the wall, absently turning the hockey stick around in his hands. He glanced down at Red Kelley's autograph, but the letters were now bleary and ran together.

He listened again for his parents' voices, but heard only silence. He didn't know what they had decided—if Noah was going to stay or not. Menashe strained to hear what was going on. They were whispering, and their voices had grown too soft to be carried up the stairs.

Menashe peered back around the wall to see what his parents were doing. He looked down to the kitchen table and was unexpectedly met with his dad's gaze. Lewis had been idly looking up toward his son's room, so Menashe backed into the shadows, out of sight. He got up and decided to go back to bed, spooked by the close call. As he softly shut the door to his bedroom he heard the low murmuring voice of his dad, continuing on as if nothing had happened.

Chapter 15
The High Life
September 1988

"Stand still, will you? Chase is going to be back any second."

Sam stood behind the bar, carefully aiming the soda gun at Paul, who was too drunk and giggly to take his job seriously.

"It'll go that far, easy," Sam was saying. "Okay, open your mouth."

Paul did—with an "ah" as if he was getting his tonsils examined—and Sam launched tonic water across the room. It seemed Sam was right about its potential distance, but his aim sent the arc of tonic water all over Paul's sweatshirt and the table where Menashe and Lenny sat, making them duck away from the spray. Lenny was yelling at Sam while the rest of them collapsed in laughter just as Chase walked in with the spare key he'd forgotten to bring Menashe.

"Sam, you piece of shit," Chase sighed, tossing the key to Menashe. "You're like a two-year-old. Seriously, I can't leave you alone for one minute."

Sam was still laughing as he made his way around the bar and helped the soaking wet and jovial Paul to his feet.

"I'm sorry, Chase," he chuckled. "But I was telling the guys, I saw this once with a bachelorette party in some bar—they shot the seltzer or whatever all the way across the room into these girls' mouths. And Lenny was like, 'No way in hell Chase's soda guns make it that far,' and then Paul was like—"

"I don't want to hear it," Chase cut him off, holding up his hand. "We're going back to the old rules: nobody goes behind the bar but me. Got it?"

"Fine," Sam said pleasantly. "Paul and I just about had this thing figured out, but that's fine. Your bar."

"Just clean it up, will you?" Chase shook his head. "Anyway," he began, turning to Menashe and stifling a smile. "I just tried it out and that key works, too."

"Thanks, Chase," Menashe said, slipping it into his pocket. "I really appreciate it."

"Don't mention it."

No one had noticed up to that point, but Lenny had gotten up and headed to the front of The Velvet Dog, and now had his hand on the door.

"Hey!" Paul called out to him. "Lenny, where are you going?"

"I'm gonna see if there's a poker game going on somewhere," he replied, and walked out the door.

Menashe was speechless, but the other guys thought it was pretty funny.

"Did he really leave?"

"Oh, yeah," Chase laughed. "That's Lenny for you."

"He likes to teach us little lessons sometimes," Paul explained. "I'm sure he does think we're idiots, though."

"Do you think he went home?"

"He'll probably find a poker game," Chase smiled.

"Well," Sam sighed, "now that we've all calmed down, let's deal the cards."

Chapter 16
Austin Scares Murray
October 1988

Austin had been dejectedly wandering the streets since dawn. He had the stubbly beginnings of a silver beard and wore a tattered, gray flannel shirt and frayed jeans. He carried a large bottle of gin, knowing he wouldn't be able to get a drink anywhere that early, and not wanting to chance another Vietnam mind-fuck without one. At nearly eight-thirty, when he feared the violent thoughts clouding his brain would soon be too much for him to handle, he made his way to West Tenth Street, hoping to find Menashe at home.

He walked down the narrow staircase and knocked gently on the door. There was no answer. Austin's heart rate quickened and he knocked again, louder this time. Silence. He set his bottle down on the concrete and began desperately pounding on the door, not really sure what he'd do if Menashe didn't answer. After a few minutes, when it became abundantly clear no one was home, Austin stopped pounding. Only then did he realize his face was wet with tears. He sat down on one of the corrugated iron steps and drank deeply from his bottle. *What the fuck's wrong with me? I shouldn't be here.*

Another hour passed and Austin was still on the step, drinking and thinking he shouldn't be there. But he needed Menashe to come home. Menashe was the only one who knew what was going on inside his head. Austin slumped down with his arms resting on his knees, his head bowed miserably. A few minutes later, he heard feet shuffling behind him and looked up. He turned around to see a kid, maybe twenty years old, with nice clothes and a blue backpack, standing behind him, apparently shaken from finding him there.

"I'm sorry," the kid said automatically. He looked dead tired. "I didn't see you."

Austin got up carefully, using the staircase railing to steady himself. He stared at him with hazy eyes.

"What are you doing here?" he asked gruffly. He climbed up one step toward him, which made the kid take a step backward. He hadn't meant to sound harsh, but it had been days since he had spoken aloud to anyone, and his voice was gravelly.

"I came to see Mr. Everett. I guess he's not home?" he ventured, trying to see around Austin.

"No," Austin responded. "Who are you?"

"My nuh–name's Murray," he stuttered, glancing at the gin bottle on the ground. "I'm sorry, I'll just come back later."

"No, wait," Austin said quickly, in a softer tone. "You don't have to go."

"I should really get to class soon anyway."

Austin frowned, sorry he had scared the kid. "You want to leave him a note?"

Murray looked thoughtful for a moment, and then took off his backpack and opened it up.

"Yeah, that's a good idea," he said, pulling out a piece of paper and a pen. He sat on the top step above Austin and began to write. Austin watched him carefully, running his hand over his eyes in an attempt to get his vision to stop jumping.

"So," he began, "do you—well, I mean, you . . . see Ash?"

Murray stopped writing and looked up. "Yeah." He paused. "Do you?"

"Yeah." Austin took out a cigarette and lit it. He exhaled a large cloud of smoke and then held out the pack to Murray. "Want one?"

"No, thanks."

Austin shrugged and put them back in his pocket. "So does it help?" he asked, looking back up at Murray.

"What?"

"The whole thing," he replied, waving an unsteady hand toward Menashe's apartment. "Does it work for you?"

Murray's face reddened. "I'm not really sure yet. I think it will, though."

"Good. Ash is a good guy."

"He is." Murray turned back to his note.

"But I don't know," Austin continued. "Sometimes I think nothing's ever gonna help, you know? That all of this is just a waste. I mean, I'll feel better for an hour, maybe two, but then it wears off and I'm right back where I started. Right back here."

"Yeah."

"You ever feel like you could get better if just one thing would go right?" Austin laughed. "Like a shot in the arm."

Murray looked up, startled. *I scared him again*, Austin thought, confused.

"I'm sorry," Austin said. "You must think I'm crazy." Murray shook his head politely, indicating that he didn't think so. "I just don't talk to many people, you know?"

Murray nodded. "It's not that easy for me either."

Austin smiled. "Now, I know I've got no right, but can I ask why you come here?"

Murray paused. Austin breathed deeply from his cigarette and took a drink of gin while he waited.

"I think—I think maybe I'm depressed," he said with rising inflection as though he were asking a question. "I don't know. I just feel bad most of the time."

Austin nodded and set his bottle down once again. "I hear that," he muttered.

"What about you?"

Austin sighed and shook his head. "I just fucking hate myself."

Chapter 17
The New Kids
August 1969

Menashe stood outside the empty classroom, reading an art show flyer that was taped to the door. *Showcasing student work every Thursday night at the university gallery, Garrett Hall.* He wasn't looking for activities this early in the year, but it seemed like a good thing to keep in mind, so he got a pen and paper to take down the information.

"Hey, you early, too?" a twangy voice asked, suddenly next to him. Menashe looked up to see another freshman, given away by his orientation t-shirt, with long, light-brown hair and a friendly smile.

"I'm sorry?"

"You're here for Intro to Psychology, right?"

Menashe shook his head slowly. "It's over."

"Really?" He laughed a little as he dug out his crumpled schedule and flattened it against the wall. "Well, damn," he replied, still smiling. "I guess we'll be in it together on Wednesday, then."

Menashe smiled. He wasn't generally comfortable around new people, but there was something disarming about this guy. And he sounded like he'd come right off the set of *Andy Griffith*.

"What're you looking at, there?" He gently pulled the flyer off the door.

"I'm thinking of going to that, sometime," Menashe said, returning his paper and pen to his backpack. "Looks kind of cool."

"You into art?" he asked, still reading the flyer.

"Yeah. I'm going to major in art history."

"That's great." He stuck it back on the door. "I'm John, by the way."

"Menashe."

"Menashe?" He said it again, slowly. "Menashe. Do people ever call you Ash?"

"Not really."

"Okay," John nodded. "Nice to meet you."

"You, too."

"Well," he began, rubbing his hands together and looking around, "You want to get something to eat? I guess I don't have anywhere to be."

Menashe laughed. "You want to double check that?"

John rolled his eyes and smoothed out his schedule again.

"See?" he said, pointing. "Nothing until eastern mythology at three."

"All right, let's go," Menashe replied, checking his watch. "I don't have anything else until two."

They went through the line at the dining hall, piling grilled cheese and fries and sodas and cookies onto their trays, before making their way to an empty table.

"I've been dreaming about the all-you-can-eat college life," John said with a sort of reverence as he surveyed his tray. They set their bags aside and ate silently for a minute or two.

"So," Menashe began, "you're from Cleveland, then?"

John laughed suddenly and started coughing on his food. "That's a good one," he smiled, after he'd regained his breath. "Houston."

"How'd you end up here?"

"I really just needed to get out," he replied, shaking his head. "I've got a big family and they're all in everybody's business. So, I started looking around for schools with good English programs, where I could maybe get a scholarship. I decided to try Ohio."

"Fair enough."

"What about you? Where are you from?"

"Toronto."

"No kidding? A Canuck? That's crazy."

"Why is that crazy? You were like ten times farther away from here in Texas."

"Hey," John laughed, his light eyes shining, "no need to get testy about your illegal status."

"I have a visa," Menashe smiled. "I'm actually applying for citizenship."

"Good. That makes me feel better." John leaned back, looking painfully full. "Why'd you pick John Carroll?"

"I went on a trip here with one of my friends last year. It was a college visit for him, but he didn't end up coming here. I just really connected with it, though. It felt like a good fit."

"And what's with the art history?" he asked shortly.

"What do you mean?"

"What do you want to do with it?"

"I haven't completely figured that out yet," Menashe began, feeling his face heat up. "I know I'd like to work in a gallery. Maybe a museum. Something like that."

"But what's the draw?" John pressed. "I mean, do you paint or sculpt or something? Do you want your stuff in a gallery someday?"

Menashe laughed. "No, it's nothing like that. I did paint a lot, when I was younger, and I would sketch and that kind of thing, but I could never work at that level. Not even close. It was more for fun and sometimes for stress relief. But I think I want to work with art because I know it's important—to see and be around every day. I know I'm not the one to create it, but I want to help people experience it, you know? I'm not sure what that really means yet, or what it will look like, but I just know it's important."

John sat back for a moment, looking thoughtful.

"That's really interesting," he said finally. "And really selfless, when you think about it. I mean, most people out there are trying to sell their own stuff, or get somebody to listen to their idea and pay attention to them, but you're doing the opposite. You want to help people see what's already out there, even if it has nothing to do with you. That's pretty cool, man."

Menashe smiled uncomfortably. "Well, we'll see what happens. I'll probably end up selling insurance or something."

"You never know, I guess."

"So, do you have a plan?"

"For my English degree?" John laughed. "No way. I just know I want to spend the next four years reading. I'll figure the rest out later."

Menashe laughed and shook his head. He really admired how genuine John seemed, and how easily he expressed himself. Part of him also wondered why John was choosing to spend time with him.

John shifted in his seat, wrapping a lock of hair around his finger. Menashe thought he looked a little mischievous, like he was planning something.

"So, listen," he said finally, leaning forward on the table. "I was thinking about doing this thing tonight in town, but I wouldn't want to do it by myself."

Menashe made a face. "Oh, hell, what is it?"

"Sort of a karaoke, open mic night kind of deal. It should be really low-key, though."

It seemed that, even though they'd known each other only an hour, John knew he'd have to soften the impact of such an idea.

"I don't know," Menashe said doubtfully. "It's the first day; I really wasn't going to go out."

"When's your first class tomorrow?"

"Eleven."

"You didn't even have to check your schedule," he teased. "You've got the whole thing memorized, don't you?"

"What's your point?"

"My point is, you can sleep in tomorrow, and I promise I won't make you go on stage. I just feel like getting out a little bit—getting to know this place."

"Don't you have a roommate you can sucker into this?"

"I'll pick you up," John offered sweetly. "I've got a brand-new Chrysler Newport." He grinned. "The girls will love it."

Menashe laughed. He supposed this was going to be the nature of their relationship. And, for some reason, he was okay with that.

"All right," he agreed. "But only because of the Newport."

Chapter 18
Ohio Savings, Student Loan Dept.
October 1988

Menashe arrived early for work that day. He wasn't able to sleep, so had spent the night finishing paperwork and listening to the muffled music that blared down from The Velvet Dog. Sometimes he just let the rhythm of the club beat a steady pulse into his brain.

"Rough night?" Larry asked with a smile as he swiveled around in his cubicle to face Menashe.

"My neighbors had a party," he replied wearily.

"And you didn't go?" Larry chuckled. "Well, the next time they bother you, let me know and I'll help you give them a scare." He smiled proudly. "My oldest son's a cop, you know, and I'm sure he'd help out."

He laughed again and even managed to get a weak chuckle out of Menashe. He then swiveled back around, returning to his work. Larry was a lanky black man of about sixty-five and had worked at Ohio Savings for nearly three decades. He always had a kind word and funny remark for everyone, and his sense of humor was largely how Menashe got through the day.

Menashe dragged his feet over to his cubicle and summoned the motivation to finish his work from Friday. He mechanically sorted through the Master Promissory Notes, the Notices of Loan Guarantee, and the Evidences of Disbursement, letting his mind drift. The interest rates were changing that day, which would keep everyone busy with complaints from customers who were expecting to get last year's lower rate. Menashe didn't talk to many customers, though. He sorted through forms, sometimes ten or fifteen years old, and prepared stacks of paperwork to be sent to the bank's storage archives and to the guarantors.

By the time his lunch hour came, Menashe had just finished his work from Friday. He collected the paper bag that held his ham and cheese sandwich and walked heavily into the break room to find an unoccupied table. Two women from his department were talking loudly over their fast food meals. He and Larry were the only two men in the department who were not management.

Menashe suddenly felt incredibly conspicuous. It was a sense he occasionally had—that people could tell what he was thinking or at least know more about him than he wanted to share. More groups of people began filing in. No one seemed to notice him, but the feeling intensified. He shivered. Turning away from the tables, Menashe took his sandwich and walked out of the bank, intending to spend his lunch hour at home.

He was about to walk in the front door when a note taped to the front of it that had been folded many times caught his eye. He pulled it off and carefully removed the tape. Written on it were the words, "Mr. Everett." He knew at once who had written the note; only one of his clients still addressed him as Mr. Everett. He unfolded the paper and read it through.

> Mr. Everett: I'm really sorry to ask you this, and it's okay if you can't do it, but I was wondering if I could move my appointment to tonight at 8:00 instead of tomorrow. I'm sorry, but I was up all last night thinking about quitting school, and I really don't know what to do. If you could call me at the dorms sometime that would be great. Thanks a lot. Murray.

Menashe felt his eyes get hazy and he frowned intensely, waiting for the stinging to subside. Murray was having a hard time and it wasn't getting any easier. He called him back and left a message, assuring him eight that night would be fine.

Menashe went back to work, but for the rest of the day his thoughts drifted away from him. He'd often felt discouraged working with clients like Austin, whose problems were so severe and engulfing. But if Austin made little progress during his sessions, there could be a million reasons why. With Murray, Menashe questioned his own abilities constantly. If he couldn't help a smart, eager kid in the prime of his life, maybe he just wasn't good enough.

Chapter 19
Strong and Silent
May 1970

"So tell me about this scholarship," Noah said, releasing a heap of salad from the tongs onto his plate. Menashe sat across from his uncle at their dining room table, keeping fairly quiet. He glanced at his father. "Yeah, your dad was telling me about it. You wrote a paper that got you early admission to the art program and a semester of free tuition?"

"It wasn't a big thing. They give those out to lots of people."

"Yeah, yeah," Noah rolled his eyes. "Lew said they give them out to ten people a year. It's a big deal, Menashe. I'm really proud of you."

"Thanks." Menashe moved awkwardly into a new position, pushing lasagna around on his plate.

"Oh, I meant to ask you—how's the new location working out, Noah?" Charlotte piped up, saving him.

"It's all right," Noah replied. "Now I'm incredibly busy, which is great, but I'm still getting used to it. Man, though, I'm really glad we left Lethbridge when we did; some of my buddies back home have been out of work for a long time. And I don't think it's getting any better." She nodded. "That reminds me," he said, standing up and walking toward Lewis' office, "I've got to call Jackson— tell him I'll be out tomorrow." Noah winked at his brother and left the room.

"What's tomorrow?" Menashe asked his dad, getting up and clearing his plate.

"Oh, just a little family thing," he replied. "We thought it'd be nice since you just finished your first year and Rebecca's going into high school, you know, to have a kind of celebration. Maybe check out the Glendon Gallery."

"Thanks, that's really nice." Menashe moved from the sink and pointed toward the front hall. "I'm just going to grab my stuff."

Lewis followed him, touching his arm gently as they reached his bags. "Are you okay?"

"Yeah, just a little tired."

"I believe it. I'm glad you're back."

"Me, too."

"And how's John?"

"Oh, I don't really know," Menashe sighed, hoisting his heavy backpack onto his shoulders. "I mean, I kept up with him all through basic training, but I haven't heard from him since he got sent over. I hope he's okay."

Lewis nodded, picking up his son's duffel. "I'm sure he is. He's a smart kid. He'll take care of himself."

Menashe smiled but felt sick inside. In his mind, all he saw was a gruesome war that never seemed to end.

"It'll be over soon," Lewis reassured him, as if he understood the thoughts plaguing his son's mind. "I know it."

"I hope so."

His dad nodded. "Should we take these up to your room?" he asked after a moment.

"Thanks," Menashe replied, walking with him to the stairs. "How's work?"

"Great. Everything's great."

As they all sat in the living room and relaxed over coffee and *The Bob Newhart Show*, Noah carried on as he always did, downing several beers and telling great stories about the past. But Lewis was strangely reserved. He didn't interrupt Noah's stories to say he was telling them wrong, and he didn't ask Menashe much at all about his classes. But what struck Menashe more was that rather than sitting with his wife on the loveseat as they had every evening since Menashe was young, his father sat alone in an overstuffed recliner, gazing in the direction of the television.

"Ma," he whispered, having followed her into the kitchen to get more coffee. "What's going on with Dad?"

"What do you mean?"

"He's been so quiet, it's just weird. Is it the job? Is it not going well?"

His mother smiled dismissively. "You need to stop worrying about everything. He's doing fine, the hours just take a lot out of him."

"But he's different," Menashe protested. "He doesn't seem happy."

"I know it's hard for you to understand. Your dad's job does come with a lot of stress, and that's not easy. But he loves what he does—making all those important decisions, being a leader. He is strong, Menashe," she said, looking into his eyes. "You don't have to worry about him."

From the living room they heard Noah's booming laugh and a subdued chuckle from Lewis at something on the television. Menashe felt a little better as they rejoined the brothers, but a bad feeling still nagged at him.

Part of him wished his dad would quit—just find something else. Something better. He knew his father well, and the long hours weren't the only thing getting to him. It was like he'd gone too far into this new life and he couldn't take it back. And sometimes Menashe wondered if his father thought he owed the family something he wasn't able to give them. He saw the strongest man he knew falling, and it scared him.

Chapter 20
I'm Not Charlie
October 1988

"I don't know what the problem is," Austin muttered, slamming his glass down in frustration. "It's just not fucking working, all right?"

"Well, it really hasn't been that long—"

"No, it's been too long," he snapped. "I can't keep doing this. I just want one night, okay? One fucking night of peace." He glared at Menashe, his leg jittering as he spoke.

"So, what, you want to quit?" Menashe asked, getting irritated himself.

"I'm telling you, I still can't sleep, still can't talk to anybody, can't do anything without a fucking drink." He shook his head. "I'm forty years old and I still wake up in the street now and then. The only difference is now I do everything with cuts all over me and glass in my clothes. So, yeah, I guess I want to quit."

Menashe closed his eyes and took a long breath before answering.

"Austin," he began, "I want to help you, but you have to give this some time. It's not a quick fix. I've got an idea you should think about, though."

"I'm not going to that vet group. John's already tried that so you can just save it, all right?"

"No, I'm talking about here. You need to let yourself go. I think you've been holding back—that you're not completely comfortable yet. I want you to know that anything you do or say here . . . it's safe. Don't be afraid to go crazy in those rooms."

"Ash, that's what I've been doing. Nothing's changed."

"No, you haven't. Listen to me: during these sessions, you've got to lose yourself. That's what it takes to get back to those places—to feel that pain you've blocked out. You need to feel it or you're not going to get better."

"You gonna tell me how to do that?"

Menashe shook his head. "I wish I could."

"Great." Austin leaned back. "You know what?" he smirked. "You're a goddamn phony, man. You just make this shit up as you go along, don't you?"

Menashe felt his face getting hot. "I never said I was a professional."

"Yeah, I know."

Menashe watched him for a moment before he spoke. "So, will you try it?"

"Going crazy?"

"Yeah."

Austin sighed. "Why the hell not? Sounds pretty easy."

He nodded and stood. Austin followed suit and they both walked down the hall to the first room of the museum.

"All four?" Menashe asked, opening the door.

Austin nodded.

"You know where I am if you need me."

"Thanks," he replied wearily, trudging into the room.

Menashe closed the door and walked back to his office. He stood in the doorway for a moment, surveying the room thoughtfully before moving to his desk. He pushed some paperwork aside and turned on the small television set. Thursday night. *L.A. Law.* He poured himself a mugful of whiskey and listened to the familiar sounds of breaking glass competing with network television. It made him feel good—like something productive was going on even though he was no longer a part of it.

Nearly an hour passed before he thought of Austin again. His show was over and he still heard the sounds of destruction coming from the museum. That was fine. Sometimes Austin took over an hour with four rooms. But something was different.

Menashe got up from behind his desk, frowning. He was halfway to the door before he realized what was wrong: the ragged breathing, the pounding bat, the fury—they were too close. They were coming down the hall.

He stood there, paralyzed by fascination and terror as Austin threw open the office door and charged inside. His eyes were cold.

"Austin!" Menashe cried. "What—"

But Austin didn't hesitate. He swung the bat and hit Menashe hard, knocking him to the floor. Menashe yelled in shock and held his stomach. The searing pain took his breath away and caused tears to instantly spring from his eyes.

"Jesus, Au—Austin!" he stammered. "What are you doing?"

Austin tossed the bat aside and threw himself on top of Menashe, pinning him to the floor.

"You," he growled.

"No," Menashe gasped. "Stop! Pl—"

Austin punched him before he could finish. His vision jerked and blood spurted from his lip.

"Austin! Stop!" he shouted, trying to break Austin's trance. "Listen! It's not real."

Austin's eyes narrowed as sweat rolled down his face.

"It's not real!" Menashe repeated. "Please—you're seeing things."

"No!" Austin shouted. "Fucking liar!"

He punched Menashe again and again, his fury seeming to grow with each hit.

Menashe yelled in pain, his heart pounding from shock as he tried to breathe, but Austin was gone. He ignored Menashe's cries, letting the blood coat his fists as he hit him relentlessly.

"Fucking Charlie!" he roared. "You did this! You killed him, you fucking pussy!" He grabbed Menashe's throat. "You set the fucking jungle on fire!"

Menashe tried to shake his head. He could no longer see straight. There was blood in his eyes and blood everywhere.

"It's Menashe," he choked desperately. "I wasn't there. I'm not Charlie."

He started coughing violently. Austin shook his head. He shook his head and brought his fist up again.

"I'm not Charlie!" Menashe shouted. He felt an explosion under his eye and groaned miserably. "Please, it's Ash."

Austin raised his fist to hit him again but looked like he was close to breaking down. Menashe watched him warily, breathing hard. He didn't say anything else and didn't try to struggle free. A siren wailed faintly a few blocks over.

Austin lifted his head and let his hand relax. He remained silent but also loosened his grip on Menashe, finally letting go.

"Ash?"

Everything was quiet. The room seemed to darken and Menashe wondered if he was going to pass out. Austin sat there, staring at him. Just staring, emotionless.

Austin looked around the room. He looked down at Menashe, smeared with blood and breathing raggedly. He got off of him and sat heavily on the floor. He looked down at his shaking hands. He didn't move, but that strange, numb look in his eyes was fading.

With great effort, Menashe sat up. He leaned his back against the wall and coughed, splattering several drops of blood onto his shirt. He felt half-dead and didn't know if anything had been broken. He touched his stomach, wincing.

Austin got up and stood over him, holding out his hand. Menashe took it cautiously and Austin bent down, gripping him strongly around his back and pulling him to his feet. He helped Menashe into his chair and then just stood, watching him curiously.

"Ash," he murmured again, as if they were meeting for the first time.

Chapter 21
Aftermath
October 1988

It was ten to nine that Sunday night. Menashe still hadn't made his mind up about the poker game. His hands shook as he got dressed; it was impossible to pull his shirt on without touching the bruises. He'd decided against going to the doctor once he was fairly convinced nothing was broken. It would just take time.

He went to the bathroom to check the mirror. At least his hair covered up one of the worst-looking injuries. Menashe gingerly smoothed back the hair above his left temple, exposing some of the scabbing purple and black wound. He looked at the rest of his face. He thought about each hit and its resulting mark.

You.

Menashe's chest tightened and he took a few steps back, trying to force himself to draw in slow, calculated breaths. But it was too much. He had to keep up with his pounding heart. He heard a sound—a startling crash. *No.* It was too loud to have been outside, so he slammed the bathroom door and locked it, leaning his back against it, shaking. *He's here.* Menashe saw his reflection in the mirror again. He wanted to leave, to get away from that terrible image of himself. But it wasn't going away. He slid to the floor and cried roughly, his hands leaving sweaty imprints on the concrete.

After a few minutes he was able to catch his breath. Then he heard a voice. It sounded like Sam's; he was talking and laughing outside the nightclub. Menashe checked his watch. 9:12. He managed to stand, wincing at the effort, and washed his face in the sink without looking up at the mirror. He walked to the kitchen where his half-empty glass of whiskey remained on the counter and downed it rapidly. He saw the toppled stack of plastic dishes on the floor. Menashe let out a deep breath and made his way out of the apartment.

They were all inside, at the usual table, when Menashe walked in.

"How can you be late?" Sam cried as the door closed. "You live ten feet away."

Everybody laughed, but as Menashe came closer they stopped laughing. Chase stood up slowly.

"What the hell happened to you?" he murmured, walking over to him. Paul and Sam stood as well and came closer. Only Lenny remained at the table, watching.

"Jesus, Ash," Paul breathed. "Are you okay? Have you seen a doctor?"

Menashe shook his head. "It's fine, guys. Thanks. I just, I fell the other day. Down those steps out there."

"You see!" Sam yelled, smacking Chase in the arm. "Your place is a fucking deathtrap!"

"No, no," Menashe stopped him. "I was carrying a lot of shit and wasn't watching. My fault."

"Well, you still need to see a doctor," Chase said, frowning. "I'll pay for it, absolutely."

"Wait, you got that bruise falling down the stairs?" Paul interrupted, peering at Menashe's throat.

"He said he was carrying shit," Sam explained. "He probably landed on it after he tripped, you know—"

"Man, look at this one," Chase broke in again, gently pushing back Menashe's hair on his forehead and grimacing. "That's just awful. You might have gotten a concussion."

Sam was muttering to himself while he attempted to reenact the scene. He crumpled in slow motion, pretending his arms were full.

"That's about how it went, right, Ash?" he asked from the floor.

Menashe shrugged and was about to say that was pretty much it when Lenny finally rose from his chair.

"Fellas," he called gruffly. "Time to back off and give Ash some space. And a drink. Let's deal the cards, Chase."

Menashe smiled gratefully at Lenny and took his seat. Chase brought him a whiskey and began to pass around the snacks. As he dealt the cards, Sam started telling them the details of another lurid date he'd gone on that weekend. Menashe looked around the table and felt his pulse even out. At first he worried that Paul would press him for more details about his flimsy excuse, but he didn't. Nobody said another word about it.

Sam and Paul were full of their usual extroversion that night. Paul told them of his daughter's latest triumphs over anxiety, which reminded Sam of a story about his last girlfriend who had a number of bizarre phobias. Chase confided in them that his sister was sick, and it had been preoccupying his thoughts for a few days. Lenny didn't give up much about himself, but he put his hand on Chase's shoulder as he spoke and gave Paul a thumbs-up when he talked about Riley. He mostly watched Sam with disdain. That night Menashe just listened. It was all he needed.

Everyone seemed tired, so it was only eleven when the guys started to leave. Menashe didn't mind; although the evening had raised his spirits considerably, he looked forward to taking a handful of ibuprofen and going to bed.

He stood up and said his good-nights to Sam and Paul, but Lenny remained, watching him thoughtfully from the table.

"You going home?" he asked as Menashe walked back from the door.

"Chase'll be back in a second," he replied, indicating the back room. "I was going to wait to say good night."

Lenny nodded. "Come sit, then."

Menashe did, hesitantly.

Lenny felt around his back jeans pocket until he came up with a pack of cigarettes. He drew a lighter from his gray canvas jacket.

"Now, I've been around, Ash," he began, pulling out a cigarette and lighting it. "I can see that whatever happened to you, it was no accident." He paused. "Cigarette?"

"Yeah. Thanks." Menashe took it anxiously, allowing Lenny to light it.

"I've seen this kind of thing before," he continued in his low, husky voice, the cigarette dancing in his mouth as he spoke. "Maybe you owe somebody money, or a deal went bad, or maybe you just crossed the wrong guy. I don't want to know." He looked up with a faint smile. "But you're a real fighter. I mean, you come to the game like usual and you hold your head up. I wanted to tell you, that takes something."

Chase walked back in the room before Menashe could say anything, but he didn't think he could have found the words anyway. He rose to his feet and shook Lenny's hand warmly before the three of them left The Velvet Dog. That night he felt a tremendous lightness and contentment that was so familiar, but it took him hours to place the feeling: it was as if he'd spent the evening with his father.

Chapter 22
The Family Business
February 1974

"No," Noah said, tilting his chair back at the Everetts' kitchen table. "I can't do it. I really—I just can't do it."

"You're just scared," Lewis reasoned. "You can do it. You have been doing it. Noah, listen to me, you're not thinking straight."

Noah, who had been shaking his head the entire time Lewis was speaking, got up and filled a glass of water from the kitchen sink.

"It's too much. I mean, just being home now I can see how much better May is with the kids. It's like—it's like I don't really know them. I don't know . . . I'm just not cut out for this."

"But you'd really leave your family? Leave them with nothing? That doesn't make any sense. I know you're crazy about them."

Noah returned to the table and sat down, massaging the muscles in his shoulder. Lewis saw he was having trouble looking him in the eye.

"Lew, I've been out of work for six months. I never thought this would happen here, but I've got to face it. You're right, I'm crazy about my family, but I'm not doing them any good now."

"How can you say that? You think the only good you've done them was making money?"

"No, not exactly. But it's like all this responsibility with the kids and everything is hitting me now and, I know it's terrible to say, but it was better when I was working a lot, you know? I knew what to do when we only had a little time together, but now it's all the time. Elena and Rebecca are practically adults now and Danny's almost twelve. I have no idea how to talk to them." Noah ran his hands over his eyes and sighed deeply.

"That's so selfish," Lewis murmured. "Things start to get hard and you take off—is that how it goes?"

"Jesus, Lew, I'm thinking of them, too. They'd be better off, believe me."

"Oh, cut the bullshit, man. Stop pretending you're looking out for your family when you know this would tear them apart. You don't know what you're talking about, all right?" Lewis slammed his hand down on the table. "Look, when I took that promotion at the hotel I was gone a lot. Long hours, travel, all of it. And I never thought it affected Menashe, but it did."

"What are you talking about? You're still so close."

"Yeah, but it hurt him. He started having more trouble at school and with the other kids. He wouldn't talk to anybody and turned into a nervous wreck if anybody talked to him. And the only time he'd actually want to leave the house was for the art museum or a hockey game. I know Menashe was always sort of an anxious kid and Charlotte constantly worried about him, but it never seemed to be a real issue until then. Until I stopped being there." Lewis looked down. "If you leave, your kids will grow up differently. The responsibility you have to them—the responsibility you think you can't handle—is so much more than paying the bills. I swear to God it wouldn't matter to them if you were out of work for the rest of your life." He sighed and leaned back in his chair. "Listen, I made a mistake and I hate that I couldn't see it then. I thought I was helping the family more by affording the bigger house and the better schools, but I wasn't. I just don't want you doing the same thing."

Noah stayed quiet and avoided his brother's eyes. Lewis could see his hands fidgeting under the table.

"Are you all right?" he asked, his tone softening. "I mean, is this all that's bothering you?"

"What, this isn't enough for you?" Noah laughed weakly.

"You just don't seem well."

"I haven't been sleeping much."

"I bet. How much have you said to May about all this?"

"I haven't said anything."

This time it was Lewis who got up and filled a glass of water from the tap. He drank it down as he stood there, trying to think of a better way to tell his little brother how much of a jackass he was being. But, as he thought back over what Noah had told him, he knew there wasn't anything malicious in his intent; he was just scared. He was scared and overwhelmed because for the first time in his life, he had to be a full-time father.

"Are you okay?" Noah asked, eyeing his distracted brother nervously. "You're going to tell me I'm being an idiot, aren't you?"

"No, I was just thinking about Menashe again."

"Yeah?"

Lewis nodded. "It's hard, not having him here. Especially now that he'll be a father soon."

"I'm sure they'll visit a lot."

"Oh, they will," he agreed. "It's just such a great time, right when you start a family. I wish I could be there with him."

"Yeah. He's a good kid," Noah murmured. "You've done a real good job with him."

Lewis smiled and walked back to his chair at the kitchen table.

"Noah, none of this is supposed to be easy," he began. "But I'm sure you'll find work soon, and you have to understand that now is the time when your family needs you the most." Noah nodded but looked unconvinced. "Just promise me you'll give it some time before you do anything crazy."

"I really wouldn't be happy about leaving. I'm just not sure yet."

"I know. Just wait and see if things settle down a bit, okay?"

Noah nodded, still fidgeting. Lewis watched him carefully.

"Can I ask you something?"

"What?"

"Have you given any more thought to what I said the other day?"

"Ugh," Noah groaned. "The program? Where you sponsor me, or something? I wish you would let that go."

Lewis shook his head. "I can't," he replied simply. "We're family and this is a serious thing."

"It's not a serious thing," Noah said evenly. "I can handle myself."

"Listen, it wasn't easy for me either. Nineteen years sober and it's still not easy. Every day is a challenge, but I want to help you. I really think you should try these meetings."

"It's really not like that, Lew. I told you; it's under control."

"I don't think so."

"Well, I really don't care what you think," he shot back angrily. "This time it's not your call, big brother. I'm fine."

Lewis's ears reddened. "You know who always said he was fine?" he snapped. "Dad. Remember? You really want to go down that road?"

"Hey, I don't want to go down any road," Noah retorted, holding up his hands, "but you're not letting this go. I'm not Dad and I'm not doing anything wrong. Will you just lay off? Please?"

"Fine." Lewis breathed in deeply. "Another time."

Noah rolled his eyes. "Fine."

Lewis got up and set his glass in the sink. His brother looked around the room restlessly.

"It's gotten late."

"You want to call it a night?"

"No," he sighed. "Not really. Want to go for a drive or something? I'm just not ready to go home yet."

"Yeah," Lewis said, looking at his watch. "Can we take your car? Charlotte took ours to her sister's."

"That's fine," Noah replied, getting up. "Just let me hit the head first."

Menashe was awoken early Thursday morning by the sound of the telephone ringing. The clock read 2:09 in bright-red numbers and he glanced at it as he reached over to grab the phone before it woke Jamie. She was six months pregnant and it was frequently hard for her to get to sleep. But she had slept through the ringing and Menashe answered the phone with a hushed "Hello?" It was his mother. He could barely understand her, but she was saying something about a phone call. Someone had just called her. A doctor. Or a policeman. Maybe a lawyer. It didn't matter, though, because he heard nothing past the next sentence she sobbed hysterically into the receiver.

"Menashe, it's your dad . . . there was ice on the road and they, he—I just don't know what to do," she cried.

Her voice went on but all Menashe could hear was his own wheezy breath and the metallic clank of their old radiator. He knew what was happening. He knew his father was dead. He didn't know what to do either, so he told his mom he'd be on the next flight and let Jamie sleep while he paced the kitchen in his flannel pajama pants and John Carroll sweatshirt, a glass of whiskey in his sweaty hand.

Chapter 23
Papers and Numbers
October 1988

Menashe's mother sent him most of the modest inheritance she collected upon the death of his father. He and Jamie had saved as much as they could, intending to use it for Wesley's college tuition. After the divorce, Menashe used it to begin work on the glass museum. It was his father's money that enabled him to buy many of the pieces for his museum. They otherwise would have been far too expensive for him to afford. In his precious free time, Menashe would spend hours at auctions and galleries acquiring pieces for his collection. He bargained with dealers, gallery owners, and private collectors like Dr. Johnston in the hopes of buying fine works for well under their appraised values. He often bought from professors at the local art institutes. He'd settled on a system in the beginning, when he realized how expensive the museum could get: each room would hold one premium work—what Menashe called a "top piece"— that needed to be of high quality and respected within the art world. The rest he filled in with all kinds of discount glass pieces. For Menashe, he needed the top piece to show that the suffering of his tormented clients was worth something, but his bottom line was to provide them with an outlet he could sustain.

It was eleven-fifteen on Sunday night and Menashe was restless. He couldn't stop thinking about Austin. There was more he could be doing—more he should be doing.

He threw a few empty bottles into the trash can, grabbed his thin green jacket, and left the apartment. He drove the short distance to Case Western's campus and parked outside the library. He sat in his pickup for a few minutes, waiting until he didn't see any students, before walking up to the door. A young guy at the front desk wanted to see his faculty ID.

"Here," Menashe said, handing him his driver's license. "I just want to look at a few books. I won't be very long."

He nodded, clearly trying not to look at the cuts and bruises on Menashe's face. "You won't be able to check anything out."

"That's fine. I'll make copies if I have to."

He felt around in his jeans pocket as he spoke, and was surprised to find three quarters and a dime. He really could make copies.

He walked over to the card catalog, feeling conspicuous. His injuries were finally beginning to fade, but he would have felt out of place even without them. Anyone there would most likely mistake him for a professor, just as the kid at the front desk had, but still he felt like a fraud. He didn't belong anymore. College had been his peak, and it was hard to face the truth of what his life had become since—a descent beginning, it seemed, only moments after walking out of that safe and familiar place to which he'd dedicated himself for five years. Had he known, he never would have left.

A few girls were talking excitedly at a nearby table, but Menashe didn't look at them. He scanned the catalog's subject headings, pulled opened a drawer and ran his fingers over the cards until he found what he wanted. *Post-Traumatic Stress Disorder.* He scribbled a few numbers down then went to the second floor. After about ten minutes of searching, Menashe emerged from the shelves with eight books and made his way to Independent Study. He found an empty table and dropped his heavy stack of books loudly, causing the kid a couple tables in front of him to jump.

"Sorry," Menashe whispered, rearranging the stack to keep it from toppling.

"That's okay," he said without turning around.

With a sigh, Menashe opened the first book and skimmed through it. After about ten minutes, he could already tell it wasn't going to help Austin. He tossed it aside (causing the kid to jump once again, and Menashe to apologize once again), and picked up the next one. He read for the next hour, but found nothing useful. He read about the same symptoms over and over—symptoms that described Austin perfectly—but he still had no direction for his treatment. He read about combat fatigue and shell shock. He knew the factors that lead to continued symptoms of PTSD years after the initial trauma. He saw Austin in countless case studies. He understood that, more than anything, soldiers need to talk and be listened to, but Menashe felt it was too late for that. He wanted to do more. He needed Austin to get better, fearing that if nothing changed he would only get worse. And, more selfishly, Menashe wanted to avoid becoming the target of another violent episode.

But with every article and narrative he read, he became more afraid for Austin. The odds had been stacked against him—his age, his background, his family history—setting him up to be fucked over by Vietnam.

At ten till one, the library lights went off, then back on. Menashe looked at his watch. He didn't have the answers he wanted but would have to leave. He took the two books he found potentially helpful to the Xerox machine and made all the copies he could afford. He walked back down the stairs and looked over at the front desk guy on his way out the door. The guy smiled as if to say, "I thought you weren't going to be long."

Menashe got into his truck but sat for a moment before turning on the engine. His stomach hurt and he could feel the beginnings of tears tickling his eyes. Looking down at the stack of papers lying on the seat next to him, he felt an intense urge to tear them up. He was absolutely nowhere.

Chapter 24
Ends and Means
January 1983

Menashe sat in his office, watching *Magnum, P.I.* on his tiny television set when a strong knock on his front door caused him to jump. It was Tuesday night and no one was scheduled to come in. He frowned and switched off the set, walking cautiously to the door with the names of potential visitors running through his head. Since it was dark and his apartment had no outdoor lighting, he couldn't tell who it was by looking out the peep hole, so he called out.

"Who is it?"

"A friend of a friend," the person called back.

"Who?"

"Can you just open the door? It's cold."

Something strange was going on, but curiosity got the better of him and he opened the door anyway.

"Can I help you?" Menashe asked the stranger leaning against his iron railing smoking a cigarette.

"You bet," he replied with a smile.

The guy flicked away his cigarette and walked up to the doorway. He was young and good-looking, with lustrous black hair, clear, dark skin, and thick eyelashes. He wore what looked to Menashe like very expensive clothes: pristine brown leather shoes, dark jeans, and a tan sweater over a white Oxford shirt. He shoved his hands into the pockets of his gray wool coat.

"Can I come in?"

"Who are you?"

Instead of responding, he pulled one of Menashe's cards out of his pocket and handed it to him. Someone had handwritten "Velvet Dog" on the back.

"This is you, right?"

"Who gave this to you?" Menashe asked sharply.

"Listen, it's really cold. Will you let me in?"

Menashe led the stranger down the hall to his office, unsure of what to expect from him. With his youthful cockiness and obvious wealth he didn't fit the general description of a potential client. But he had a card. And Menashe was pretty careful about that.

"So, what can I help you with?" he asked, sitting down behind his desk.

"I want an appointment," he replied plainly. "To use the museum."

"What?"

"This is where you come to smash all the expensive glass, right?"

Menashe was speechless. In a wave of panic he saw everything he'd worked for over the past five years disappear. The business he tried so hard to keep secret had been compromised. This kid had a card. He knew someone.

"Who the fuck are you?" he demanded.

"Roger Maldonado," he said. Menashe's anger did not appear to faze him at all. "I really like your place," he said, taking off his coat and looking around.

"Listen, Roger," Menashe said calmly, resisting the impulse to jump over his desk and throttle the rich bastard, "I need to know who gave you that card."

"Sure," he agreed. "I understand. In fact, it's a pretty interesting story. A couple days ago I was having a drink with a friend of mine. Well, actually, I wouldn't really call him a friend—I see him every couple months or so out at the bars. Anyway, we're talking about what we've been up to and he spills that he's been in this kind of alternative therapy with a guy who lets you break glass. Real nice shit, too, he said."

Roger paused. "You should know, though, this guy, he was pretty trashed and didn't really know what he was saying. I mean, he did tell me this glass business was all top secret and everything, but I know he wouldn't have given you up if he'd been sober."

"And your friend is . . . ?"

"Man, I have no idea. Probably lying in an alley somewhere at the rate he was going."

"His name, Roger."

"Liam Jones."

"Son of a bitch!" Menashe exclaimed, slamming his fist down on the desk. "I knew it! I knew it must've been that asshole."

Roger laughed and leaned back in his chair. "You're not going to have him killed or anything, are you? I'd feel kind of bad."

"Well, he's definitely not coming back here."

"Right," he nodded solemnly. "So you've got a spot open, then."

It was Menashe's turn to laugh. He couldn't believe this guy thought he could just come in and Menashe would hand over the museum to him.

"This isn't for you," he said. "Believe me."

"It might be."

"Yeah? Tell me, then; why would you need this?"

"Well, I wouldn't say I *need* it."

"Most people don't go looking for therapy unless they need it."

"Oh, I don't want the therapy," Roger explained. "I just want the glass part. I want to wear the hockey gear and get the bat and smash your shit in there."

I'm going to fucking kill Liam Jones.

"Because it sounds like fun?"

"Yeah. I know it'll be fun."

"Okay, get out," Menashe said flatly, shaking his head and getting up from behind his desk. "There's no way you're getting anywhere near the glass, all right? Just get out."

Roger didn't move and Menashe wasn't surprised. He knew what this guy was about—the self-assured type who'd been handed everything his whole life and whose enormous sense of entitlement extended to the property of others. He would never let a kid like Roger destroy his museum.

"I'll pay you triple what these other guys do," he said, looking Menashe directly in the eye. "I'll commit to a year and pay in advance."

"Forget it."

"I've got friends and they'll pay, too. I know they will. Come on, Menashe, this must get expensive."

Never before had Menashe so intensely hated the sound of his own name.

"How old are you?"

"Twenty-three."

"Why wouldn't you and your rich asshole friends rather blow your money on drugs and booze? Or college?"

"Because," Roger smiled, "this is different. This is something you can't get anywhere else. I want to try it."

"There's no way you're getting in."

"You sure about that?" he asked, taking the business card off the desk where Menashe had tossed it. He began writing on the back of it.

"Positive."

"Okay." Roger handed him the card. "That's my number if you change your mind."

Menashe tore up the card and threw the pieces into the trash. He stood up. "Get out."

Roger rose to his feet, smiled, and left.

It was nearly three a.m. and Menashe was under his desk on his hands and knees, trying to piece together the torn-up business card. He thought it must surely have been the low point of his career. *Ends and means, right? This is what I've worked for.* He'd been through it over and over, and even though he hated giving Roger what he wanted, he knew he couldn't let the opportunity slip away.

He sighed and taped the card back together. He dreaded the call he was about to make, especially since his words had exuded such outrage earlier that night. But he had to think about the museum—about how long he could afford to keep it. With the kind of money Roger was offering him, Menashe could charge his real clients next to nothing—something he'd wanted to do from the beginning—and still remain financially stable. That realization made the idea of Roger and his bastard friends using the museum almost bearable. And he could always take out the top pieces whenever one of them came in. Menashe rubbed his eyes. He knew he'd always feel some regret if he gave into this. But it would be better in the long run. He could help more people. He could make it work.

"Roger? This is Menashe Everett. Yeah, we're on. Come by tomorrow night at nine and we'll set the rules."

Roger arrived at eight-thirty the next night, dressed as well as he had been the day before, with another cigarette in his hand.

"I wore long sleeves," he said with a smile when Menashe opened the door. "That's part of it, right?"

"Yeah," Menashe muttered. "That's part of it. Get in here."

They went back to the office and Menashe sank heavily into his chair, wondering if he'd made the right decision. *Don't think about it. It's done.*

"You want some coffee?"

"Instant?"

"Yeah."

"No, thanks."

"All right, let's get down to it: you get two friends, all right?"

"What?"

"You can only tell two people—people I check out and clear before they come in—and they've got to pay triple just like you."

"You got it."

"When somebody leaves we can talk about replacing him, but I've got to approve. And nobody talks about this." Roger nodded. "You'll get one session a month," he continued. "And you've got to be in and out within an hour each time."

"Fine, fine," Roger agreed eagerly. "Can we start now?"

"You got money?"

He smiled and leaned forward, digging his wallet out of his back pocket. He pulled a wad of cash from between its folds and tossed it on the desk in front of Menashe.

"That seem fair?"

Menashe counted the money and nodded, transferring it to his own wallet.

"Just give me a minute to set up a room, okay?"

Menashe led him into the first room. He'd removed the top piece to put back in storage. And instead of retreating to his office as he always did when someone began a session, Menashe listened at the door. He felt no need to respect Roger's privacy.

At first there was silence. He waited about ten minutes before he heard glass break. There was a startling crash followed by laughter, and after that he heard constant noise for about fifteen minutes. When the room once again grew quiet, Menashe went back to his office.

It took about ten more minutes for Roger to finally walk through the door to Menashe's office, drenched in sweat. He held his tan sweater loosely by his side and bits of glass sparkled from between the fibers of its fabric. His hair hung in strings and his face was flushed. He collapsed into the chair across from Menashe.

"Man," he said, breathless. "What is this?"

"I thought you didn't want to talk," Menashe replied. "Just the glass, right?"

Roger smiled. "Right." He pushed his hair back off his forehead and stood up. "I'll see you next month."

* * *

Menashe sat in his office for nearly an hour after Roger left. What finally drew him back into the real world was the understanding that he could no longer put off going to the grocery store. The only food left in his apartment was a half-empty box of freezer-burned toaster waffles and week-old Chinese leftovers that hadn't been very good to begin with. *At least now I can get some decent food*, he thought, feeling the wad of cash in his wallet.

He gathered his keys from the bedroom and shut the door behind him. Throwing on his coat, Menashe walked out the front door and up the stairs, stepping on some kind of toy that nearly caused him to trip and fall onto the sidewalk. He scowled and kicked the object aside, its shiny red paint shimmering in the streetlight.

"Fucking kids!" he shouted aloud, although, as he looked down the street, no one was around.

Only then did he take a good look at the toy he'd tripped over. He felt his blood pressure elevate as he walked toward the overturned fire engine that lay with its small wheels spinning wildly in the air.

Chapter 25
Wesley
June 1978

"Oh, Menashe," Jamie got off the phone, crying. "I've got to go out to Fletcher tonight. Aunt Tracy had a heart attack."

"Oh, Jesus," Menashe breathed. "How bad is it?"

"Bad," she said, shoving her checkbook and keys into her purse. "I just have to get out there now."

"Don't worry, we'll be fine here."

Jamie eyed him cautiously. "So you're not going out to Jeffrey's tonight?"

"No, no. I'll cancel, definitely."

"And you'll, you know . . . be careful?" she asked, nodding toward the living room with a pleading tone in her voice.

This annoyed him. He knew what she was thinking, what she hadn't stopped obsessing over since it happened. A few weeks ago Menashe had taken Wesley to pick up a few things at the grocery store and, at some point, lost track of him. He'd stopped to read the label on a peanut butter jar while Wesley pattered over to the display of crazy straws, and a moment later he was gone. It took a lifetime to find him—about four minutes—during which a kindly employee had asked the little boy if he was lost, then led him up to the front of the store to make one of those announcements. What Jamie didn't understand was that Menashe's heart had stopped at that moment. He was ready to tear the place apart to find him, just as she would have been. And had the roles been reversed, Menashe would have understood.

"Jamie, we will be fine," Menashe answered shortly.

She looked at him again carefully, slightly narrowing her left eye in a manner that always aggravated him, but no doubt remembered the phone call and collected her things to leave. He hugged her goodbye and walked into the living room. Wesley was asleep on the couch with a tired old tape of *Robin Hood* playing on the television. Menashe sighed and sat down next to his son, rubbing his back as he slept. After a few moments he got up and went to the kitchen to call Jeffrey.

"Hey, Jeffrey, what's going on?"

"Oh, nothing, just getting ready for tonight. It looks like we're going to end up with way more shit than we'll need."

He laughed and started to say something else but Menashe cut him off.

"Jeffrey? I'm actually not going to be able to make it tonight. My wife's gone out of town for an emergency and I've got Wesley. Sorry, man, another time, I hope."

"No, Ash, listen, you've got to be here. Really, you need to get out," he pressed. "Just bring little Wes. We can put him in front of *Captain Kangaroo* or something."

"I know, but I really think I should just stay in tonight."

"Is it because of the people? I know how they scare you."

"Shut up."

"No, really," he laughed, "most of the guys I invited are going down to that music festival in Columbus, so it's just going to be me and you and three of my new co-workers. No big crowd, no crazy party. Right up your alley."

Menashe had to admit that Jeffrey's offer was looking better. And it might be the best way to shake off the shitty day he'd had at work.

"You'll keep it clean, right? Kid-friendly?"

"Absolutely," Jeffrey promised. "No jokes or anything."

"All right, we'll come for a bit," Menashe conceded, looking back at Wesley, still asleep.

Jeffrey was not a very close friend, but Menashe couldn't resist an evening that included the promise of a bottomless tap. And Jeffrey was a good guy. He and Menashe liked many of the same pastimes and each enjoyed the other's company. They had met three years before at an Indians game through a mutual friend who worked with Menashe at Ohio Savings. Menashe had originally thought of Jeffrey as obnoxious—he was one of those loud drunk guys who always seemed to sit behind him at the ballpark—but by the end of the evening, Jeffrey's ridiculous charm had started to grow on him. He was loud and talkative, but because Menashe was naturally introverted, it took the pressure off him having to find things to say. Many of the things Jeffrey said aloud would be the same things Menashe thought to himself anyway.

At the age of twenty-nine, Jeffrey had what many would call a frat boy's dream job: he was a media consultant for a brand new microbrewery called Great Lakes Brewing Company. He organized promos, worked on ad campaigns, and generally did all he could to make its name known. Jeffrey often came home with giant cases of beer to "test," and these were the times when he would call up his friends to come over and help.

Menashe arrived with Wesley just before nine o'clock, set in his mind to stay no longer than an hour. Jeffrey's home was incredible. He had an expansive and beautifully maintained lawn, a pool, a gazebo, a barbecue pit, and a fancy patio. Around the patio table sat a man, two women, and a young boy, maybe seven or eight years old. Judging from the empty bottles, Menashe supposed they had already been there an hour or so. The boy was rocking his chair back and forth with his head tilted back, idly blowing at a few bugs that hovered over him. The adults smiled at them and one of the women waved hello.

Jeffrey then emerged from the house with a six-pack of dark beer and two bottles of wine under his arm.

"Ash!" he exclaimed, nearly tripping over a slightly raised flagstone paver as he made his way toward them. "Hey, man, I'm so glad you made it. And the little man!"

Jeffrey placed the assortment of alcohol on the patio coffee table before turning to Wesley.

"How's it going, Wes?" he asked jovially, mussing Wesley's still baby-fine hair.

Wesley looked up at him and smiled, but also looked nervous. Menashe knew his son was still wary of Jeffrey—his tall, sturdy build combined with his curly, dark hair and full beard made him look like some kind of wild mountain man. With some effort, Jeffrey lowered himself to face Wesley, his hands balanced on his knees.

"Well, Wes, I thought maybe we'd let your dad play some poker with the big kids tonight. What do you say we find you a good movie to watch inside?"

Wesley looked guardedly around the yard, and then up at his dad. He shook his head.

"I want to stay here and play with you. I'm not going inside by myself."

"Oh, but there's a friend here for you," Jeffrey interjected in a high-pitched voice, clearly unused to talking to children. He pointed to the boy at the table. "That's Damien. I'm sure he'd love to play something with you."

Damien did not look thrilled. He whispered something to the woman Menashe assumed to be his mother, looking back at Wesley with disdain.

"I want to stay out here!" Wesley repeated in a whinier, more pitiful voice. His brown eyes began to water and well up to what seemed like twice their size in what Jamie called his "hurt Bambi look." Looking at him now, Menashe saw just how striking a resemblance Wesley bore to Jamie: he had her naturally straight blond hair, delicate features, and pale complexion. His eyes were also large and warm like his mother's, but they were brown like Menashe's rather than blue.

"Nobody would even be inside to watch him," he told Jeffrey in a low voice.

"He can't watch himself?"

"Jeffrey, he's four years old. And that kid is what, seven?"

"He's nine, I think."

"All right, we'll just let him stay out here with us."

"Sure," Jeffrey agreed. "We'll be cool."

It was a warm night and Menashe leaned back in his chair on the patio, breathing in the summer air. Jeffrey's new friends were nice enough. All in their twenties, single, careless. Even Damien's mother, Liz, had an air of recklessness about her that motherhood hadn't quelled. It seemed they all liked to party, to have a good time. And they all liked to drink.

By the third hand of poker and his fourth beer, Menashe was finally starting to loosen up. He was glad Jeffrey had pushed him into coming. But an unpleasant feeling still nagged at him. He shook his head. *The fucking bank.*

His boss had threatened to fire him that day. He'd lost a stack of forms. He'd been thinking about other things, about Jamie and Wesley and how they were going to afford another year of preschool and if he really needed it, and then couldn't find the promissory notes he'd organized just a moment before. His heart raced as he ransacked his desk, and when he came upon the pile of terminated contracts he sank into his chair, wondering if he was going to throw up. This time there was no fix. He'd shredded the wrong stack of papers. Menashe was surprised Kevin had let him keep his job at all, but still, the threat had badly shaken him. He saw how easily he could ruin his family.

Menashe glanced over at his son, who was sitting cross-legged and running his toy fire engine around on the patio. The other boy, Damien, was playing with him now, lining up an assortment of Matchbox cars and letting Wesley plow into them. Wesley mimicked a siren sound as he drove away from the crash site.

"Your son is adorable."

This voice brought Menashe back to the table. It was Cali, the twenty-five-year-old receptionist from Jeffrey's brewery.

"Thanks," he smiled. "Do you have kids?"

"Oh, no," she laughed. "I couldn't imagine."

Cali scooted her chair around toward Menashe, giggling as her sandal got stuck under its leg. Normally an interaction with a pretty girl would make him uneasy, but she was drunk so it didn't much matter if he said something stupid. He set down his fifth beer, half full. He'd started to feel fuzzy—not too much, but he didn't want to overdo it with Wesley there. Menashe again looked toward his son.

"You work at a bank, right?" Cali asked.

He nodded, turning back to her.

"Do you like it there?"

"Not really."

"Oh?" She seemed genuinely interested. "And what would you rather be doing?"

Wesley was now lying on his stomach and propelling swirled glass marbles down the concrete path and into the pool. Damien laughed and ran to the edge to watch them sink.

"Here, give me one," he called. Wesley brought his remaining marbles over to the side. Damien took a green and yellow one and held it calculatingly over the water.

"What are you doing?" Wesley asked.

"I want it to get stuck in the drain." He let the marble drop and both boys watched it descend. "Too bad," he said after a moment.

Wesley then threw the rest of them in with a flourish, as if to impress the older boy. None of them went close to the drain. Wesley knelt down and stuck his hand in the pool.

"How do we get them?"

Damien shrugged. "Maybe they've got one of those nets." He put his hand in as well. "Whoa! It's heated." His eyes glimmered with delight. "Want to get in?"

Wesley shook his head. "I don't have any trunks."

"Neither do I. We have shorts; it's like the same thing." Damien was already taking his shoes off.

Wesley looked down into the water again. The lights were on, which gave the pool a magical glow. He looked back at the table where his dad sat, laughing with his friend.

"I don't want to get in trouble," he said finally.

"*Look,*" Damien said sharply, gesturing to the adults, "*they don't even care what we're doing. If we have to play here we should at least have fun.*" Wesley shifted uneasily. "*Here,*" he said in a softer tone, "*you can hold my hand and we'll go down the stairs together. We can even just stay in the baby end if you want to.*"

"Wow, so did you have, like, moose in your backyard?" Cali laughed, touching Menashe's hand briefly.

"You know, Canada does have real cities."

"I guess."

He smiled. "I lived in downtown Toronto my whole life, until I moved here. No moose."

"And you like it here?"

"For the most part."

"What would you change?"

"Well, I guess I'd like to be closer to my mom."

"Oh," she sighed, as if she'd caught sight of a cute puppy. "That's so sweet." She touched his hand again, but didn't retract hers as quickly.

Menashe had spent the better part of their conversation trying to figure out if he was doing something wrong. He'd gone ahead and finished that beer plus one more, so he wasn't sure if this girl was attracted to him, or if the alcohol was making him think she was. Either way, he felt guilty. It would have killed him if he knew Jamie was off flirting with some guy while he was out of town. But he liked the attention. And Cali was allowing him to finally forget about work. He glanced over to the other end of the table. Jeffrey was telling Liz and the other marketing guy, Nate, another lively tale from his college days. He scanned the yard for Wesley and saw him sitting on the edge of the pool with Damien, dangling his feet in the water.

"Hey, Wesley!" he called down. "Be careful, all right?" Both boys waved and he turned his attention back to Cali.

"So," he sighed, feeling thoroughly relaxed, "what about you?"

"What do you mean?"

"What's your family like?"

She shrugged. "I don't really talk to them much."

Menashe frowned. "I'm sorry to hear that."

Just then, Damien came running up to the house and started digging around in his mom's canvas bag.

"Hey, hey, what's going on?" Liz called to him. "What are you looking for?"

"My jellyfish. It must be in the very bottom," he said, starting to overturn the bag.

"Damien," she snapped. "Do not dump my stuff out. I think you had it in the house when we got here. Remember, you were showing it to Jeffrey?"

Damien ran inside and she shook her head. "I swear, you guys—that kid fucking wears me out."

Jeffrey laughed loudly and stood to pass out the next round of beers. Everyone accepted except Menashe, who held out his hand in refusal.

"What?" Jeffrey gasped dramatically. "Ash, I don't even know who you are anymore."

Nate laughed and pushed aside a few empty bottles. Damien's voice rang out from inside the house.

"Mom!" he called. "Where's the bathroom?"

Liz looked at Jeffrey apologetically. "I'm so sorry," she said. "Do you mind helping him?"

"No problem," Jeffrey chuckled, heading inside.

A moment later Menashe again turned toward the yard, but this time did not see Wesley. A knot immediately formed in his throat.

"Wesley!"

He looked more carefully, urgently, but part of the yard, including the shallow end of the pool, was hidden from view.

"Wesley!" he called again, jumping to his feet and trying to control the shaking of his hands. "Wesley, answer me, please!"

The others had stopped talking and were now looking out at the empty yard as well. Menashe ran down the slight hill toward the pool. When the shallow end became visible, he felt intense heat, like an electric shock, run through his body and he let out a cry. His mind felt detached, seeing his son floating in no more than two feet of water. He sprinted over to the stairs, fear causing the blood to pound in his temples, but he was unsteady. As the darkening world wobbled in front of him, he tripped over an uneven paver, scraping his hands and face as he fell on the hard stone. The others had followed him, running now, too, but he was first to reach Wesley, pulling him out of the pool and laying him gingerly down on the side.

"What do I do?" he choked through his tears, desperately looking from face to face, but they had no words. Menashe leaned over his son, trembling. He forcefully blew air into his mouth.

"Jeffrey!" he coughed, turning toward the group. "Jeffrey, call them! Call 9-1-1!"

The women were crying now and Nate stood dumbly with his hand over his mouth, but Jeffrey did it. He ran back to the house as Menashe fumbled through his resuscitation attempt. He desperately forced air into Wesley's lungs, his rapid breaths causing white specks to dance in front of his eyes. Nothing was happening. Menashe struggled to wake his son, but the panic took hold of him. He couldn't catch his breath. He saw Jeffrey running down the hill, but then blackness seeped across his vision.

Menashe had a faint memory of waking up in the ambulance, lying on his back and squinting at the lights that lined the ceiling. The bumping of the ambulance made him queasy. There was a woman talking on a radio. He panicked because he didn't understand what she was saying; it sounded like she was talking in code. He closed his eyes.

Menashe opened his eyes to more lights. Big fluorescent rectangles. More hushed code-talking. The smell of stale food and chemicals. It was the hospital.

He suspected he blacked out again because he couldn't recall anything with lucidity until hours later. He had the strong taste of stomach acid in his mouth and was listening to a doctor try to soften the reality of what was happening. It had taken Wesley under four minutes to drown, they concluded.

"Little kids," he sighed, "they just can't swim that long. And they're rarely able to call for help."

Menashe was numb at that point and had to remind himself to nod and blink and breathe at appropriate intervals.

"My wife," he mumbled after a moment.

"We've called her. She should be back in town within the next few hours."

They just can't swim that long.

Menashe suddenly thought back to the day Wesley was born, how he had held him for the first time, fearful he would drop him or squeeze him too tightly. How he had driven him to preschool so many mornings, and would reach back at the red lights to hold his hand.

* * *

He didn't break down until he was in the car the next morning, ready to go home. He instinctively checked the rear-view and saw the empty car seat. He cried until his ribs hurt and his breath could no longer escape his chest. He thought of crashing his car on the way home, but he knew he was too afraid. He heard a plane taking off from the airport down the road and thought about running away. He shook as he lit a cigarette, not bothering to crack a window. He knew he had no way to live.

Chapter 26
Close to Home
April 1978

It was on a cold overcast morning that Menashe drove his family out to Cleveland Hopkins International Airport. There were still patches of snow on the ground, and when the Everetts piled out of their maroon Chevrolet Vega, Wesley exhaled deeply to watch his ghostly white breath linger in the frigid air.

"Come on, Wesley, let's go inside!" his mother called, dancing in place to keep warm.

Wesley followed his parents and walked with his head tilted toward the sky, undoubtedly hoping an airplane would fly over him. The Everetts strolled leisurely through the airport, unencumbered by luggage or flight schedules. They were not going on vacation, but rather had come to Cleveland Hopkins so Wesley could watch the airplanes land and take off. This was one of his favorite activities and one his parents were happy to indulge. Jamie would often pack lunches for the three of them and make it into a real event.

"Look!" Wesley cried, catching sight of a blue and white plane taxiing up to its gate. He ran over to the window and put both his small hands against the glass, peering at the plane to catch a glimpse of the pilot. Menashe and Jamie walked over to him, holding hands and smiling at their son's enthusiasm. "Do you know what kind of plane that is?" Wesley asked, turning to them excitedly. Menashe shook his head.

"No, I don't. What kind is it?"

"It's a seven-twenty-seven! That one's easy," Wesley admitted. "And that one!" he continued, running along the window with one hand still touching the glass. "Do you know that one?"

"Is it a seven-forty-seven?" Jamie guessed. Wesley looked at her authoritatively.

"It's a DC-nine."

"Great job, you know them all."

He began racing around Gate F-40 with his arms spread out like wings. Menashe and Jamie sat in the hard plastic seats connected into rows and watched, talking softly to each other.

"I talked to Elena today," Menashe began in a low voice.

"Really?" Jamie asked with surprise. It had been several months since their last conversation.

"Yeah. She's still with Noah, but she said he's not any better."

"You think you should go see him?"

"No," Menashe snapped. "Definitely not."

"I'll go with you if you want."

"Jamie, I'm not going to be in the same room with him. I don't give a shit what his problems are."

"What about her?"

Elena Everett, Noah's younger daughter, spent most of her time with her father at Riverdale Hospital in Toronto. Since the accident in which Noah crashed his car into a utility pole and killed Menashe's father, he'd lost all control of his alcoholism, leading him to develop advanced liver cirrhosis. He'd been in and out of the hospital, trying numerous programs to overcome his addiction, but they would never last. After his second drinking relapse, his wife received the divorce she had been seeking and, with their elder daughter Rebecca and young son Danny, went back to Lethbridge. Elena, however, at eighteen years old, wanted to stay with her father.

Menashe wanted nothing to do with Noah, but couldn't shut his kindhearted cousin out of his life. He and Elena spoke every few months, giving each other updates on school and work, and also on her father's condition, which never seemed to change.

"Elena knows I won't see him, Jamie. She understands, all right?"

"But she's still alone. I'm just saying it must be hard."

Then her goddamn family should come back from Lethbridge, he thought bitterly.

"Shit," Menashe muttered suddenly, rising from his chair. "She said they moved Noah and got him a new doctor and I forgot to get all that information. Just in case there's an emergency with Elena," he added. "I'd better go call her back."

"Why don't you wait till we get home? It'll be so expensive."

"I'll call collect."

Jamie nodded and Menashe walked over to the pay phone. Wesley had completed his loop around the gate and was heading back.

The phone rang eleven times with no answer. Menashe stood there, watching his son as he waited for Elena to pick up. There was a look in Wesley's eyes that left him unsettled. He wasn't running or bouncing anymore, but talking seriously with Jamie, and looking over at Menashe every so often. After seven more rings, Menashe gave up and walked sullenly back from the pay phone. Jamie put her hand on top of his. He sighed, resting his forehead in his other hand. Aware that he hadn't heard Wesley's voice for a few minutes, Menashe lifted his head again and blinked a few times to clear his vision. He glanced across the terminal briefly, and in that moment locked eyes with his son. Wesley had been watching him carefully.

"How's Wesley?" Menashe asked Jamie cautiously, still holding his son's gaze.

"He said you always look tired," she replied, digging around in her bag for their sandwiches. "I think he worries about you."

Chapter 27
The Day After
June 1978

Five days after Menashe left the hospital, he received Jamie's divorce papers. She had not come back to the apartment but there was, in addition to the papers, a request that he begin separating their belongings.

He supposed Jamie had told her lawyers to fix it so she never had to see him again. After the funeral, they dealt exclusively through legal firms, and Jamie would only go to move her things out of the apartment once they had reached an agreement stating that Menashe would not be present. He didn't believe he would ever see her again. He had asked her lawyer once where she was moving, but he wouldn't say. It could be anywhere. Menashe slammed his fists against the kitchen table in his empty apartment. He knew she was upset, and he had even assumed she would leave him, but he never thought Jamie would cut him out so completely or instantaneously.

Although it wouldn't last long, Menashe quit drinking the day after he finalized the divorce. Instead of waking up and reaching for the bottle of whiskey he kept in the nightstand, Menashe would wake up and think, *what can I do to make sure I don't kill myself today?* And whatever it was, he would do. Six months after his son's death, Menashe came up with the idea for his museum. It was a thought that came to him after returning home from Las Vegas, thinking back to that lonely hotel room. It came from what he was vaguely aware was a dark and disturbed part of his mind, but he had a strong feeling that it was a good thought. It had to be, because he couldn't afford to fail again.

Chapter 28
Lost Time
November 1988

Murray had been walking up and down West Tenth for about half an hour. He was early for his appointment and needed to think—he'd passed the pay phone a few times but wasn't ready to use it. A homeless man watched him curiously, blowing air into his gloved hands, probably wondering what a clean-cut student was doing in that part of town. Murray didn't mind the neighborhood and was usually caught up in his thoughts when he came to the museum anyway.

"Hey, Honor Roll," the man called when Murray passed again. "You lost or something?"

"No," Murray smiled. "I'm just a little early to see somebody."

"Got any spare change?"

"Yeah, I think so." Murray unzipped his backpack and dug out his money. He held onto a couple dollars and a quarter, and then handed the rest to the man.

"You keep out your bus fare?"

Murray nodded. "And a quarter for the pay phone."

"Smart kid," he smiled. "Thanks."

Murray smiled in return and picked up his backpack. He walked past The Velvet Dog again, but this time he stopped at the pay phone at the end of the street. He took a breath and resignedly pushed a quarter into the slot. *She might not even be there.* He dialed the number. *What if it's her roommate?* he thought uneasily. He almost hung up on the third ring, but a voice on the other end stopped him.

"Hello?"

"Hi, uh, Emma?"

"Yeah, who's this?"

"It's Murray."

"Oh . . ." she said flatly. "What's going on?"

"Are you, well, are you going to that thing tonight at school? The concert?" He closed his eyes. *Stupid.*

"Murray, why are you calling me?"

"I'm sorry," he said with a sigh. "I know this is weird. I just really felt like I should talk to you. I have for a while now. I've wanted to tell you that I'm getting help. I'm seeing somebody."

"Good. That's—that's really good, Murray." She sounded tired. "I should go."

"Wait, Emma. Are you okay?"

"Fine."

"You sure?"

She laughed. "I don't really know how to answer that."

"I mean, have you been doing okay?"

"Well, today I felt pretty good. Today was all right."

"But in general . . ."

"You mean since we broke up."

"I guess."

She sighed heavily. "Yeah, you know what, Murray, I've been doing great. My grades are really high, I'm sleeping well, and I've just never been happier. It's almost as if I didn't spend a semester with a guy who'd hit me when he had a bad day. Is that what I'm supposed to say?"

Murray's stomach sank.

"Jesus, Emma, I really was just checking in. I worry about you."

"Well, don't, okay? It doesn't make any sense. You wouldn't have to worry about me if you hadn't been like that." Her voice shook. "What you did, do you even get it?"

He looked toward The Velvet Dog, wondering if maybe he didn't get it at all. His stomach was now churning ruthlessly.

"I'm sorry. I really am sorry. Listen, I won't call you again."

Murray hung up before she could reply and ran to the trash can just outside the nightclub. He threw up onto discarded Styrofoam take-out containers, newspapers, and liquor bottles. He coughed and lifted his head to the sound of laughing. It was the homeless man down the street.

"Way to be, Honor Roll!" he called cheerfully. "You're ready for those frat parties now."

Murray lowered his eyes and drew his coat around him. He stumbled down to Menashe's apartment, worried he was going to vomit again. He sat down on the steps for a few minutes, taking calculated breaths and thinking he was getting in too far over his head.

"I had a good amount of friends in grade school, but I was usually more comfortable by myself, you know?"

"Mm hm," Menashe nodded. "And when was it that your parents separated?"

"I was thirteen."

"But your father came back after about a year?"

"Yeah, a little over a year."

"Do you know why they separated?" Menashe asked.

Murray shook his head. "I don't really remember."

"Okay," Menashe murmured. "How about games you played as a child? What did you like to do with your friends?"

"Well, I know we played outside a lot. I was always dirty and running around," he smiled. "My friends and I would climb trees all the time. My dad said that's how I broke my arm one summer."

"So that's another instance you can't remember?"

Murray nodded, wondering how Menashe got those marks on his face and trying not to stare at them. He looked worse than usual that day, Murray thought. His long-sleeved shirt had a hole in the pocket and a cigarette burn on the sleeve, and his hair seemed unwashed, nearly matted.

"Was it your left arm?"

"Yeah, that's right."

"Sometimes it seems like it bothers you."

"It does. It starts throbbing sometimes, or I'll wake up and it's really sore."

"Do you remember anything from around that time?"

"Yeah, I mean, I remember lots of things about that summer. I know one of my friends got a new basketball hoop we played with a lot, and I remember that's when Jake made the tryouts for select soccer. I just don't remember breaking my arm. Maybe because it hurt," he laughed anxiously.

Menashe smiled. "Maybe."

"Some things like that," he continued, "it's like they didn't even happen. Or not to me, anyway." He shifted in his chair and frowned, concentrating. "Like, I know we went on this big family trip once, camping I think, and—" Murray stopped and rubbed his eyes roughly. "Damn it. It's like, the more I concentrate on remembering, the harder it is."

"Don't worry. You're doing fine." Menashe leaned back in his chair and put Murray's file back in the cabinet. "Have you ever asked your parents about things you can't remember?"

Murray shook his head. "God, they'd think I was crazy," he said. "I mean, who doesn't remember stuff like this? It *is* crazy. I've just got to pretend I'm on the same page as everyone else. And really, it's not so bad. The bits and pieces I can't remember don't really come up, I guess."

"So you get by all right?"

"Yeah, I think so."

Menashe looked thoughtful. "One more question?"

"Sure."

"Do you drink at all?"

"No," Murray answered. "Never. And not just because I'm not old enough, either. It's like . . . it's like I really don't want to get out of control, you know? I feel it too much already. I don't even like seeing my friends drink."

"Okay," Menashe nodded. He sat silently for a moment, and then rose from his chair. "Ready?"

"Are you okay?" Murray asked, unable to quell his curiosity any longer. "Your face, I mean. Looks like it hurts."

"Oh, no, I'm fine. Another couple of days, this'll all be gone."

"Was it . . . no, I'm sorry. It's none of my business."

"No, what were you going to say?"

"Well, was it somebody from here?" *Murray, how did—*

"What?" Menashe frowned, looking startled.

"I mean," he stammered, "I mean, did somebody from here do that to you?" *How did all this happen?*

"No, Murray, it was nothing like that. Just an accident. I wasn't thinking and tripped coming down the stairs out there."

Murray nodded. "Okay."

He followed Menashe to the hallway and waited while he opened all the doors but one.

"Are you okay with three rooms this time?"

Murray nodded and took a breath.

"Wait." Menashe stopped suddenly and looked at him. "Do you have a long-sleeved shirt on you?"

"No, sorry; just my coat."

"Okay." Menashe looked thoughtful and then retreated to his office. "Hold on," he called.

He returned with one of his long-sleeved knit shirts. "Is this okay?"

Murray nodded and thanked him, slipping the larger shirt on over his own. He put on the protective gear and told Menashe he was ready. He felt that he was. Menashe walked back to his office to wait and Murray heard the lock click behind him.

He stepped into the first room, his hands quivering badly as they picked up the bat. He didn't know what was happening. He raised the bat cautiously to strike a large, dimpled vase and everything after was surreal. He didn't yell or cry, but Murray tore through the rooms with fury and panic. His arm was killing him now.

This isn't happening, this isn't happening.

He couldn't even hear the glass breaking. The bat sliced through the air, leveling an entire table of serving bowls. His heart pounded in his ears and his breath came in labored gasps, but his stomach was finally calm.

Images of his past flashed into his mind. He saw a bike, a basketball, a gun. He heard shouting and crying, and felt a stinging warmth shoot through his body. As he put the memories together, he smashed the glass harder and faster, sending sprays of clear flecks into the air.

Chapter 29
Murray's Flash
July 1979

It was a beautiful Sunday morning in early July, and Murray was eager to go outside and play with his friends. Greg's dad had just put up a new basketball hoop in their driveway, and Murray was supposed to meet Greg and Shaun over there by lunchtime at the latest. He rushed around the house, trying to finish his weekend chores as quickly as possible. He made his bed, cleaned up his room, returned Matthew's records and Jake's soccer ball to their room, and hauled the two giant trash cans up from the curb. It was eleven-fifteen. Murray grabbed his baseball glove, just in case, and yelled to his mom that he was going to Greg's house. She was upstairs sewing and called back, telling him to have fun and stay out of the street. Murray ran through the front hall and out the storm door, nearly crashing into his father who was walking up the front steps.

"Jesus, Murray, watch out!" he said gruffly, grabbing his chest.

Adam Henderson was forty-three years old, but looked young for his age. He was a tall man, lean and very muscular from his years in the army. He had light-brown hair he wore in a crew cut and a clean-shaven face. He stood there for another moment, wiping his tanned forehead and taking in slow breaths. His sons knew that, more than anything, he hated to be startled.

"Sorry, Dad. Hey, I did all my chores so I'm going to Greg's, okay?"

"Sure," he replied, glancing at the stack of paperwork he was holding. "Did you eat?"

"Greg said his mom would make us lunch."

His dad nodded. "Just be home by dinner. I should be back about then, too. I've got to finish some more paperwork at the station, then Officer Wilkins and I are going running." He climbed up the last step then turned around. "You ever see his boy around school? James or Justin, I think."

"No, I don't think so."

Murray did know Jack Wilkins, but he couldn't tell his father that Jack was one of the bullies Murray and his friends had grown to fear. He was constantly cornering them at recess, wanting money, homework, or just to give them a good pummeling before the whistle blew.

Murray stuck his baseball glove in the back of his jeans and hopped on his bike, pedaling fast down his street toward Greg's house. Greg lived in a brown, split-level house about half a mile away from Murray's neighborhood. When he arrived, Greg and Shaun were already taking shots at the new basketball hoop.

"Murray! Hey, what took you so long? You get lost again?" Greg laughed and tossed the basketball back to Shaun.

"Very funny, smart ass," Murray replied, throwing his glove at Shaun's head. He bobbed away, letting it fall on the ground next to the hoop. "What were you playing?"

"Nothing, just messing around," Greg answered. "You want to play HORSE?"

"Sure."

Greg beat them both viciously at the first game but won the second by only one letter. They decided to play two-on-one for a while until Mrs. Crowley called them in for lunch. She set chicken salad sandwiches on the table and asked the boys if they'd like chocolate milk or plain milk to drink, wiping her hands on a pink dishtowel hanging over the sink.

"Chocolate, please," Murray and Shaun answered.

"Plain," Greg replied a few seconds later.

Probably just to be different, Murray thought. Mrs. Crowley filled their glasses, then left to finish cleaning the upstairs of their house. The boys sat at the table and talked about forming a basketball game with other kids they knew from school.

"Yeah, it's kind of dumb with only three," Greg admitted. "But everyone else I know is at camp or on vacation."

"Me, too," Shaun said, and turned to Murray, who was staring thoughtfully into his chocolate milk.

"I know something else we could do," Murray said. The boys leaned in. "A couple days ago I saw where my dad keeps all his police stuff—badge, nightstick, all of it. And he's going to be gone until dinner if you guys want to go see it."

Shaun's eyes lit up immediately.

"Real cop shit? Yeah, let's go."

"Okay, I call nightstick!" Greg shouted.

The boys finished their lunches hurriedly and then rode their bikes to Murray's house. His mom had left a note saying she was going to the grocery store and a few other places before dinner. Murray's brothers were at soccer conditioning and wouldn't be back until around five. The house was theirs. Even so, Murray spoke in a whisper.

"Upstairs, you guys."

He led the way, creeping up the stairs and into his parents' bedroom. It was very clean and still, which made Murray nervous, but the desire to impress his friends pushed him on. The three of them crept over to the closet, and Murray opened the door. He dug around and emerged with an unmarked cardboard box.

"Greg, close the door, will you?"

Greg did, and then came over to where Murray and Shaun were peering inside the box. Murray pulled out his father's orange reflective vest and his belt, which had two holsters and places for the nightstick and walkie-talkie.

"Whoa," Greg breathed, "he can hold two guns at once?"

"Yeah, I guess," Murray said, smiling. "Pretty neat, huh?"

Before Greg could answer, Shaun pulled his dad's badge out of the box.

"Check this out!" Shaun slipped the vest on and held the badge open in front of him. "Excuse me," he said, approaching Greg haughtily, "but do you have a permit for that belt?" Greg giggled and put the belt on, tightening the strap.

"Why, yes I do," he mocked back. "And I can hold two guns in this thing, so you'd better watch it!"

Shaun lunged forward, holding the badge like a fencing sword and jabbed it at his friend.

"Guys, guys!" Murray cried. He was trying to be serious but couldn't help breaking down into laughter at their skit. He lifted the nightstick dramatically from the box, and made as though he was going to beat them both. "Your badge means nothing next to *this*."

"Haha!" Greg exclaimed. "It's perfect! Hand it here, will you?"

Murray gave him the nightstick and Greg dropped it into the proper space. "Now I'm ready."

"Oh, definitely," Murray laughed.

There was nothing left in the box, so the boys just sat around it, admiring their official police equipment.

"You know," Shaun began sweetly, "this stuff is really cool and everything, but . . ." He trailed off, a big grin resting on his face. Murray held his breath. ". . . I want to see the gun."

"Yeah," Greg breathed, his eyes widening.

Murray had been afraid of this. "No, we can't," he stated as firmly as he could. "My dad would kill me. Probably you, too."

"But he won't be back till dinner."

"It's dangerous," Murray protested. "It's not a good idea."

"Listen, Mur," Shaun said, standing up and walking toward the closet, "we're not little kids. We can hold a gun without pulling the trigger, right?"

Murray shrugged. "My dad says kids shoot themselves all the time playing with guns."

"Yeah, stupid kids," Greg piped up. "You don't really think we're that stupid, do you?"

Murray looked from Greg to Shaun, then back to Greg again. "I guess not."

"Right!" Shaun replied cheerily, clearly encouraged by Murray's weakened response.

Murray had to think fast to come up with a compromise, otherwise he feared the pressure would get to him.

"Okay, but I'll hold it and you guys just *look* at it, okay?"

The boys agreed.

Murray reluctantly got the chair from his mother's sewing table and dragged it over to the closet. He knew the gun was kept in a shoebox on the top shelf—he had seen his dad take it down once before work. He was standing on the chair, balancing on his tiptoes as he tried to reach the box, when he heard the front door slam and the sound of heavy footsteps trudging up the stairs. Murray's eyes widened in panic, and in his haste to get down off the chair, he tipped backward and fell hard onto the floor with the chair pinned underneath him. His father must not have seen the note on the counter, because Murray heard him yell to his mother that he'd just come back for his running shoes and Officer Wilkins would be waiting at the park so he had to hurry.

Adam had not even finished the end of his sentence when he opened the door and walked into his bedroom, finding his son and two other boys playing with all his off-limits police equipment. Hot blood reddened his cheeks as he looked from one boy to another, his gaze finally resting on his son, sprawled out on the floor with a stunned look on his face.

"What the fuck are you doing in here?" Adam bellowed, coming at them with terrifying fury. He suddenly seemed huge to Murray, like a bear towering over his feeble prey. His face was flushed and sweaty, but his eyes were still cold. Even in that moment, Murray knew his father was planning his punishment.

Greg and Shaun shrank back in horror, and Murray felt a pang of envy to remember they had never seen an adult behave this way. The boys shed their gear with impressive agility and were out the door in a flash, leaving Murray to face his enraged father alone. He grasped the overturned chair, using it to pull himself up. He had hurt his knee when he fell and could now only stand unsteadily, but the injury was far from his mind as he began an apology to his father.

"Dad, I'm sorry. I just thought the guys would be really imp—"

Adam slapped his son hard against the side of his face, knocking him back down. Murray scrambled to get up, his heart pounding fiercely. *It's okay*, he thought frantically. *That's fine. I deserved it. Maybe he'll just stop this time. Maybe that'll be it.* But Adam grabbed him by the collar and slammed his back against the wall.

"What the hell were you thinking!" he shouted into Murray's face, pounding on the wall to accentuate his words. "You can't just go into my room and take whatever you want! What's the matter with you?" Adam hit him again, harder, and blood began to trickle out of his nose.

"I know, I'm sorry! I'm so sorry," Murray sobbed, choking on his breath.

"What were you doing in here?"

"We were just playing. I wanted to show them your badge and . . ." he trailed off. "I'm sorry. I won't come in here again."

Adam took a breath.

"Oh, I know you won't, son," he said menacingly. "But I also know you have trouble remembering the rules around here."

He suddenly turned away from Murray and looked toward the closet, as if a thought had just occurred to him.

"Murray?" he began, speaking in a calm voice that scared his son far more than shouting.

"Yes," he answered miserably, wiping onto his sleeve the mixture of blood and snot that ran out of his nose.

"What's that chair doing over by the closet?"

Murray's heart slammed savagely against his chest to the point where he thought he might suffocate.

"I . . . I . . . I don't know."

"Come on, Murray," Adam coaxed with a nauseating smile. "I'm pretty sure I saw you lying on top of it when I came in. Now tell me what you were doing."

Murray's tears now flowed freely.

"I . . . I wuh-wasn't, I—"

"Stop stuttering, you little asshole! You were getting my gun, weren't you?"

"Dad, please—"

"Tell me! Were you and your little asshole friends getting my gun?"

Murray nodded. "I wasn't going to let them touch it, I—"

His dad slammed him against the wall again, and Murray moaned as pain shot through his shoulder blades.

"Goddamn it, Murray! You just don't learn, do you?" He let go of his son, allowing him to crumple sadly to the floor. "You did something very stupid today and I don't want it to ever happen again."

"It won't, I promise," Murray murmured.

Adam was pacing the room. "I know."

Murray tried to stand, but his nausea and blurred vision caused him to collapse again.

"I'm, I just—"

Murray stopped, realizing nothing he could say would matter. It was as if his dad wasn't even there. Adam approached him again, still glowing with anger.

"Get up," he instructed, kicking Murray lightly in the ribs.

"I can't. I really can't."

Adam looked down at him with disgust. "Get up," he repeated gravely.

Murray knew he was serious, so he tried his best to rise, planting his flat palms on the floor as though he were going to do a push-up, but his arms and legs were shaking too violently to support his weight and they ultimately buckled.

"You just need a shot in the arm," Adam said matter-of-factly, reaching for his belt that lay on the bed.

Murray found that the words he wanted to say caught raggedly in his throat, so he turned and looked desperately at his dad, hoping their eye contact would bring him out of whatever spell he was under. But looking into his father's eyes, Murray knew he only saw a display of intolerable insubordination. Murray summoned all his remaining strength and gripped the wall, slowly rising to his feet. Adam dropped the belt and grabbed Murray's left arm, holding it behind his back as he pushed him harshly against the wall. It was a move he used on criminals resisting arrest. Murray's face was pressed against the bland taupe wall of his parents' bedroom, so he couldn't see his father, but over the years he had come to understand that a punishment lasting this long was serious and would not end well for him.

"I don't think you understand what you've done."

Murray could feel the full weight of his father pushing against his back, wrenching his arm at an excruciating angle and suffocating him.

"I'm sorry," Murray desperately attempted.

"You're not!" Adam roared, pushing Murray's twisted arm farther up his back and causing him to shout in pain. "You are *never* to come in this room again! Do you hear me?"

He gave Murray's arm a final punctuating thrust. They both heard the sickening sound that caused an immediate silence in the room: a harsh and rapid crack letting them know Murray's arm had been broken. It took a moment for Murray's brain to get beyond the sound of his injury and to register the pain, but when it did, he shrieked unabashedly.

"My arm!" he cried, horrified. "Dad!"

"Shhh," Adam hushed, unperturbed. "You'll live."

Adam drove recklessly to the hospital. Murray guessed he was trying to pretend it was a real emergency—pretend he cared about the injury his son had suffered at his own hands. They rode quietly for most of the journey, Murray shivering from the pain.

"Now, Murray," his dad began, breaking the silence as he checked his rearview mirror, changing lanes, "how did all this happen?"

A cold feeling crept over Murray's skin.

"What?"

"Well, it looks like maybe you had a nasty fall. I mean, you've got bruises all over and a broken arm. Did you fall out of that big tree you and your friends like to climb out back?"

His father's false sensitivity made his stomach ache. Adam took his eyes off the road to look at his son closely.

"That *is* what happened, right?"

"Yeah," Murray agreed uneasily. At the mention of his friends, he now pictured Greg and Shaun, back at Greg's place playing basketball. They had probably already forgotten about him. "I guess I should be more careful."

Adam smiled. He put his right arm around Murray and held the steering wheel with his left.

"Don't worry about it, son. You can't tell a ten-year-old boy not to climb trees."

Chapter 30
Fathers and Sons
November 1988

Menashe waited in his office for twenty, thirty, forty minutes. Finally, after nearly an hour, he got up from his desk and went out into the hallway. He found Murray in the third room, collapsed and sobbing amid the destroyed art. Menashe's shoes crunched on the glass, and Murray looked up with bloodshot eyes.

"Please, I want to go back," he begged. "I want to forget, just like before. I need you to undo it. Please."

"I'm sorry," Menashe said, helping him to his feet. "I'm so sorry, Murray, but there's no going back. Please believe me, though; it's better this way. It will be better."

"I know now," Murray sniffed, struggling to stay balanced. "I know it was my dad." Menashe nodded, and Murray looked at him curiously. "Did you know?"

"I thought."

"Why didn't you say anything?"

"It's really tricky," he sighed, "uncovering parts of your past like this. I didn't want a suggestion of mine to plant false memories."

Murray shook his head. "That's why he had to leave," he continued. "I remember they were only separated, but Mom was ready to divorce him. I remember everything now," he said with wonder. "He was crazy. He would beat me to hell just for getting in his way. My brothers, too."

The anxious look in Murray's eyes made Menashe sick. He frowned. Murray didn't even look like the same person. His blond hair was messy and wet, and he pulled at it nervously as he stammered though his words. His normally neat clothes were rumpled and snagged with cuts. He looked deranged.

"But he went through all that anger management shit and came back," he laughed, wiping his nose roughly, "and that's the person I remember, not who he really is."

Murray looked around with astonishment at the rooms he had destroyed, as if he had no recollection of doing it. He suddenly got a wild look in his eyes.

"That's who he really is, isn't he? Oh, I can't go back now." He grasped Menashe's arm, shaking. "I can't go back there—I won't. Please, Mr. Everett."

"It's okay, Murray, just calm down," he soothed, gently holding Murray's arm, which still gripped his own. "Everything's different now, right?"

"I don't know. I mean, I duh-don't know how long it'll last."

"But he obviously wanted to change badly. He left for a year to try to deal with his problems," Menashe reasoned. "He probably still hates himself for what he did." He tried to steady Murray, who was having trouble staying on his feet. "I'm sure there isn't a day that goes by where your dad doesn't wish he had done everything differently. I'm sure he wishes he could tell you how unhappy he's been over the years and how sorry he is for what he did to you. And how much he loves you. I'm sure—"

Menashe stopped, noticing that Murray was eyeing him cautiously. Menashe's face flushed.

"Listen," he began again, forcing out his own troubled thoughts, "I just think you shouldn't hide from it anymore." He looked Murray in the eye. "Really."

Murray's palms were covered in small red dots where the crumbs of glass had gotten under the gloves and cut him. He had calmed down a bit and walked with Menashe to his office. Menashe brought him water and motioned for him to sit.

"Would you be willing to talk to your father with a professional?"

"You?"

"No, I'm afraid I'm not a professional. I mean a trained psychologist."

Murray looked uneasy. "Maybe, but I feel like I shouldn't even mention it, you know? I mean, what if I bring it up and he loses it again?"

"You don't have to do anything you're not comfortable with, but you have to understand your feelings aren't all worked out yet." Menashe thought for a moment and then looked pensively at him. "Murray, everybody makes mistakes—even huge ones like this. People can be helped through anger problems, and you said yourself he's different now."

He looked closely at Murray for understanding, feeling he had made a connection that wasn't strong, but was good enough.

"Okay, I'm going to give you this business card for a great counselor I know, and I want you to talk to your father and see if he'll go with you to see him. And if he won't, I strongly suggest you see him by yourself. Is that okay?"

Murray nodded, taking the card obediently and reading it. He looked like he was going to cry again. Menashe got up and came around his desk, so Murray stood and prepared to leave. Menashe was going to try to say something comforting but instead put his arms around the distressed young man and hugged him.

Menashe watched him walk out of the museum toward the bus stop. Murray turned to wave, and he nodded in return, turning back toward the museum. *It should have been me.* He paused for a moment, letting his eyes rest on the train tracks that paralleled West Tenth Street.

Menashe lay in his bed, exhausted. He was worn out, but still he couldn't sleep. He felt a gnawing sense of self-disgust for how he had left Murray. There had been nothing but fear and weariness in his eyes when he left the museum. Menashe hadn't done him any good, and his selfishness had forced him to attempt a reconciliation that would be unlikely at best and dangerous at worst. He sighed and felt utterly lost. His vision was starting to waver and he knew a migraine wasn't far off. He picked up the phone and dialed Murray's dorm room number. He got the machine and left a message asking Murray to call him in a few days, just to let him know how everything was going. Menashe thought this would make him feel better, but he drifted into an uneasy sleep wishing his whole life would just go away.

Chapter 31
Dr. Rao
May 1974

"What about Dr. Rao?" Menashe asked his mother tiredly, thumbing through her enormous Rolodex.

"No. I really can't understand a word he says."

"Ma, he's a good doctor."

"I don't need a doctor."

Menashe set aside the Rolodex and ran both his hands through his thick hair.

"If I come with you, will you talk to him?"

Charlotte sighed. "Menashe, this is ridiculous. Why is it so hard to believe I'm doing okay?"

"Because Dad just died!" Menashe practically shouted. "I'm sorry, but I can't believe it's that easy to forget about someone you spent, what, twenty-five years with? It's insane!" He pulled a card roughly out of the Rolodex and handed it to Charlotte. "We're seeing Dr. Rao, all right?"

"Menashe," his mom murmured, "I haven't forgotten your father. I'm just not willing to completely fall apart because he's gone."

Menashe's right knee jittered fiercely under the table. "Do you blame Noah?" he asked in a strained voice, focusing hard on the grain of the kitchen table.

"It was an accident."

"I know, I know," he muttered. "Ice. Inclement weather. Don't you ever wonder, though, if there was something else going on? I mean, the man was a complete drunk!"

"Menashe!" Charlotte said sharply. "Calm down and think about what you're saying. I admit, I worried about his drinking at first, especially around you, but Noah did the best he could, and always thought about the family first. He was like a second father to you."

They both sat silently but Menashe's leg continued to twitch.

"Are you seeing a therapist? In Cleveland?" Charlotte asked.

"No. I wanted to go with you."

Charlotte nodded and Menashe looked at his watch.

"I need to call Jamie soon. I probably shouldn't have left her; she looks about ready to burst."

"I'm sure she's taking care of herself."

"Yeah," he answered distractedly. "I should be back by Wednesday, though."

"That's fine," his mom replied. She took a deep breath. "Then we should probably call now to schedule an appointment."

"What?"

"With Dr. Rao. I'm sure he's really busy," she said with a faint smile.

"Really?" Menashe asked, visibly relieved.

"Really. I think it's important. So here," she said, sliding the card across the table to him. "See what he's got open."

Dr. Vijay Rao's office was in the new medical building downtown. His waiting room was furnished with Navajo print couches and chairs, and the gray linoleum floors were cold and clean. Menashe sat on one of the Navajo chairs reading a surprisingly recent edition of *Life* while his mother sat on the couch opposite him, sorting through the contents of her purse, which were spread out on the cushion next to her.

"Did you know I had two of the same lipstick shade in here?"

"No."

"It's because this thing is way too big. I can never find anything," she complained. "I probably thought I'd lost it and bought another one."

"So get a smaller purse."

Charlotte looked up at him in surprise. "But I *need* everything in here."

"Okay," he replied, turning back to his magazine.

"Really, what would you have done if I didn't have those emergency Wash 'n Dris handy? You'd probably still have that little boy's ice cream all over you."

Charlotte's lecture was cut short as a young man opened the door to the waiting room and told them to come back with him.

Vijay Rao was an Indian man in his late twenties with thick, square glasses and a youthful face. His native language was Malayalam, which gave his accent a soft, sing-song quality Menashe liked. He wore a burgundy striped button-down shirt with no tie and dark brown suit pants that exactly matched his eyes. When

Menashe and Charlotte entered his office, he smiled and rose from his chair, greeting them warmly.

"Ah, the Everetts!" he exclaimed genially. "So nice to see you again, Menashe."

He nodded and they all sat down—Rao in his chair and Menashe and Charlotte on the large, suede couch across from him.

Menashe had seen Dr. Rao on the afternoon immediately following his father's funeral at the request of Isaac Dashkoff, Temple Sinai's head rabbi. Though Menashe resented the fact that he had been forced into therapy, he couldn't deny the genuine respect he felt for the doctor. But today wasn't about him; Menashe had come only as a means of support for his mother, who was obviously in denial over her own grief.

"So, Menashe," Rao began, settling himself into his black leather office chair, "you are having some more trouble about your father's death?"

"No, no," he began slowly. "I'm here for my mother. She hasn't seen anyone about it yet."

"And you are having trouble, Mrs. Everett?"

"Not really," she answered. "Menashe's worried about me, though. He thinks I'm hiding something," she said, patting his leg and smiling.

"I just think she's taking all this a little too well," Menashe said defensively.

"Okay," Dr. Rao replied. "Mrs. Everett, may I ask you a few questions?"

"Sure."

"Have you had trouble sleeping, or felt overly lethargic during the day?"

Charlotte shook her head. Rao glanced at Menashe. "What about when your husband first passed away?"

"Well, for the first few weeks I was tired a lot and didn't have much energy, but it's gotten better."

"And you have not seen a therapist before now?" he asked.

"That's right."

"Okay. Have you developed any habits since the death of your husband, such as drinking, smoking, or any sort of drug use?"

"No."

"Menashe, what about you?"

"What about me?" he asked, startled.

"Did you develop any habits?"

"No."

"Nothing?"

"Listen, I just told you," Menashe said, the unevenness of his voice giving away his frustration, "I haven't. I mean, I'll smoke a few cigarettes now and then, but that's nothing. It's nothing."

"All right," Rao agreed, turning back to Charlotte.

"Mrs. Everett, do you ever have sudden and overwhelming feelings of anger?"

Charlotte thought for a moment, but ultimately shook her head.

"No."

"Now, think back again to the time of your husband's death. Was that true then as well?"

"It was hard, definitely. And there were times when I felt so sad I wasn't sure what to do, but I wasn't angry. I just missed him. I still miss him, very much."

"Any thoughts of suicide?"

"No, never."

Menashe was astonished. "How is this possible?" he blurted out, unable to contain himself. "How is any of this possible? I mean, you haven't even lost sleep?!"

"I'm just answering his questions," Charlotte said with a frown. "I'm not going to lie."

"But why are you acting like nothing's changed?"

"Menashe, that's not what I'm doing." She put her hand on his arm in an effort to calm him down. "We're just dealing with this in different ways."

"You're not dealing with it at all!" he yelled, throwing off her hand. Sweat was beginning to break out on his forehead, and he could feel the blood coursing through his temples.

"Menashe," Dr. Rao broke in gently, "why did you come back here?"

"To Toronto?" he asked, confused.

"No, why did you come back here, to my office?"

"I told you already."

"For your mother?"

"Right."

"Why didn't you let her come alone?"

"Because she wouldn't have come."

"But you think it's necessary for her to be here?"

"Of course!"

Menashe held both hands against his head. He was beginning to think maybe Rao wasn't so good after all.

"I think you came back because you still don't feel better about your father. Could that be it?"

"No, it couldn't," Menashe retorted. "I feel fine."

He could see out of the corner of his eye that his mother was staring at him, noticeably worried.

"But you are still angry."

"With good reason!" he said, turning back to Charlotte. "I just don't get how you can take this so well."

"Menashe," Dr. Rao said softly, redirecting his attention, "on the day of your father's funeral, you were so upset you drank to excess and punched a mirror in the bathroom of your synagogue." Menashe shrugged ruefully. "You required two security guards to help you sit quietly through the service and stanch the bleeding of your hand." Rao leaned forward in his chair, resting his forearms on his knees. "Are you upset because no one else had such a violent response to his death?"

Menashe once again turned to his mom. "I'm leaving. I'll see you back at home, all right?"

Charlotte looked at Dr. Rao desperately, but said nothing. Her green eyes were large and anxious.

"Why are you leaving?" Rao asked.

He glared at him. *Why did I ever like this asshole?* "Because this meeting was supposed to be for her."

"I began asking her questions and you interrupted in a fit of anger," Rao reminded him.

Menashe was severely close to losing the remainder of his temper but didn't want to give Rao any new material, so he remained silent. Charlotte said something about coming back another time, but he barely heard it. All he could think about was how strange he had felt in that bathroom—how desperately he had wanted to hurt someone, but thankfully took his misery out on a mirror. Menashe held his breath and stared at the ground. With a great deal of effort, he took a deep breath and pushed away the feelings that threatened to get him in trouble. He looked up at Dr. Rao and smiled.

"You're right. I'm sorry I got so upset," he said. "I'll stay."

Chapter 32
Just the Glass
November 1988

Menashe leaned against the door, listening. He supposed Roger had just exploded the tacky St. Basil's sculpture he'd recently found at a thrift store, and was now pounding its fragments. He looked at his watch. He waited a few more minutes. Everything was quiet. Roger's sessions all ended the same way, Menashe had come to realize; after all the glass had been broken, and smashed, and powdered, Roger would stay in the room for at least fifteen more minutes, just breathing.

Finally, Roger emerged, muttering to himself, with his coat over his arm.

"What's the matter?" Menashe asked.

Roger looked up, surprised.

"Oh, nothing," he said, looking down at his pants leg. "Just cut a hole in these new pants. You can't keep anything nice."

"Yeah."

"So, I guess I'll see you next week, then?" He turned to leave before Menashe could answer.

"Hey, Roger, wait. Did you know Lehman is quitting?"

"Yeah. Why?"

"Can you come into my office for a minute? I just want to ask you a couple things."

"What things?" he asked suspiciously.

"Just come in, will you?"

Roger followed Menashe into his office and sat down. "Don't you have another appointment coming in?"

"I moved him to later tonight. I've wanted to talk to you for a while now, but you always manage to slip out before I can."

"So what were you doing, listening? Waiting outside the room till I was done?"

"Roger," he began, taking out a new folder from his file cabinet, "I want you to fill out some forms for me."

"What forms?"

"Just some questionnaires and a personal statement."

"That's not part of our deal."

"I know. I think we should change it."

"No, no. We agreed, man, I give you the cash and you let me break the shit in there," he explained, gesturing to the rooms behind him. "You can't change that."

"It'll be better this way. Trust me."

"Why the hell would I do that?"

"Because I think you want to talk."

"No. No, no," Roger said, shaking his head and getting up. "I know what you're doing and it's not going to happen. I've said from the beginning I don't want any therapy, just the glass, and that's how it's going to be. You're not getting any more money from me."

Roger turned and began to walk out the door, then stopped. Menashe was laughing.

"Wait," he called. "Roger, I don't want to charge you any more money. I'm talking about giving you the other part of the treatment for what you're paying now."

"This isn't treatment for me, Ash!" he shouted. "Forget it, man, I'm quitting. I hope you can afford it—me and Lehman in the same week—but that's how it goes. See you around."

Roger arrived for his appointment the next week as if nothing had happened. He didn't answer when Menashe questioned him, but rather pushed past him down the hallway, mumbling that he wanted to be left alone. Menashe had expected that. Roger went into the first room and closed the door behind him. Menashe waited, wondering how long Roger could keep up his act before he needed to talk. Maybe a long time. He listened and soon heard the familiar sounds of destruction. But it was different; Roger was tearing through the museum. He was crying and yelling and smashing furiously. *What's he hiding?* Menashe leaned back and frowned. *Why does he need this?*

Roger destroyed the room in ten minutes. And once again, when he emerged, Menashe was leaning casually against the opposite wall, waiting for him.

"Were you going to tell me you broke my helmet?"

"What?" Roger panted.

"There's a big crack down the side of it and now I've got to replace it. What'd you do, throw it against the wall or something?"

"I didn't break your goddamn helmet."

"Is that right?"

"Yeah, that's right," Roger said irritably. "Sounds like something one of your nut jobs would do."

Menashe flushed. Without warning, he hit Roger hard across the face, knocking him back against the doorframe. He gripped Roger's shoulder with a strong hand.

"Don't call them that," he said in a low voice. "Not ever, all right?"

"All right, man, shit," Roger cried. "I didn't mean anything."

Menashe released him and he touched his face cautiously. Menashe closed his eyes, running his hands through his hair. He hadn't meant to react so strongly. He wasn't a violent person by nature—he had never actually hit anyone before—but hearing Roger talk about his clients that way, and seeing the dismissive look in his eyes, he just couldn't handle it.

"Come back to the office for a minute, all right?"

"No, listen, I don't want to do this again."

"Just hear me out. If you're still not interested, I'll drop it, okay?"

Roger agreed hesitantly and once again followed Menashe down the hall to his office.

Menashe poured him a glass of water and set it on the desk. Roger tenderly rubbed the side of his face. *Now I've traumatized him*, he thought regretfully.

"Do you want some ice for that?" Menashe asked, watching him closely.

"That's okay."

"I'm really sorry."

"Really, it's fine."

"Okay." Menashe turned back to his papers. "I want to talk about Lehman."

"Lehman?"

"Yeah. He was coming for, what, eight or nine months before he quit?"

"Sounds right."

"I know he thought it was pretty fun—really fun, for a while—but he's gotten bored and now he's moving on."

"So?"

"So, this is what all your friends have done. Joe, Dominic, Scott, Mario, Dylan—all of them. They come and mess around for a few months, sometimes as long as a year, but eventually they all get bored and move on."

Roger took a drink of his water and shifted in his seat.

"What's your point?"

"Roger, you've been coming here for five years," Menashe continued, leaning forward. "You did three years at just one session a month, the next year at twice a month, and this past year you fought till I let you come every week. You've never missed an appointment. Why? Why are you still coming?"

"'Cause it's fun, man, I told you."

"Bullshit."

"Really, that's all it is!" Roger protested. "So I'm not doing the same thing as my dumbass friends—that doesn't mean anything. I'm doing it just like we agreed."

"Yeah, but there's something else going on and I think I know what it is."

"You're wasting your time."

"I think you've been coming here for five years because the glass is only half the process. You do have a problem; I can see that. You've got something bothering you and maybe you thought you could fix it yourself just by 'breaking shit,' as you call it, but that's not how it works."

Roger glared at Menashe but remained silent.

"I have time now," he continued, "and I'll talk with you about it, but you need to stop kidding yourself. What you're doing, it won't get you anywhere."

"But there's no problem! Jesus, man, what do you want me to say—that I'm a drug addict? That I'm a fucking fag? Sorry, but it's not true. You're just looking for something that's not there."

"I don't think so."

"Then what are we doing?" Roger shouted. "Talk about not getting anywhere! You won't be happy until you've invented me a problem."

"I don't want to invent anything," Menashe said calmly. "I just want you to know you can talk to me."

"This is crazy! I told you there's nothing wrong."

"Then just tell me what's been on your mind lately."

"No!" Roger yelled at him. "There's nothing wrong with me!"

"I didn't say there was something wrong with you."

"You did! You said you could tell. You said you've known it for a while now."

Roger's hands were shaking and his voice wavered. Menashe hoped he wasn't about to cry.

"I'm sorry, I didn't mean it to sound like that. I just meant I thought you were struggling with some kind of problem."

"But that *is* the problem!" he shouted hysterically. "I don't fucking know what's wrong with me, all right?"

Roger rubbed both hands over his eyes and sighed heavily. Menashe refilled his water and waited a minute before speaking. He saw something familiar in Roger that he eventually came to see in all his clients: a frantic, frightening sense that they're not normal. He saw Roger trying to fit in with his friends, wearing the right clothes, knowing the right clubs and the right restaurants, caring about the right things. But that started to fall apart whenever he came to the museum.

"Okay," Menashe said finally. "So whatever's bothering you—it's not something specific?"

"No," he said, taking a deep breath and a long drink of water.

"Is it like a bad thought?"

"It's more like a feeling that won't go away."

"What kind of a feeling?"

"Well, I mean, it's not—it's not really concrete," he stammered. "I just feel . . . lost."

Menashe was silent. He watched Roger thoughtfully for a moment, then brought out his yellow legal pad.

Chapter 33
Because It Works
November 1988

Menashe stood on the sidewalk in front of Lopez Bar and Grill and lit a cigarette. It was cold, but he didn't like to wait inside. After about ten minutes, he saw John's old, precious Newport go by as he looked for parking. Menashe leaned against the side of the restaurant, trying to control his shakiness. He knew he looked worse than usual. He hadn't slept at all the past two nights and had no idea how to conceal the evidence of it.

"Hey," John greeted him a few minutes later, walking over. He looked good, as usual, with his long hair nicely combed, and wearing a new Cavs jacket. He rubbed his hands together.

"Hey."

"You always pick Lopez," he laughed. "What a hole."

"Yeah, but it's cheap and nobody else goes here," Menashe smiled.

"You've got that right."

Menashe tossed his cigarette and they both went in, moving through the neon-lit darkness to the bar. Menashe ordered whatever the special was—some Mexican beer on tap—and John ordered a Coke.

"When do you have to be back?" Menashe asked, shaking off his coat. He checked his watch. It was almost nine.

"Whenever," John shrugged. "The kids are asleep. I've got time."

Menashe nodded, settling into his seat. "So how's the writing going?"

"Pretty good, I think," he replied. "I've had to make myself stick to a strict schedule, though, otherwise I can't focus."

"That doesn't sound like you."

"I know. It's weird, but it's the only way I can get the ideas flowing."

"And you like it?"

John nodded. "I can't even tell you how happy it makes me."

"That's really great. And I'm proud of you for going for it. That takes some guts."

"Thanks. We'll see, though. I can't do it forever unless I figure out a way to make money at it. But Abby's been great. We've done a lot of cutting back and her extra shifts are really making this work."

Menashe nodded and took a long drink. "So what are you writing about?"

"It's hard to tell. I've started going off of some of the free writing you had me do after my sessions. That's actually been a great motivation. You want to read some?"

"Sure."

John reached into his back pocket and pulled out some folded papers.

"You mean it?" he laughed. "I was going to ask you for your opinion on this, if you were interested."

"Absolutely. Now?"

"No, no," John shook his head, handing the papers over to Menashe. "That'd be weird. Just anytime you feel like it."

"Great," he said, transferring them to his own coat pocket.

"So," John began, letting Menashe know he was shifting to a more serious subject, "I'm glad you called to get together, but I was a little surprised."

"Why?"

"Because you called to get together."

Menashe nodded slowly. John was right. He always was the one prodding Menashe into getting out, having some kind of human interaction.

"Are you doing okay?" John asked gently.

"Honestly," Menashe paused, "I don't know. I just don't know what I'm doing anymore."

"You mean the museum?"

"Yeah, everything. It just seems like a failure sometimes."

"A failure? You've kept it going for ten years," John said emphatically. "That's really incredible. And it's something you just can't get anywhere else."

"I guess."

"Menashe, you are helping people who have nowhere to go."

"I don't know," he said again, leaning his elbows on the bar. "I want people coming because it works, not just because it's different."

"You think they're not getting better?"

"Well, clearly you've gone to shit."

John laughed. "I can't blame you for that. So, what, is it Austin? Or can't you talk about it?"

"No, I can't talk about Austin. There's another guy, though, who's really been worrying me. I'm afraid I sent him down the wrong path."

"Oh, yeah?"

"Yeah." Menashe rubbed his face with both hands. "I'm not sure if I should talk about it. It's not like you'd ever see him or know who he was but . . . I don't know. I really might have fucked him over."

Menashe looked up and saw John was watching him closely.

"Have you been sleeping much?"

"No."

"Because of this client?"

"That's part of it, I'm sure. I just feel like I mess up everything I touch. So maybe I should just stop touching stuff."

John shook his head. "You are doing something really important, okay? I know it's hard to see right now, but it's important."

"Thanks," Menashe muttered. "I guess I'm just overwhelmed."

"So, do you—I mean, have you ever done it?"

"Done what?"

"Used the museum."

Menashe laughed at the unexpected question. It made sense, but no one had ever asked him that before.

"No," he smiled. "I mean, I've done it, but not at the museum. And not for a long time. But . . ." he trailed off, searching for the words. ". . . It wasn't like anything I've ever experienced. It's funny, you know? How there can be so much relief in something so simple."

What he couldn't tell John was that he didn't trust himself to use the museum; that he was afraid of what he might unlock.

John nodded. "Do you ever want to talk, you know, about . . . anything else?" he asked carefully.

"No," Menashe shook his head immediately.

"If you ever think it would help—"

"Ash? Ash Everett?" came an excited, squeaky voice, interrupting their conversation.

Menashe turned to the man who was now sitting beside him. He was short and lean, with a genuine smile and bright brown eyes. He was in his mid-thirties, like Menashe and John, and was conspicuously overdressed in an expensive-looking black suit.

"It's me! You don't remember me, do you?" he asked good-naturedly. Menashe shook his head.

"It's Charlie Kavanaugh. From Ohio Savings."

"Charlie, wow, I can't believe it," he said slowly, getting up and shaking his hand. "I'm sorry, you just look so different."

"Yeah," he chuckled, "I've lost a lot of weight over the past few years." He patted his flat stomach.

"Charlie, this is my friend, John. We went to school together."

"Nice to meet you, John," Charlie smiled, firmly shaking his hand. "Your buddy and I were interns together." Menashe thought Charlie would move on, but he instead sat back down with them and waved to the bartender.

"So, how have you been?"

"Oh, good," Menashe replied hazily. "Are you still in loans?"

"No, no," Charlie said. "It just wasn't for me, you know? I always wanted to be in radio, so after I left Ohio Savings, I decided to finally get my degree in broadcast communications."

"That's great. So you work for a station now?"

Charlie nodded, beaming proudly. "Yeah, it took a while to work my way up, but I actually just got promoted to station manager for WNCX. You guys know it?"

"Cleveland's Source for Nonstop Classic Rock?" Menashe asked slowly.

"That's the one! I'm glad to know you're a listener."

Menashe strained a smiled and downed the rest of his beer. "Oh, definitely," he said, gesturing to the bartender for another.

"So what do you do, John?" Charlie asked him cheerily.

"Well, right now I'm unemployed and writing stories in my basement, but I'm optimistic." John stood up and stretched. "Be right back, guys," he smiled, going off toward the restroom.

Charlie laughed. "Well, what have you been up to?" he continued, with that same intense glee. *He could be on something*, Menashe thought. *I think speed does this to people.* "Still hang around with Jeffrey?"

"Yeah, I see him around now and then."

In truth, Menashe hadn't seen or heard from their mutual friend in nearly a decade.

"That's good. He's a fun guy. I haven't really seen much of the old gang lately," Charlie admitted. "I mean, once I got out of student loans, I just never wanted to look back, you know?" he laughed. Menashe didn't respond, so they sat in silence for a minute or so. "So where are you working now?"

"Ohio Savings, still."

"Great," he exclaimed. "So, what, department supervisor? Manager?"

"Not exactly," Menashe began, edging slightly away from Charlie and pulling out his pack of cigarettes. "I'm a junior loan rep."

"Well, it's a great place to work."

Menashe laughed and lit a cigarette. He offered one to Charlie, who declined.

Charlie frowned and both men feigned interest in the television. Menashe thought maybe he should feel embarrassed, but he just didn't care. *Charlie wants to leave. Why doesn't he just walk out?*

"How's the family?" Charlie asked brightly.

"I'm actually on my own now," Menashe replied, looking toward the restroom, hoping John would emerge. "Jamie and I divorced a while ago, but it's okay, you know?" He smiled. "These things happen."

"I'm really sorry. I would never have said anything—"

"No, don't worry," Menashe stopped him. "It's really okay."

Charlie rubbed his forehead and stood up. "Well, I've got to run, but it's been nice talking to you. I'm glad we ran into each other."

"Yeah, me, too," Menashe said, working on his next drink.

"I'll give you a call sometime." He tossed a couple bills onto the bar.

"Sure, just look me up."

Charlie walked out the door of Lopez Bar and Grill into the eerily blue-lit night, leaving Menashe alone with his beer and another sleepless night ahead of him.

Chapter 34
No Direction
April 1975

Jamie was taking forever to pick her outfit. Menashe called up again from the kitchen where he was giving Wesley some applesauce and hot dog bits in his high chair.

"Seriously, Jamie!" he yelled. "Just wear whatever's comfortable!"

"I'm going with the full pantsuit," she said, walking into the kitchen. "I can take off the jacket if I need to. I just think it's more professional than the other one, right?"

"Probably," he nodded without looking up. "Just don't get all sweaty. Nobody hires the sweaty reporters."

"Check." She walked over and kissed Wesley. Menashe noticed for the first time she was still in her street clothes.

"Jamie, what the fuck? I thought you were getting dressed!"

"Hey," she frowned, "take it easy. I'm going to change after I nurse Wesley."

"Fine," he muttered. "At least he seems tired tonight. I think he'll go down easily."

"Good." Jamie checked her watch. "I've got about half an hour." Menashe was silent. "Are you okay?" she asked after a moment. "You're being kind of weird."

"Yeah, I'm fine," he replied, standing up and clearing the dishes.

He cleaned Wesley up and brought him out of the high chair, giving him a final hug and kiss before sending him off with Jamie. They retreated to Wesley's room for bedtime, leaving Menashe alone in the messy kitchen. He looked around at the piles of dishes and bits of toddler food all over the floor. He just didn't have the energy.

Menashe went to the cabinet above the fridge and reached down a tan bottle. He poured himself a glass and sat back down at the kitchen table. *What if she gets this job?* He took a long drink. The house was silent except for the ticking clock.

When Jamie came back into the kitchen she was dressed for the interview.

"All right," she breathed nervously, gathering her purse. "I'll be back." She smiled at Menashe, who had stopped doing dishes and was now turned toward her. "Love you."

"Love you, too. Good luck."

The door closed and Menashe inadvertently sighed. Jamie had been trying for months to move up at the local business magazine where she worked as an assistant. It was slow going, but this was the closest she'd ever been: final interview. The magazine was doing very well—and busy enough that it needed to squeeze all its finals into evening interviews over drinks. She was up against two other people for a reporting job Menashe knew she'd kill for, but it didn't feel right to him. And he wasn't sure why.

After finishing up in the kitchen, Menashe poured himself another drink and sat on the couch, unsure of how to use his free evening. He switched on the television. He wanted something mindless. It was always his first instinct to look for sports; he found their impersonality comforting. He never liked football much, so he clicked past a college game. *There should be something better. Baseball or soccer or—*

Hockey. His face darkened as he saw the familiar blue and white jerseys, the agile skaters tearing around the rink and spraying thin walls of ice. North Stars/ Maple Leafs. Of course it was personal. He turned it off and took another long drink, his eyes wet and glistening. The house was quiet again. It seemed so empty. *Jesus, Dad, where are you?* He squinted at the clock above the television. Jamie should be leaving the interview soon. Might even have an idea about the job. *A real job.* He looked down. His glass was empty.

Half an hour later, he was lying on the couch with his eyes closed, thinking it was as good a place as any to try to sleep, when he heard Wesley cry. It wasn't the hollow, tired cry that usually faded back into stillness, but rather a harsh, panicked cry. Like a nightmare. Menashe got up, too quickly, and rushed toward Wesley's room in a dizzy fog. In his haste, he stumbled into an end table, knocking it over with the lamp that sat on top, shattering its base and bulb. Wesley cried louder and Menashe cursed himself as he slipped into his son's room.

"Shhh, it's okay," Menashe whispered, easing Wesley back down onto his stomach and rubbing his back. His racing heart slowed as he felt his son's breath slide back into a calm rhythm. Even after Wesley was asleep he stayed, lying next to the crib, murmuring parts of nursery songs that he could remember.

The next thing he knew Jamie was shaking him, forcing his mind out of its hazy dream and back into Wesley's room.

"Menashe, come on," she whispered. "You fell asleep."

She helped him stand up slowly and make his way out of the room. The brightness of the rest of the apartment assaulted his eyes, forcing him to squint.

"What time is it?" he rasped.

"Almost ten."

"Did you get the job?"

"I don't know. Menashe, what the hell happened here?" She indicated the broken lamp on the floor.

"Wesley was crying," he began, rubbing his forehead. "I ran over to check on him and just didn't watch where I was going."

"How much did you drink?" she asked sharply, looking toward the glass and bottle on the coffee table.

"That had nothing to do with it," he said coldly. "I was nearly asleep when I heard him."

"No, Menashe, no," Jamie cut in anxiously. "I mean, it was fine before, when it was just you and me, but with a baby now, I'm not going to let this go. You cannot drink like that around him, okay? It's not safe."

Menashe felt his temperature rising.

"That's bullshit, Jamie. I had two fucking drinks. You think I can't watch my own kid? That I'm not safe enough?"

"That's not what I said."

"But you don't trust me," he pressed. "You think I'm—I don't know, irresponsible. That you'd be better off with a fucking babysitter."

Jamie didn't say anything. Maybe she was too angry to put her thoughts into words or maybe she just didn't want to start a fight. He couldn't tell.

"Maybe," he continued, "you shouldn't take this job. I mean, if you're so worried about me being around Wesley, maybe you shouldn't get a full-time job. Hell, maybe you shouldn't even have the one you've got."

He turned away from her, storming off toward their room and muttering under his breath. He sank into the bed and lay on his back, closing his eyes. He'd overreacted, again. But there was no way to make Jamie understand what was going on in his head when he didn't even know half the time. He wished he knew what to do. And he wished his father were there to tell him.

Chapter 35
Step Nine
November 1988

It was nine-thirty on Saturday morning when a firm knock at the front door interrupted a bad dream and sent Menashe groggily down the hall.

"Holy shit," he whispered to himself upon looking out the peep hole. He opened the door. "Jeffrey, what are you doing here?"

"Hey," Jeffrey replied, staring at Menashe's tattered gray sweatpants and equally worn-out thermal t-shirt. "I'm sorry, did I wake you?"

Menashe drew in his breath. He looked just the same—imposing physique, curly dark hair and lumberjack beard. If he'd been holding a beer and making a joke, Menashe would have thought they were still at one of his parties. He just couldn't believe it. And he didn't want to.

"It's fine, don't worry. Come on in."

They sat around his tiny kitchen table on yellow folding chairs Menashe had saved from one of his neighbor's trash piles. He poured them both some orange juice into plastic cups. Jeffrey had been staring off distantly until Menashe set the cups on the table. The sound seemed to bring him back to reality.

"Thanks, Ash." He took a drink. "That's got kind of a zing, doesn't it?" he remarked, squinting a bit.

Menashe took a drink and winced. "I'll say." He got up and checked the bottle. "Yeah, that expired a long time ago. Sorry." He motioned for Jeffrey to hand him his cup.

"It's growing on me, actually."

Jeffrey took another drink and shifted in his chair. Menashe shrugged and sat back down.

"So, why the visit?" he asked pointedly, nervous to even be in the same room with him.

"What," he laughed anxiously, "I can't just come over to say 'hi'? See how everything's going?" He paused and looked around. "What's with this place anyway?"

"What do you mean?"

"You're in the basement of a nightclub."

"Yeah?"

"So how'd you get it as an apartment?"

"The owner was pretty desperate to get some money out of it—I think he hadn't been in the business very long when I was looking, and I asked if he'd rent it out to me."

Jeffrey nodded.

"But really," Menashe continued, looking quizzically at his former friend, "you came over just to see how things were going—after all this time? I don't get it."

"I know, I know," he nodded. "It's just—this is kind of hard to talk about . . . what I came for, you know?"

"Talk about what?" *Do it now. Just tell him to leave.*

"And I'm sorry to just stop by like this," Jeffrey continued, idly running his finger around the rim of his cup, "but I want to talk about that night—the last night I saw you."

Menashe looked at him with a sharp, frightened expression.

"Listen," he began in a hard voice, grinding his fingernails into his palms under the table, "I really appreciate what you did, trying to help and everything, but there's nothing to talk about."

"I'm sorry, Ash," he broke in firmly, "but there's something I've got to say."

"I don't want to talk about it."

"I know, and I understand. But just listen then, okay?"

Menashe strongly considered leaving his own apartment just to get away from him, from hearing about that night. Just seeing Jeffrey again made him feel closer to the whole terrible chapter of his life—Wesley's death, the hospital, the divorce, everything. But he had already started talking.

"Well, I'm actually in AA now. I'm sure you noticed even back then how out of control I was." Menashe frowned slightly. "Anyway, there are the twelve steps, you know, that help you get better, and I'm on nine right now."

He stopped, as if he assumed Menashe would know about step nine—as if all the steps were common knowledge. Menashe looked at him blankly for a moment, but his expression quickly turned harsh when he assumed what Jeffrey must be getting at.

"Did you come over here to tell me I need to go to AA with you?" he asked incredulously. "What the fuck makes you think I still even drink?"

Jeffrey started laughing, which was, in Menashe's mind, completely inappropriate, but seemed to lessen his nervousness. He started to sound more like himself.

"No, no, I'm not interventioning you or anything," he chuckled. "Step nine is when you find all the people you've done bad shit to while you were drunk and say you're sorry."

Menashe suddenly felt cold. "Really."

"And it's not just about things you did while you were actually trashed, it's every bad decision you made during the whole time you were drinking. And I made a lot of them. Anyway, that night you and Wesley came over," he began, avoiding Menashe's eyes, "I've always felt real bad because, well, because you tried to get out of coming over and I talked you back into it. I mean, you knew it was a bad idea but I kept hounding you. So, I'm really sorry, Ash. I was wrong."

Menashe felt a strong nausea churning up his stomach, threatening to send the expired orange juice back up his throat.

"Listen, Jeffrey," he said, "I'm not going to get into it. I told you I don't want to talk about that night. If I had my way, I'd never even think about it. But since you're here, you should know I don't blame you for what happened. It was me. I made the decision to come over and I was the one who didn't think."

This response seemed to further sadden Jeffrey. "I just hope you haven't been beating yourself up these past ten years," he said.

"No, I've been fine. Really."

"And I just want you to know, I've never talked to anybody else about what happened. I figured it's nobody's business, and I don't want you thinking it turned into some gossipy story, because it didn't."

"Thanks." Menashe tapped his fingers edgily against the table to give Jeffrey the sense he was done talking about it.

"Okay. So what've you been doing with yourself?" Jeffrey asked.

"Well," he sighed, "I guess I'm finally putting that art history degree to work." His muscles relaxed slightly. "I've got a sort of museum in this place now."

"Wow, that's great," Jeffrey said, leaning in his chair and trying to catch a glimpse of one of the rooms. "Do a lot of people come in?"

"They keep me pretty busy," Menashe nodded.

"You know," he began thoughtfully, "you might want to think about getting into one of those storefronts on West Huron. Your visibility would be a lot better. They've got three up for lease right now."

Menashe smiled for the first time since Jeffrey's arrival. "Jeffrey, if you haven't noticed, I'm kind of on a budget."

"All right," he said. "I won't pry into your affairs. But can I get the tour?"

"Sure."

He led Jeffrey down the hallway and into the rooms already set up for Menashe's next appointment.

"I should warn you: some people find it a little boring. All glass, you know."

"Oh, no way," Jeffrey replied with wonder. Menashe smiled, sensing that Jeffrey was humoring him. "This is amazing. Really."

He was especially captivated by a large bowl with a detailed school of fish etched into its side. It was the top piece.

"My little sister would love this one," he remarked. "Remember how obsessed she was with fish?"

Menashe nodded and said he remembered. Jeffrey continued to walk slowly around the room, carefully peering at each piece with interest.

"I'm glad you like it," he said, showing him back to the kitchen after they toured all the rooms. "It's pretty much been my life for the last decade."

They sat down at the table again.

"What about you?"

"Still doing the marketing thing, but not for Great Lakes Brewing, obviously," he remarked, reddening. "For the last couple years I've been working for a consulting firm. It's pretty good work."

Menashe couldn't stop watching him as he spoke. There was something odd about Jeffrey and something odd about their whole encounter, but he couldn't pin it down. It was probably just the peculiarity of seeing him again after all those years—after all that had happened.

"How'd you know where to find me?" Menashe asked suddenly.

Jeffrey laughed. "I used to know Chase Stephens."

"My landlord?"

He nodded. "He owns this bar I would go to—a real shitty place called The Diamond. We'd get to talking on the nights he was managing, and one night your name came up. He told me he had a tenant by that name: a serious guy who kept to himself." Jeffrey smiled. "I guess that was . . . maybe three years ago." He looked down. "I'm sorry I haven't come by before now, I just wasn't sure if you'd want to see me."

"Don't worry about it. I'm glad you're here now." Menashe wasn't glad, but he saw no harm in telling Jeffrey what he needed to hear.

Jeffrey stayed for only a few minutes more, assuredly sensing Menashe's discomfort. After he'd gone home, Menashe went into the kitchen for something he couldn't remember and ultimately stood leaning on the counter, staring off into space, unsettled. He felt as though he'd traveled back in time but hadn't been able to change anything while he was there.

Chapter 36
Ghosts
November 1988

The harsh ring of Menashe's telephone jerked him awake. His thoughts immediately went to Jeffrey because he'd so unexpectedly reappeared in his life a few days before, but when he answered the phone he was surprised to hear a woman's voice on the other end.

"Menashe?" she asked hesitantly. It sounded as though she'd been crying.

"Yeah?"

"I'm really sorry to call so late. This is Elena."

He sat up slowly. He hadn't spoken to his cousin in nearly a year. Whatever it was, it had to be bad. And he knew he didn't want to hear it.

"Menashe? Are you there?"

"Yeah. Sorry."

"Listen, I need to talk to you about my dad."

He sighed. Nothing was ever really over. Communication between himself and Elena had lapsed when it seemed like Noah was getting better. Menashe had just figured she didn't need him anymore and understood that he wouldn't want to see her father, regardless of his condition.

"Are you okay?"

"Yeah, I'm fine. It's just—" She paused and Menashe could tell she was trying to keep it together. "Dad's not good."

"What happened?" he forced himself to ask.

"Well, it looked like he was going to be okay, you know? I mean, he'd been out of the hospital for a while, and he even seemed to get a handle on his drinking, but . . ." she trailed off again, this time unable to hold back her tears. "It's just so awful. He had another relapse and we've been back at the hospital for a week now. We just got the new test results and it looks like his liver damage is more extensive than they thought."

"I'm sorry, Elena."

She took a breath and whimpered, almost like a child. "They're doing surgery the day after tomorrow, but the prognosis isn't good."

"What are they saying?"

"His risk of infection and other complications is just so high," she explained. "But they need to try it; it's the only chance he has left. They told me to prepare for the possibility that he might not wake up."

"Shit. I'm sorry."

"I need your help."

"What do you mean?"

"Can you come to Toronto?"

"No, Elena, I'm sorry. It's not something I can do."

"Please, Menashe. I'm so sorry about your dad and I know there's nothing anyone can do to take that back. I feel terrible even asking you, but I need you here. I really think you can help him. Please think about it."

"How could I even help?"

"Because he talks about you all the time. The guilt is killing him and I think talking to you would at least put his mind at peace before this surgery. It might even motivate him to recover somehow."

Menashe groaned and desperately wanted to slam the telephone receiver back into its cradle. He knew he was reaching the limit of what he could take and wondered how many more people from his past could re-emerge before he cracked.

"What is it you expect me to say?" he demanded. "If I come up there and talk to him now, I might end up making things worse."

"Then lie," she said desperately. "Pretend to forgive him, I don't care. Menashe, I can't begin to imagine what it's been like for you since Uncle Lewis died. But now, I'm afraid my dad is going to die, too, and I know it's selfish, but if you could come to Toronto and try talking to him, at least I'll feel that I did everything I could for him."

Silence.

"Shit," he muttered finally, looking over at his alarm clock. Elena sure did have a way of getting to him. "Yeah, I'll be there."

"Thank you, Menashe. It means so much to me that you're coming. And I'll pay for your ticket, so don't worry about that. Just call when you have your flight information so I can pick you up."

"Okay, El. I'll call you."

Menashe didn't call the bank to tell them he wasn't coming in for work. He thought he'd probably change his mind anyway and show up. But he couldn't do that to her. He just numbly smoked a few cigarettes, packed a bag, and reserved a seat on the next airplane out. An MD-80.

When Menashe walked through the gate into the Pearson International Airport, he was not at all surprised to see his mother waiting for him. For reasons beyond his understanding, she had been a source of support for Noah and Elena over the years, and had no doubt been informed of his arrival in Toronto by her niece.

"Hey, Ma," he said, giving her a hug and managing a smile. *I know I look like shit.*

"Good to see you, sweetie. Is that all you brought?" she asked, indicating his beat-up duffel bag.

"Yeah. I don't plan on staying that long."

She nodded. "How have you been?"

"Not bad," he shrugged. "I'm working a lot."

"And you still see John around?"

"Yeah," he replied distractedly. "Are you coming to the hospital?"

"No, I thought I'd just drop you off if that's okay."

"Sure." *If I do this, I sure as hell don't want anyone there.*

"And I fixed your room up at the house," she continued, smiling, "so stay as long as you can."

"Thanks, but I think I'm going back home tomorrow." He sighed and wiped his palms on his coat. "I really don't want to do this."

"I know." She gently rubbed his back as they walked through the terminal. "But I think it's important—for your health, especially."

"My health is fine."

"Do you see a doctor?"

"Ma, my health is fine."

"Okay," she said in a wistful tone that let Menashe know she was giving up to avoid a fight. "But you're the only son I've got. I just want to know you're all right."

Menashe felt his body shudder as he walked into Riverdale Hospital. He hadn't been inside a hospital in ten years, but that familiar smell jerked *they just can't swim that long*

him back instantly—bad food, industrially cleaned linens, and medication. It radiated hopelessness.

He walked briskly down the hall and got on the elevator. He took a deep breath, overcome by the inevitability of the unbearable task awaiting him on the fourth floor. *Elena said she'd be waiting. I'm not doing this if she's not there.*

But she was there. She hugged him and told him how wonderful he was for coming all that way, when he knew there was nothing wonderful about it.

"Should I go in?" he asked, anxious to get it over with.

"Sure," she replied. "He's awake. I told him you were coming."

"What did he say?"

"Nothing."

He walked into the room. The only light came from a dim table lamp sitting on the nightstand. Once his eyes adjusted to the darkness, Menashe could see the thin figure of Noah Everett, sitting up in bed with matted gray hair and pale, papery skin. He was, at fifty-eight, still young, but his condition had aged him dramatically. Menashe never thought he could look so fragile.

"Uncle Noah," he said as evenly as he could. "I'm here."

"You're here," Noah repeated weakly.

"All the way from Cleveland-fucking-Ohio."

Menashe thought his uncle might be crying, but it was too dark to tell. And he needed to focus on keeping himself together so he stared at the ground, trying to gather his scattered thoughts.

"Elena's lucky to have you," Noah replied softly.

"Yeah," he murmured, feeling his temperature rise. "It's pretty bad if I'm this family's best shot."

"You've always been a good kid."

"Thanks."

"Are you all right?" Noah asked, scrutinizing him with dull, gray eyes.

"I'm fine."

"How are things in Cleveland?"

"Okay, I guess."

"You got a girlfriend?"

Menashe began to tremble. "Are you trying to have a normal conversation with me?"

"I just want to know how things are going."

"Well, stop, all right?" He only then realized he'd been pacing the floor in front of the bed. He rubbed his eyes. "I don't even know why I'm here."

"I know."

"Why?"

"Elena. You've always been so kind to her. I appreciate that."

Menashe nodded and walked over to his uncle, sitting down in the stiff chair by his bedside. Noah watched him carefully, narrowing his eyes as they crossed the path of the lamplight.

"You can say anything you want," he murmured. "I know this can't be easy."

Menashe closed his eyes. "You're right. I only came here because Elena said she needed me, but now, I don't think I'm going to be much help."

"Why do you say that?"

"Because I can't forgive you."

Noah turned away and remained silent.

"Menashe," he began after a moment, "I really did want to see you, and I'm very grateful to you for coming to Toronto, but I never expected you to forgive me."

"What?"

"It's okay. You don't have to."

Menashe sat back, bewildered. "But Elena . . . she said you talk about me all the time. She said if I forgive you, you might get better."

Noah smiled slightly. "No, son. I'm not getting better. I really just wanted to talk to you."

"But you don't want me to forgive you?" he asked, frowning.

"Menashe, you have to understand. What happened," he began, his voice shaking, "that's something I live with every day. And every day I pray God will forgive me, but I can't ask that of you. All I can do is tell you how sorry I am. I know Elena's told you I've been having a rough time," Noah continued, "but I also know that it can't compare to what you've gone through. I—"

"Uncle Noah," Menashe broke in, blinking rapidly. "I need to ask you something."

"Of course."

"That night you and Dad went out," he said, trembling again, "you had been drinking, right? That's what caused the accident."

"No." His uncle shook his head, his eyes suddenly sharp. "No, Menashe, that wasn't it at all. In fact, that night I was closer to quitting than I'd ever been before. Because of your dad. He told me I needed help and I blew him off, of course, but I kept thinking about it. You know," he said, "I had always admired him for going sober, though I never admitted it. I just never found the strength he had."

"Wait," Menashe stopped him. "What do you mean 'going sober'? Dad never drank."

"Well, no, not that you would remember. I guess you were about four or five when he quit. . . . You mean he never told you?"

"No."

"Oh, I'm sorry, son," Noah sighed. "I don't mean to cast him in a different light for you. But in a lot of ways, he's so much stronger for what he was able to do."

Menashe sat silently for a moment, wiping his eyes with his sleeve.

"What made him stop?"

Noah smiled. "You did."

"What do you mean?"

"There was something really important to you—your first soccer or t-ball game, something like that. Anyway, you were so excited for him to be there. But the night before, Lewis drank so much he couldn't get out of bed the next morning to go with you. I remember he said he'd never forget how disappointed you were. You told him you didn't want to keep it up if he wasn't going to be there. And that was all it took. He got himself the help he needed and never looked back." His voice was soft and unsteady. "You gave him his life back, Menashe. You were his guy. Always."

Menashe nodded, unable to speak, as he could no longer keep himself from crying. He hadn't allowed himself to really think about his father in a long time. And he wasn't disillusioned by what his uncle had told him. He was relieved.

"I have to go," he finally whispered, unused to such a flood of emotion. "I have to, I have to get back home. I—"

Noah reached out and grasped his arm weakly, forcing Menashe to look into his eyes.

"I am so sorry I took him away from you."

Menashe shook his head, rising from his chair as new tears began to fall. He had the strange and unsettling feeling that he had no idea what he was about to do. There was pressure building inside of him, and he could just as easily punch the wall as he could puke his guts out. He turned back to Noah, who was watching him closely, small and frail but still looking so much like the man he remembered. And the man he'd lost. He leaned down and hugged him, letting the memories escape through his sobs and for a brief moment, feeling like the child of a family again.

Chapter 37
Good Try
December 1988

Menashe sat on the ground outside The Velvet Dog, about half an hour early for the poker game. He watched a few kids, maybe high-schoolers, throwing rocks and messing around on the train tracks across the street. *I'm twenty years older than they are.* He took a long drag from his cigarette and leaned against the brick wall. It was starting to snow. He closed his eyes. He couldn't stop thinking about Noah. He'd felt so good at first, learning that he'd helped his father through the biggest struggle of his life. But after coming home, he started to think about his own role as a father. And how badly he'd failed. He blinked a few times, trying to clear his thoughts, and stared out into the snow. A few minutes later, Chase came walking down the sidewalk to the club, carrying his briefcase.

"Hey, Ash," he said, slowing his pace. "You get locked out?"

Menashe shook his head. "Just needed some air."

"It's like twenty degrees out."

"I don't mind the cold." He smiled.

"Whatever," Chase laughed. "You want to come in yet? The guys should be along soon."

"Sure."

He extended his hand and Menashe took it, pulling himself up.

"I don't know how you can smoke in this weather anyway," Chase continued, unlocking the door. "It kills my chest, makes me hack up all kinds of shit."

"Yeah, me, too," Menashe admitted. "I guess I'm pretty addicted."

"Well, we all have our demons."

Chase heaved the overflowing briefcase onto a table. "I have to work out a better system for all this." He sighed deeply, pulling off his coat. His club shirt was purple that night. It was a good color on him. "Taking on that third bar might have been a mistake."

"You've got three now?"

"Indeed I do. It's called Aquilon . . . or The Aquilon. Anyway, nice place, just south of the Center Street Bridge."

"That's great," Menashe replied, collapsing into a chair. "I'm sure you can handle it."

"Yeah," Chase said doubtfully, looking around the room. At that moment the club's door swung open and all three of the others came trudging in, stomping their feet on the mat.

"You guys came together?" Menashe asked.

Sam laughed. "No way, man. I was almost here when I saw Paul's cab go by, so I waited for him. And Lenny wasn't far behind, skulking around."

Lenny gave him a sour look as he took off his coat.

By the time they got their drinks and found their places around the table, all the guys were eager to start playing. But Menashe couldn't focus. He found himself losing track of the game, slipping off into his own thoughts and missing parts of the conversation. When he once again missed his turn to bet, Paul spoke up.

"Ash, what is going on tonight? Are you sick or something?"

Menashe looked at him, surprised, and saw that the others were looking at him, too, waiting for the answer.

"I'm sorry," he mumbled, rubbing his bristly face. "I guess I'm just tired. I'll try to keep up."

"Well, wait a minute," Sam frowned, holding up his hand to prevent Paul from continuing the game. "Tell us what's going on. You've been weird all night—something must have happened."

"It's been a long week," he acknowledged. "You guys don't want to hear about it, though."

"Sure we do," Chase said.

Menashe glanced around the table again and it seemed they were interested. *Make something up.*

"I went out of town a few days ago," he began reluctantly. "To see my uncle. I hadn't talked to him in years, but he's really sick, so I went. For my cousin, really. And it was all right," he said thoughtfully. "I mean, better than I expected, but . . . I don't know, it was just strange, being back home and seeing him after all that time. So," he held up his cards, "mystery solved, and I will try to keep my head in the game, okay?"

"Sure," Chase nodded, and the others all murmured in agreement.

"Great."

They continued quietly for a while, placing bets and stacking chips, passing around the pretzels Chase kept stocked. Menashe wanted to give them more, but he didn't know how. He couldn't explain himself without bringing in too much of his past. *What would I say—that everything with Noah just made me think of what I did to my own son? They don't even know I had a son . . .* His heart just wasn't in it that night.

"So," Sam began, stacking his chips casually, "why did you stop talking to your uncle?"

Paul coughed into his drink. "Sam! Mind your own business, will you?"

"What? I am," he replied. "Ash is my friend and my friends are my business." He turned to Menashe. "You can tell me to back off if you want. I just want to help, that's all."

Menashe shook his head, reddening. "I don't mind you asking. But I really don't think I can talk about it."

"Sure. It just doesn't seem like you have a lot of—"

"Leave it the fuck alone, Sam," Lenny growled. "I'm serious."

Sam looked surprised, then held up his hands. "Okay. You're right. I'm sorry, Ash."

"Don't worry about it."

Menashe looked at his watch. It was only ten but he needed to get out of there. To be alone. He needed to think about his sessions for the coming week. And he needed to forget.

"Hey, I'm sorry to do this," he said, rising from his chair, "but I've got to be up really early. I think I'm going to go get some sleep." He frowned. He was sorry; it was the first time he'd left the group early since he started going.

They all said good night but Sam followed him to the door.

"Listen, is this about what I said?" he asked in low voice. "I'm really sorry. I'm going to start working on some boundary issues—"

"No," Menashe smiled. "It's not that. You were great. And thanks for calling me a friend."

As he walked out of the club, Menashe drew his coat around him and hurriedly descended the steps to his apartment. He then caught sight of a figure, slumped down in the corner of the landing.

"Austin?"

Austin lifted his head slowly, then jumped up when he saw it was Menashe. "Christ, Austin. What happened?"

Even though the temperature that day had been in low twenties, he was dressed as though he were going to the beach. Austin wore an unwashed white shirt, muddy khaki pants, tan canvas thong sandals, and his same faded purple baseball cap. He was obviously hung-over, with a dark-red burn stretching across his throat. He shook badly, which caused him to lean heavily against the doorframe.

"I want to talk about Vietnam."

Chapter 38
Austin's Tour
October 1968

The air in An Khe was thick and humid. The rainy season was winding down, and Austin supposed the heat was only going to get worse. He would soon find out, anyway. He'd been in Vietnam for eight months and expected to be there for many more.

Austin had fallen behind his platoon when the sergeant asked him to stop a group of locals for questioning. This didn't bother him; he'd gotten a reputation for connecting well with the local people, and he preferred it to most other duties. They were rice farmers, and when Austin asked them a few questions about the VC, they'd given him a typical response: "America number one, Viet Cong number ten!" When he saw nothing more would be said on the matter, he let them continue on their way and hurried back onto the path, hoping to catch up to his unit before nightfall.

Austin had not been drafted into the army, but rather signed up voluntarily. It was an unusual occurrence at that point in the war, and caused him to be ostracized by those in his company who had grown to resent America's involvement. Before going to Vietnam, Austin lived with his family in Edina, Missouri. His parents were farmers, but his father also managed a local grocery store, for which Austin and his three sisters worked as part-time cashiers and grocery baggers. Bill Gendron had served as a Sergeant Major in the army for twenty years, including active duty for the entirety of the Korean War. He was quite modest regarding his accomplishments, however, and rarely spoke about the war. Austin admired everything about his father: his kind and gentle demeanor, his incredible work ethic, and, of course, his selfless service to his country. So in early February of 1968, when Austin was not quite twenty years old, he offered to fight in Vietnam. The army eagerly accepted.

It was still bright out, but Austin was worried. If darkness fell and he was alone, something would surely happen to him before he made it back. He trudged along with his immense pack and M16 strapped to his back. With eight months in-country, he had more experience than most guys in his company but wasn't used to going out by himself. He assumed Sergeant Ellison had asked him to stay back alone because their squad was down to four men and replacements hadn't shown up yet. A full squad was rare to find, but Austin's had been drastically reduced by a week of heavy combat. He walked as quietly as he could, making sure none of his gear clanked together. The ground was squishy with wet plant matter and thick mud. His right boot sank into a patch of deep mud and he made a face. *Why does it have to fucking rain all the time?*

His thoughts were interrupted by rustling he heard on the path up ahead. He automatically fell to one knee and pulled the gun off his left shoulder, aiming it carefully at the sound. He stayed low to the ground and crept forward silently. The path curved sharply to the left and he couldn't see around the corner, so he stood up and inched his way along, hugging the inside edge. When it straightened out again, he saw it was just a stray dog running through the underbrush that had made the noise. What he saw next made him cry out. It was a man from his company. Austin tried to breathe but his chest felt torn apart. Steve Wells, a twenty-five-year-old private, lay dead in the middle of the path.

"Steve?" Austin called out softly, carefully approaching him.

As he got closer, he could see the severity of Steve's injuries. He turned and pitched toward the edge of the path, falling to his knees and vomiting into the jungle. He saw that metal shrapnel was lodged in what looked like every part of his body. *Jesus, he hit a claymore.* Steve's left eye had been pierced by a triangular sliver of metal, and blood mixed with yellowish pus oozed down his face. The shards gleamed brilliantly in the sunlight and the horrible sight made Austin think of a pincushion. But the piece of shrapnel that had most certainly drained Steve's life away was one that had firmly lodged itself in his throat. As he lay in the mud, Austin could see that a heavy stream of blood had poured out of the wound, further saturating the earth and creating a brick-red paste.

He hadn't known him very well. Steve had been closer with the older guys more his age. But they'd sat up together several nights at the LPs when Austin had only a few weeks in-country, and he remembered how Steve would try to make him feel better about the shit they would hear. He'd explain away the frightening noises and say things like, "We never get mortared here," but most of the time, all he'd have to do was shake his head or smile over at Austin to make him feel like everything was okay.

Austin sat down on the muddy ground next to him, unsure of what to do. A few minutes passed. He sat looking at Steve. It was starting to rain again.

"We're moving out tonight," he muttered, looking around, wondering if he was about to cry. "I just can't believe this."

The rain made Steve's skin shine and washed away some of the blood. *He's dead. He's not going home.* They were about five klicks from camp and it was getting dark. Austin took out his poncho and put it on. He took Steve's helmet off to look for photographs. There weren't any. He opened up his pack and found cigarettes, some ammunition, water, C-rations, a poncho, and several letters. No weed. *That's right, Steve didn't mess around with that.*

He lit a cigarette. His hands were trembling, and it was hard for him to shield it from the rain.

He knew he should be getting back to camp. Lieutenant Veneman would get on him for being so late—he wouldn't care about Steve. Austin brought the wavering cigarette to his lips and stared off into the rain. His feet were starting to itch. He looked down at Steve's body, wondering who wrote him all those letters. He didn't dare read them.

He took Steve's poncho out of his pack and wrapped it around the body. He didn't want to look at the gruesome wounds anymore. And it made Austin uncomfortable to see him getting soaked in the rain. Austin felt a knot rising from his stomach to his throat and thought he was going to throw up again. It might make him feel better.

He sat quietly next to Steve for a few more minutes, finishing his cigarette. He stood up slowly, exhausted. *We've got to bury him. I'll just carry him back to camp. It'll be okay, it'll be okay* . . . Austin stood there repeating this to himself, hoping he would come to believe the words, when he looked back down at the plastic-covered body lying in the mud. He knew it would never be okay. Nothing he had seen or done was okay. And now another man was gone.

The humiliation and horror of what it was to die in that place rushed into his brain, and the lump in his throat now threatened to choke him. He sat back on the ground, sinking into the mud next to the body. He didn't care if he ever got up again. He sat there with his eyes closed, listening to the soft tapping sound of the rain on their ponchos. The sound threatened to drive him insane.

Austin bent over to pick up Steve's body. He just had to go ahead and do it. He bent over and at that moment a bullet whirred past his head. He straightened himself, startled, and looked into the silent forest. He stooped again to lift

Steve when three more bullets flew past him. One grazed his arm and a trickle of blood ran down to his elbow. He cried out. He turned quickly in the direction he believed they were shooting from. He thought he saw the glint of a shiny black shirt button, but it disappeared so quickly it must have been a trick of the light. Or his mind. He crouched down, trying to remain hidden. Everything was still, except for the rain. He waited.

A few minutes later he moved to get up and a sniper shot him squarely in the shoulder.

"Shit!" he cried.

Blood was soaking through his green khaki shirt and poncho, and it felt as though his arm was on fire. The rain blurred his vision and he knew he was close to breaking down. Close to giving up. That soft patting of the rain was too much for him. He started shaking. He fell to his knees and threw up, coughing raggedly. The blood was running down his hand and dripping off his fingers. He couldn't stop shaking. He needed to go—to get back to camp and find a medic. He couldn't bring Steve.

Austin took a breath and lowered himself into the mud. He crawled with the most excruciating pain he'd ever known coursing through his arm. Once he reached the end of the path, he jumped up and ran through the dense jungle, reminding himself to keep breathing.

Steve.

No one would remind him to keep breathing. No one would re-read his letters or smoke his cigarettes. No one would tell the new kids that the sounds were harmless, that they'd get out of there alive.

Chapter 39
Austin's Last Session
December 1988

Austin took the handful of tissues Menashe passed him. He laughed scornfully at what a mess he had become.

"There's just so much shit in my head: the blood and the booby traps and the snipers." He took his hat off and ran his hand through his hair. "And then Steve. It's too much, you know? It won't let me rest."

"Then maybe you could take it one thing at a time," Menashe said. "When you're in the rooms, instead of letting all your thoughts come down on you, just try focusing on one thing. When you think you can let it go, focus on something else."

"I don't know."

"You don't think it'll work?"

"No. I don't think anything'll work, really. Not anymore."

"Well, maybe that's the problem," Menashe replied. "I mean, if you don't believe this can work—that you can get better—I don't think it's going to happen." He paused. "Will you try really focusing this time? I think it'll help."

Austin sat silently for a minute, squeezing his hands into fists over and over, trying to release some of the tension he felt building inside of him. But his breath kept picking up, and his face reddened as he felt something terrible rising to the surface.

"Damn it!" he exclaimed, slamming his fist on the desk.

Menashe jumped in his seat.

"Hey, calm down, okay?"

"No! You don't fucking get it, all right?" he shouted, rising from his chair. "It's not that easy!"

"I know," Menashe said, holding his hands up. Austin saw they were shaking. "I know it's not easy."

"You say I can just concentrate better and make everything go away! You think I have control over that?" he growled. "It's not going away."

Menashe looked toward the door. "Listen, do you want to step out for a minute? Get some air?"

Austin frowned, thrown off. "Why?"

"I don't know, just to cool down a little."

"What the hell, Ash?" Austin rubbed his face in frustration then threw up his hands. "What do you want me to do? You know what this is like for me, talking about all this. Why are you trying to get rid of me?"

"I'm not. I just, I guess, I didn't mean to upset you so much."

Austin smiled weakly and sat down. "That's funny, Ash. I always thought it was your job to upset me."

Menashe laughed and settled back into his chair.

"Should we keep going, then?"

"I don't know." Austin narrowed his eyes pensively.

"What do you mean?"

"I'm just thinking."

"About what?"

"Do you mind if I switch things up for a sec? You know, do a little therapy on you?"

Menashe laughed nervously. "I'm not sure what that means."

"I just think I know what's been going on with you."

"With me?"

"Yeah."

"All right," Menashe shrugged after a moment. "Go ahead."

"I think you've been watering down your therapy," he replied, leaning forward the way Menashe sometimes did. "You know, giving in, trying to avoid a fight." Menashe didn't say anything, so he continued. "I mean, we used to really get into it, remember? You'd ask me all kinds of stuff I didn't want to talk about, and at the time I'd hate you for it, but it always made me think. It made me try to figure out what my problem is. But now, you never let it get that far."

Austin sighed, taking off his baseball cap and tapping it against the leg of his dirty khakis. He looked away from Menashe.

"I'm sorry about what happened before; I really am. It's just another goddamn thing I wish I could take back. And I know you're afraid I'm going to lose my shit and lay into you again." He glanced up briefly and saw Menashe was looking down. "But I swear to God, Ash, that wasn't me. I'd never do it on purpose."

Menashe nodded slowly. "I know."

"So, is this still going to be all right? Me coming here, I mean."

"Of course," Menashe said firmly, finally meeting his eyes. "I want this to work for you. And you're right; I haven't been myself lately and that's not fair."

"Just takes time, I guess," Austin replied, absently touching the sore burn across his throat.

"You want to talk about what happened there?" Menashe asked, indicating his throat.

Austin shook his head. "No, man. Not tonight."

Menashe frowned. "Will you do me a favor?"

"I doubt it."

"Will you take my coat—when you leave tonight?"

Austin laughed. "I'm fine. I've still got mine, at home . . . just wasn't thinking. I really haven't noticed the weather lately."

"Okay."

Menashe stacked his papers. "Should we start your session, then?"

He shrugged. "Sure."

"And you'll try what I said? Really picking out the details of what's been bothering you?"

"Yeah, I guess." Austin sighed heavily.

He didn't want to try it or anything else, but he had promised his friend John that he'd give this a real shot. And Austin really owed him one. He had saved his life during the war when Lieutenant Veneman found Austin's weed and John claimed it as his own. John was from another platoon, so Veneman had to turn the matter over to his lieutenant who didn't give a fuck if his men wanted a little escape. Austin recalled that John even gave his stash back to him a few days later. He knew if he was caught again Veneman would see through their story and his punishment would be terrible, but he didn't care. It was worth it.

Austin sat back in the dim office, earnestly thinking about what Menashe had said and making up his mind to give himself a genuine chance at moving on. Menashe got up from his desk and walked toward the door to lead him down the hallway. Austin reached out and held his arm as he passed, giving him a hard look.

"Before I do this, do you think you can give me a decent drink?" he asked, holding up his empty glass.

"Sure," Menashe replied, moving back toward his desk and pulling out a bottle of whiskey from the bottom drawer.

The remaining glass bottles clanked against each other as he slid the drawer back into place. He took Austin's glass from his outstretched hand and filled it halfway. He then took his own empty Ohio Savings coffee mug and filled it halfway. He handed Austin's glass back to him and reclined in his chair, drinking from his mug.

"Thank you, Ash."

He drank his whiskey in one breath and then set the glass down on the desk. Menashe continued to drink slowly.

"So you really think it'll be different this time?" Austin asked after a long silence.

"I think you can make it different, yes."

"Fair enough."

This time Austin took two rooms. Menashe walked him down the hall and handed him the gear and the bat. Neither of them spoke, but Menashe smiled reassuringly before he walked back to his office, locking the door behind him. Austin smiled slightly before closing the door and taking a deep breath. He held the bat and started jumping up and down, getting his energy flowing. *Okay . . . Lieutenant Veneman, think about Lieutenant Veneman.* He closed his eyes and kept jumping, getting back to where he was in Vietnam. *That bastard was the one getting us all wound up—getting us ready to kill.* Austin could picture his face now. He could hear him making speeches to the boys in his camp. He could hear him orating to Bravo Company, telling them attractive lies that got the job done at Bi Quan.

As painful as it was, he kept the memories trapped in the forefront of his mind as he raised the bat. He smashed more rhythmically and methodically and felt calmer almost immediately. He didn't lose control or cry or scream or charge the other rooms. He did it just like Menashe told him—one thing at a time, one nightmare at a time, one atrocity at a time. And when a memory threatened to shut him down, and make him go numb again, he forced himself to feel it—to know it really happened.

Please, he begged as he shattered a pitcher, images of combat in Dak To flashing through his mind. *Please, let me go.*

When it was over, an unusual feeling came over him. He thought it might have been relief, but he couldn't be sure. By the time he left, he was confident he would sleep through the night.

It was nearly one-thirty that morning when Austin stumbled out of The Diamond in Cleveland's unsavory Flats District. It was bitterly cold and the wind tore at his poorly clothed body, but he felt nothing. He stood, mesmerized by The Diamond's blue neon sign for a few minutes, and then turned away sadly. *Dammit, Steve, why were we even there?*

He sat down on the curb and looked up at the bright-yellow moon, trying to clear his head, but could only see that mutilated eye staring back at him, unseeing, with a shard of shrapnel lodged in its pupil. He shivered.

"Damn, it's December—get a fucking coat!" yelled a man passing by, flicking his cigarette butt into the street.

Austin didn't even turn toward the man when he spoke, but rather continued staring numbly at the moon, allowing his tormented thoughts to shut him down. *Ash said it would be different*, he reflected, but sitting on the edge of Fall Street with the iridescent moon cruelly taunting him, mocking him, he knew nothing had changed. He shuddered, tears gleaming in his eyes, and tried to stand—to get away from his thoughts—but the sudden movement caused his head to reel and forced him back onto the curb. He sat there helplessly for several minutes, rubbing his hands together.

His vision was blurry from a mixture of his tears and his inebriated state, so when a figure approached him, he was not able to recognize it immediately. The man stood at the edge of the street, staring down at him reproachfully.

"What the fuck is this, Gendron?" the man barked. Austin stared with wet and reddened eyes, disbelieving what he saw.

"Lieutenant Veneman?"

Summoning all his strength, Austin hauled himself to his feet in an effort to properly address his superior. Inexplicably, the lieutenant looked exactly as he had twenty years before, right down to the green khaki uniform. His shadowy frame was tall and muscular, with thick dark hair that hadn't thinned or even grayed, and his stubbly face was sunburned. Austin watched Veneman with fascination and horror, as if their interaction proved he would never be rid of the chapter of his life he'd worked so hard to forget.

"So this is what you do with yourself, huh? You have some bad dreams so instead of sleeping you get shit-faced and spend the night crying on street corners?" Veneman sneered. "I guess it makes sense—I mean, you were never really cut out for the job we were doing. Your heart just wasn't in it like some of the other boys. Like Dereck. Remember?"

Austin nodded. "Yes, sir."

Veneman took a few steps closer, allowing the streetlamp to bathe him in sickly golden light.

"I know you've been feeling sorry for yourself, but that's bullshit, Gendron. You should be living up to the example your father set." He gazed past Austin and into the darkness. "As you know, I had the honor of serving with him in Korea when I was just a private. You could tell right away there was something about him. He was a born leader." He focused back on Austin. "Do you have any idea what he did for you? For all of us?"

He nodded miserably. "Yes, sir, my father was a great man." His voice caught in his throat as he looked at Veneman's stern face.

Austin lowered his eyes quickly, and noticed something that sent a cold shiver down his spine.

"You've got blood on your shoes," he said softly. *He can't be here. He looks like he just walked out of Bi Quan.*

Veneman looked down at the dried brown splotches that tarnished his black combat boots and smiled. "Cigarette?" he asked, holding out a red-and-gold pack of Lucky Strikes.

Austin reached out cautiously and took one that was jutting out of the pack. Veneman struck a match, lighting Austin's cigarette and then his own. He took a long drag.

"Nothing ever really changes, Gendron," he continued, exhaling deeply. "Like you. You will always be weak and afraid. I know the type. Now, tell me if this sounds familiar," he began. "Your stomach hurts all the time. Even makes you throw up for no reason. And you're almost always alone even though that's what scares you most."

Veneman locked eyes with Austin, his voice hardening. "Twenty years later and you wake up thinking you're still in the jungle. And I'll bet you have at least one bottle of booze in every room of your house, just in case."

Austin looked away from Lieutenant Veneman as the tears threatened to burst through his sore eyes.

"Come on, Gendron," he continued. "You pack your mind with so many worthless memories and nightmares that one day you won't be able to take it anymore and you'll blow your fucking brains out." He chuckled. "And won't that be something? You were so goddamned afraid of getting shot until you got home and decided to do the job yourself."

Austin stood silently at attention because that was how he was taught, but he wanted badly to tell Lieutenant Veneman to fuck himself—that he hadn't been afraid of getting shot in Vietnam. It wasn't death that had terrified him, it was the thought of dying in that place—dying without basic human dignity, forced to count his last seconds alone with the world rapidly growing dim around him. Even two decades later the thought made him shudder.

"Gendron!" Veneman snarled.

"I'm sorry, sir."

"Austin," he began again, in a surprisingly gentle tone, "did you really think things would be different?"

Austin again thought of Menashe, and all the time he had spent at the museum. He thought of Menashe's intense, foolhardy belief he was getting better. *I never made it different*, he lamented.

"No, sir, I guess I didn't," he conceded with a sigh. Veneman put his arm firmly around Austin's stooped shoulders.

"It's okay," he said. "Everything will be fine now."

Austin staggered blindly out of the Flats District, hurling his half-smoked cigarette into the street. After nearly a mile of walking, he was still trying to dispel the unsettling conversation with Lieutenant Veneman from his mind. *This can't be real. There's no way he could be here . . . or know what he knows.* Somehow Veneman knew he hadn't improved at all—that he was still the same frightened kid he'd been back then. But what hurt more was the fact that Veneman knew Austin had failed to live up to his father's reputation, both as a soldier and a man. It hurt because he knew himself it was true, and it was something he could never rectify.

It was now a few minutes past three a.m., and Austin found himself walking along a deserted street that ran perpendicular to the Cuyahoga River. He stopped on the bridge, holding the iron railing tightly as he swayed from side to side, his rough hands pale and chapped from the winter air. The current moved the black water swiftly, sending soft ripples rushing downstream. The moon reflected eerily off the river's dark canvas, causing his flesh to creep. He shivered and thought again of Lieutenant Veneman, deciding it couldn't have been his imagination that brought him there that night. Somehow, he knew the truth, and Austin was meant to hear it. *He was right, I know he was. I've never done a brave thing in my life—it's all just been a waste. Jesus, he was right about everything.*

Austin paced the bridge, thinking about Veneman's prediction that one day his tormented mind would be too much for him to handle and he'd blow his brains out. *Or jump off a bridge.* There was really no one left in his life to care about him: his parents were dead and his sisters were living contented farming lives with their husbands back in Edina. He had no wife or children, not even a dog to miss him. He did have one friend, John Cook. But they were too different in Austin's mind: John had been getting better.

Austin's heart began to pound fiercely as adrenaline rushed through his body. He was in control. If he said stop, it would stop.

He hauled himself on top of the thick iron crossbeam that served as a railing and looked over the calm black water polluted by streaks of yellow light. *It probably won't even hurt.* But that didn't matter because it felt right. He was home and no one was going to pull the trigger on his own life but him. He closed his eyes and drew in his breath slowly, thinking about the frigid water below and readying himself for the shock.

He stopped. *Menashe cared about me.* The thought seeped into his mind quietly, so different from his usual thoughts that assaulted his brain and left him numb.

Austin remembered there was a pay phone at the next corner, so he reluctantly climbed down off the railing and began to walk down the rough, gravelly road, swaying slightly as he went. When he reached the booth, he wedged himself inside and shut the door, even though no one was around. He pulled his wallet out of his back pocket and rummaged through it until he found Menashe's business card. Luckily, he found a few dimes in his pocket as well. He picked up the receiver and cradled it against his ear while he pumped change into the slot and dialed the number.

Chapter 40
The Phone Calls
December 1988

Menashe awoke to his phone ringing. He answered it, half asleep. He sat up and rubbed his arm across his eyes. His head was throbbing and his eyes squinted painfully as he turned on the lamp by his bed. The voice on the other end was frantic and disjointed.

"Austin, please," his voice cracked. "Austin, tell me where you are." He listened but couldn't make out half of what Austin was saying. "Wait, Veneman? No, just tell—Austin, what's the name of the bridge?" Menashe could only hear his cries now, so he slammed down the receiver and rushed to get dressed.

There were a lot of bridges in Cleveland. He drove around for two hours, checking the ones he knew, the ones close to bars, the ones close to pay phones. The few people who were out hadn't seen anyone matching Austin's description. He finally had to head home, knowing he was at risk of falling asleep at the wheel.

It was Saturday, and Menashe had no appointments. He awoke once again to the sound of the telephone ringing. It was Larry from Ohio Savings.

"Hey, Ash? Sorry, man, were you asleep?"

"Yeah, Larry," he growled, coughing a few times. "What'd you need?"

"Hell, you're a real pretty picture when you wake up," he kidded.

"Well, I'm not exactly a morning person."

"It's one-thirty."

"What'd you need, Larry?"

"I just wanted to let you know, Kevin'll be on your back next week since you've been kind of spacey lately. I've been able to cover for you so far, just don't be late or get behind again, all right?"

"Yeah." Menashe leaned over in his bed and pulled the alarm clock closer to him, squinting at it to see if it actually was one-thirty. "Thanks, Larry. I'll keep that in mind."

"All right, man. Go back to sleep."

Twenty minutes or so after Larry called him, Menashe's phone rang again. He had just been drifting back into an uncomfortable, hazy sleep when the alarming sound caused him to sit bolt upright in bed, his heart pounding.

"What?" he snarled into the receiver, past the point of courtesy.

"Menashe Everett?" a young man's voiced asked with trepidation.

"Yeah, what is it?" he asked without softening his tone. He rubbed his eyes, now bright red, with the back of his hand, causing a small fireworks display to burst inside his eyelids.

"Are you a friend of Austin Gendron's?"

"Yeah, I know Austin," he said, suddenly alert. "Who are you? Do you know where he is?"

"Well," the small voice began, "my name is Ryan Douglass and I work for the East Cleveland Police Department. I'm afraid Mr. Gendron is in the hospital. He attempted suicide early this morning."

Menashe couldn't respond.

"I'm so sorry. Are you related?"

Menashe opened his mouth and tried several times to speak, but found he could hardly breathe.

"Why did you call me?" he finally uttered.

"Your business card was found in Mr. Gendron's wallet and he'd written a note to you on the back. He had no next of kin in the state and I was wondering if you'd come down so we can ask you some questions."

"No," Menashe managed to say. "No. I can't do this—not now. I didn't, I mean . . . Wait, where did you find him? Is he going to be okay?"

"I can't give you much detail, but I know he's still unconscious. He jumped from the Main Avenue Bridge into the C—"

"Main Avenue!" Menashe cried out. "I went to Main Avenue. I went everywhere trying to find him."

"So he talked to you before he did this?"

"He called me. I knew he was on a bridge but . . ." Menashe trailed off. "How did he get to the hospital?"

"Luckily some campers saw him floating soon after and pulled him to shore. We have reports of a leg injury and head injury upon arrival at the hospital, but

I don't have much else to go on." He paused. "Do you think you could come in today?"

"Today? No, I'm sorry. I'm sorry, I just can't. This is—"

"That's fine, Mr. Everett," Douglass broke in calmly. "But if you don't mind, I'll call you back in a few days to schedule a time when you can meet with us. And I'll call you sooner if there's anything to report from the hospital."

"Yeah, fine," he agreed, needing to get off the phone.

"Again, I'm very sorry."

He sat silently in his bed for a few minutes, still holding the telephone in his hand, before he could force himself to hang it up.

Chapter 41
Who Needs Roger Maldonado?
December 1988

It was Sunday afternoon and Menashe was sitting on the kitchen counter, reading *TV Guide* and drinking directly from his bottle of whiskey when he heard the doorbell ring. Resisting the urge to keep quiet and ignore it, he walked out of the kitchen to see who it was.

"Roger," he began slowly as he opened the door, wishing people would start calling him before they came over.

"Ash, I brought you something," he started to say, but stopped when he saw his face. "Are you okay?"

"Yeah, I'm fine. Just been kind of sick lately."

"You look really bad."

"Yeah, I know. It's okay."

"Have you seen a doctor?"

"No. I don't have insurance."

"What?"

"I don't ha—"

"How can you not have insurance?" Roger cried. "You need to see somebody, man. Maybe you can go on mine."

"I'm pretty sure that's fraud, but thanks anyway."

"You don't get it through work?"

"No."

Roger just stood silently for a moment, as if the idea that people live uninsured had shaken his very belief system. Such extreme naiveté bewildered Menashe. This guy had no idea what it was actually like out in the world. If Roger really knew him—really knew what it was like to live his life—he'd probably go insane.

"What did you need, Roger?" he asked tiredly.

"Can I come in for a sec?" He smiled broadly and Menashe's stomach began to turn.

He sighed. "All right."

Back in the office, Roger set his backpack down and unzipped it. He took out some kind of box, but held it behind his back with childlike excitement. *What am I doing?* Menashe thought as he watched him. *What a joke this place is.*

"Okay," Roger said, walking over to the desk. "I brought you a replacement. You know, for the one I broke."

With a dramatic flourish, he produced a brand new, shiny black CCM helmet still in the box from behind his back and handed it to Menashe.

"No hard feelings, right?"

Menashe smiled. "Right."

"I wanted to get you an upgrade. This is the best one out right now."

Menashe turned the box around and inspected it, trying to remember the last time he'd owned something of such high quality. He supposed this was Roger's life: buying shit that was brand new, still in the box, not reduced for quick sale or discontinued or defective. It was going to bars and clubs, the doctor and the dentist, leaving town for weekend trips and friends' weddings. Roger had a good family. He had money, too, but was wasting it all. He was living in a world that didn't even exist and Menashe was sick of it. He was sick of this kid trying to tell him about fear and pain—about feeling lost. He didn't have real problems, Menashe decided, but rather petty inconveniences and delayed gratifications.

"And really," Roger continued, lowering his eyes, "I wanted to thank you for how much you've been helping me. I know I was an asshole about it at first, and I'm sorry for that. Things really have gotten better since we started this— since you started it, I mean." He stopped. "Are you okay?" he asked, watching Menashe carefully. "You seem upset about something."

"Just feeling sick, that's all," he replied. "I'll be fine."

"Want me to get you anything?"

He shook his head. "No."

"You want some of that soup from the place down on Twenty-Third?"

"No, thanks," he murmured. "I'm not really hungry. I think I might just sleep for a while."

"Well, I'll go and let you rest," Roger said, getting up. "I hope you feel better, and I'll see you next week, okay?"

"Okay. Thanks, Roger."

Chapter 42
The Abramoviches
December 1988

It was eight p.m. *Austin missed his appointment yesterday.* Menashe replaced the empty whiskey bottle at his bedside with a full one, stripped down to his plaid boxers and got into bed. He lay awake, drinking and trying to count the line of ants that stretched from the wall above his headboard to the crack under his door, when he again heard a knock at the front door. It didn't sound urgent, but when another minute had passed and the knocking didn't subside, he grew curious.

"Who is it?" he demanded. No one answered, so Menashe rose from his bed and walked unsteadily down the hall to the front door.

"John," he said, frowning as he opened the door. "What's up?" John looked at his watch with equal confusion and then back at Menashe, who was still dressed in nothing but boxers, with uncombed hair and distracted eyes.

"It's eight o'clock," he said, but failed to jog Menashe's memory.

"Yeah?"

"Have you been drinking?" he asked.

"Yes," Menashe replied impatiently. "What's the problem?"

"Ash, we have an appointment for tonight. For right now, actually."

Menashe closed his eyes and let out a groan. John was right. He rubbed his face with his hands and then brought them up through his hair, trying to think clearly.

"I'm sorry. I can't believe I forgot," he said to himself, dazed. "Jesus, I'm really sorry, John."

"No, don't worry about it. Seriously, it's fine."

Menashe thought he detected a tone of relief in his voice.

"What, you want to stop treatment?" he asked.

"Oh, no, nothing like that," John assured him, leaning against the doorframe. "I'm just having kind of an off day, and you know, with everything that happened with Austin, it was making me nervous to think of doing this now."

He nodded. "You sure you don't want to talk or anything?"

John shook his head. "Man, I'm sure you hear enough depressing shit to put you in the nuthouse forever."

Menashe winced but John continued, unaware.

"Listen, I want you to come out to my house tomorrow night, all right? I'm having a party—well, I guess Abby's having it. It'll be mostly her friends there. Anyway, I really think this'll be good for you. For both of us."

"A party?" Menashe repeated doubtfully.

"Come on, it'll make you feel better. Help you take your mind off everything,"

"What time?"

"Eight. But if you wanted to come earlier, we can all have dinner together."

Menashe pictured in his mind the sad spectacle of him eating dinner with John and his family, trying to think of something charming or at least appropriate to say to his wife and two children. John was looking at him expectantly.

"I'll just meet you there at eight, okay?"

Menashe's eyes blazed with rage and he was sweating all over as he followed John to the back of the house. He felt like the lead role in a mean-spirited tragedy.

"John, how the hell could you not tell me?" Menashe snarled, grabbing onto John's shirt and trying to keep his voice low.

They had removed themselves from the party and now stood alone in John's dimly lit bedroom.

"I swear to God, man, I didn't know. Abby didn't tell me, and besides, I forgot to tell her you were coming."

"Well, what am I supposed to do? She wants to fucking talk now!"

"I know," he whispered, waving his hands at Menashe in an effort to quiet him down. "I'm sorry. I really had no idea this would happen."

"Did you know she was pregnant?"

"No," John shook his head. "Honestly, Abby just reconnected with her. They'd only talked on the phone a couple times until tonight; she never mentioned a baby."

"Perfect," he muttered, releasing John and once again pacing the floor in front of the bed. "Seriously, what am I going to do?"

"Why don't you go talk to her?"

"What, and make small talk with the new guy? What's his name, Zack? Rick?"

"Nick," John corrected. "Abramovich."

Menashe glared at him. "Can you be less helpful? Please?"

He shrugged. "You can leave if you want. I'll make something up for you."

"I think it's too late for that."

"Well then, maybe you should just go out there. I mean, Menashe, if there's something you want to say, this might be your only chance to say it."

Nick and Jamie Abramovich sat comfortably on the living room couch with Abby, looking at pictures she'd brought out from their family trip to New York City. Menashe approached them awkwardly, waiting for a break in Abby's narrative. When she saw him out of the corner of her eye, she got up hurriedly and left the room, making some excuse about checking on the kids.

Menashe couldn't take his eyes off Jamie. She was just as beautiful as she'd been ten years before. Her blonde hair was long now and layered, with wispy bangs she parted on the side. The white cotton shirt and drawstring khakis she wore reminded Menashe of how she used to dress in college. He couldn't help noticing the outfit also accentuated her pregnant stomach.

"Menashe," Nick began politely, "you want to have a seat?"

He smiled and Menashe noticed his teeth were perfectly white and perfectly straight. Nick was perhaps five or six years older than he, with short dark hair and a distinguished mustache. He wore a black business suit and shiny black shoes. Menashe looked down at his own grungy tennis shoes, faded jeans, and pilled green sweater. He flinched slightly.

"No, thanks. I'll stand for now. And call me Ash."

Nick nodded and Menashe thought he noticed Jamie shake her head slightly. She was upset.

"So, Nick," he began numbly, "what do you do?"

This question prompted Nick to begin a long-winded speech about his important and powerful job at an important and powerful law firm downtown, but Menashe wasn't listening. He still could not take his eyes off his wife. *Ex-wife*.

"You stayed in Cleveland," he said abruptly, addressing Jamie, uncertain if Nick had even finished talking. A lump rose in his throat as he stared blatantly at her stomach.

"We moved back two years ago," she replied. "From Chicago. That's where we met." Her eyes clouded with tears.

"Hon, are you okay?" Nick asked his wife, watching her closely.

"Yeah, I'm fine," she said, smiling up at him. "Listen, do you mind if we go talk for a minute?" she asked him, nodding toward Menashe.

"Okay. I'll be right here," he added meaningfully, letting Menashe know Jamie had told her new husband everything about him.

Menashe and Jamie donned their coats and walked out the sliding glass door onto John's deck, even though it was bitterly cold, leaving Nick waiting on the couch, watching them. They sat in opposite facing patio chairs and breathed puffs of white steam into the frigid and black Ohio night. The whole thing was so surreal. Menashe still couldn't believe he was sitting down to talk with the woman he'd married fifteen years earlier. *Jamie Abramovich.*

"So, you're pregnant," he said, dumbfounded, as Jamie sat staring at the reddish stained planks of the deck.

She nodded. "Our second."

"You have two kids with this guy?"

Menashe had done his best to remain calm, but felt a terrible rage rising inside of him.

"With my husband, yes," Jamie said defensively, finally looking at his face. "We've been married six years."

"So how old's the other one?"

"Lily is three."

He shook his head in disbelief, blowing warm air into his cupped hands. "Do you know if it's a boy or a girl?" he asked.

"Yes," she said. "He's a boy." She turned her eyes to the ground again. "We're going to name him Michael, after Nick's father."

Menashe laughed. It was a strange sound that combined scorn and misery. "That's great. Congratulations."

"What is the matter with you? How can you be mad at me?"

"Did you never want to see me again?" he asked, blinking hard against the cold air. "With your lawyers. Did you tell them to make it so you never had to see me again?"

Jamie paused. "Yes."

Menashe laughed again. "So that was just, what, a nice little kick while I was down?"

"I don't want to fight with you, Menashe. I just wanted to talk."

"Now you want to talk? About what?"

She took a breath and drew her pink, faux fur-lined coat around her. "I forgive you," she said simply.

He felt like he'd had the wind knocked out of him.

"I know these past ten years have been hell for both of us," Jamie continued. "I just don't want to carry this anger around anymore—it doesn't make sense. I know how much you loved him." She paused.

"Did you know I was going to be here?" He felt his muscles tense and his face grow hot, despite the bitter air.

"No. I was actually going to send you a letter. I've written it so many times over the last year or so. But this is probably better."

He frowned. "You forgive me."

"Yes." She was looking at him cautiously.

"Well," he said finally, "I'm very happy for you."

"Why are you so angry?" Jamie asked him, frustration straining her voice. "Is there anything I could say that you wouldn't take badly? I was trying to help you, too, you know."

Menashe spat on the frozen deck. "Go back to Nick," he said carelessly. "I don't give a fuck."

"You're lying," she retorted, then looked through the glass door into the house where Nick was now standing. "And you're shutting me out, just like you always did when things got hard."

"Hey, what about you?" he snapped, his voice rising. "You shut me out and left without even telling me where you were going."

"Because I was heartbroken," she said. "I couldn't be around you. It was just too sad."

"Because it was my fault. Because I did it to him, right?"

She shook her head and began to cry.

Menashe ignored her. It didn't matter anyway. He knew what she'd thought all along. He turned and rested his hands on the railing of the deck, looking out into John's backyard.

"You can't imagine what this has been like for me," he murmured. "Wesley should be fourteen now. And every year, every goddamn year I think about what he'd be like—how he'd be growing up." He paused and rubbed his eyes. "I can't stop picturing him growing up. But it's my fault he never will and so I have to make myself stop, because after a while all I'll want to do is put a bullet in my head. I'll want to drive my car off a bridge or slit my wrists because all I can think about is this person I'll never get to meet."

He stared vacantly into the distance.

"Menashe, please don't do this," Jamie whispered.

The sound of her voice tore him away from his thoughts. "I'll do whatever the fuck I want," he said raggedly, turning around and stepping toward her.

Just then, Nick appeared and grabbed the collar of Menashe's coat roughly, spinning him around.

"Leave her alone," he said.

"Just back off, Nick," Menashe replied. "We're talking."

"You're done."

Menashe turned toward Jamie to tell her everything was under control when Nick, once again, grabbed him from behind.

"You need to leave, Menashe. Now."

"People really don't call me that anymore, Nick. I told you, it's Ash." He sat down on one of the deck chairs facing the house. "We were just fine before you showed up."

"It's time for us to go," Jamie said firmly. "Will you be okay?"

After a minute or so during which Menashe neither moved nor spoke, Nick and Jamie whispered a few words to each other and walked back into the house to say their goodbyes. Menashe sat on the chair for a long time, numb from the cold. He hadn't even noticed when it started to snow. He eventually got up and walked around the side yard to the front of his house where his pickup was parked on the street. He climbed in and drove off, not wanting to talk to anyone else.

Chapter 43
Chase Steps Up
December 1988

Menashe remained in a delirious haze for the next few days. He stopped going to work and refused to answer his telephone. Most drastically of all, Menashe shut down his museum. He felt he was starting to lose his mind and therefore believed it would be hypocritical to continue acting as a therapist to his clients. He spent most of the day in bed. He occasionally read or turned on the TV, but he mostly just drank and slept. This went on for three days. On the fourth day, Chase showed up at his door.

"Ash!" he called, pounding on the door with his fist.

It was ten a.m., an hour Menashe hadn't been awake for in over a week. He shifted groggily in his bed, the sheets twisting around him. He waited, hoping Chase would give up and go away.

"Ash!" he called again loudly. "Come on, man, open up! We need to talk—and you're a week late on your rent!"

He groaned and grabbed the nearly empty Everclear bottle off his night-stand. Still lying down, he took a big swallow and choked on it, coughing rough-ly. Menashe was never late on his rent. In fact, he usually paid Chase a day or two early for his own peace of mind.

"All right, I'm coming in."

Chase used his key to enter the apartment, and rushed down the hall to the bedroom.

"Whoa!" he exclaimed, standing in the doorway. "What the hell's the matter?"

Menashe was quite a sorry sight: he lay nearly passed out on his twin bed, half covered by blankets with the Everclear bottle still clutched in his hand. His hair had become slick with grease and heavy stubble covered his face. He looked up agitatedly, narrowing his eyes at the noise.

"Nothing's the matter," Menashe replied hoarsely. "It's just been a rough couple of days."

Chase walked over to his side and wrestled the bottle out of his hand, setting it down carefully across the room on his desk. Menashe followed him warily with his eyes as he walked from the desk to the window. He pulled the shade open with a quick, dramatic movement, blinding Menashe with sunlight.

"Holy fuck, Chase!" he shouted in surprise, throwing a pillow over his eyes. "My head is killing me!"

"Sorry," he replied flatly, "but it's time to get up."

Menashe lifted the pillow slightly and glared at him. "No, it's not. I'm going back to bed."

"You're getting up and we're going to take care of that headache."

Menashe was stunned. It was as if Mary Poppins had inexplicably entered his home.

"Why do you care?"

Chase looked at him thoughtfully. "Because you're my friend. Because you stopped coming to poker and I haven't heard from you in weeks. But mostly because you're my tenant and it's in my best interest to keep you alive. So, let's go."

He groaned as Chase helped him sit upright in bed, putting a pillow behind his back. Chase went into the kitchen for a few minutes and came back with black coffee and the bottle of ibuprofen.

"Here," he said, handing him the mug of coffee. "You want these first?" he asked, standing over him and holding out four tablets.

Menashe nodded and took the tablets, swallowing them dry, then drank slowly from the coffee mug.

"Man, I've had the worst headaches," he said after a moment.

"I'll bet," Chase replied, glancing over at the bottle on the desk.

"It's the weather."

"What made you switch to Everclear?"

Menashe lifted his head and caught his reflection in the small mirror that hung on the wall. He winced at the sight of himself.

"My wife's new husband."

"I'm sorry."

"Yeah."

Menashe gazed longingly at the bottle on the desk. *I just never found the strength he had.*

"Come on, Menashe. What's all this about?" Chase asked gently. "Seeing your ex again? That sounds pretty rough."

Menashe looked at him blankly. "No. It's nothing. It's just been one of those weeks."

"Is it about Austin Gendron?"

"What?"

"Austin Gendron. I know you two know each other. He told me a few months ago."

Menashe closed his eyes. He still hadn't gone to see that police officer. He needed to get his story straight.

"He was a regular at The Diamond," Chase continued. "Were you close with him?"

"He's not dead, you know," Menashe snapped. "And this isn't about Austin." He leaned back, worn out. "What did he tell you about me?"

"Not a lot."

"Really?" He looked at Chase carefully.

"Listen, Ash, I know you've got people coming in and out of here on some kind of schedule, but I've decided I really don't want to know about it, all right? Just keep it legal."

"Okay."

"You want to talk about Austin?"

"No, I'm really okay."

"All right," he said, getting to his feet. "You're a good guy, Ash. Whatever it is that's bothering you, don't let it get you down so much."

"Sure," he murmured.

"Okay," Chase said brightly, "enough of this lying around feeling sorry for yourself. Do you have the stuff to make pancakes?"

Menashe narrowed his eyes, confused.

"You know, flour, eggs, baking powder . . . ?"

He smiled faintly. "No, just some frozen waffles."

Chase shook his head. "Okay, that's unacceptable." He got up, put his black down coat back on and headed for the door. "I'll be right back."

Menashe pulled himself out of bed as Chase left. It was strange, having someone take care of him like that. He didn't know how he should feel, or how Chase was thinking of him. Maybe as a friend, or maybe as a charity case. It didn't really matter though; that day he could admit he just needed the help. And he was starting to feel better at the thought of eating real pancakes.

Chapter 44
Don't Get Him Wrong, Don't Get Him Mad
December 1988

By nine-thirty on Friday evening, Murray was in the passenger seat of his roommate Casey's old Plymouth Duster, leaving school behind him for three and a half weeks. He honestly had no idea how he did on his finals, but knew he wouldn't get the As and Bs he was used to. He sighed unhappily. His mind was so disorganized, and all he wanted was a starting point from which he could begin to clean it up.

"God, look at all this snow," Casey breathed, putting his windshield wipers on high and leaning forward in an attempt to see past the large wet flakes stubbornly sticking to the windshield. The snow had been coming down steadily all day and the roads were completely covered. "It's going to take forever to get home."

Casey and Murray lived only a few miles apart and about forty minutes away from the university, but it would probably take them triple that time to make it home in the snowstorm.

"Thanks for driving," Murray said apologetically. He didn't have a car, so Casey generously drove him to and from school on many weekends and whenever there was a break.

"No problem." Casey turned on the radio. "What're you doing over break?" he asked.

"Just seeing family."

He nodded. "Me, too. We're going to see my grandparents in Lakewood," he sighed glumly. "Seriously, we do this shit every year and nobody ever has a good time. It's kind of weird," he added, looking over at Murray. "I mean, we're family. You'd think we'd have figured out a way to get along by now." Murray smiled. "Are your brothers coming in?" Casey asked, looking over his shoulder to see if he was clear to change lanes.

"Yeah, they're both getting in next week."

The car slowed down rapidly as Casey saw that an accident was blocking the road. Blue and red lights flashed crazily from the police cars, fire trucks, and ambulance. The darkness made it hard to see what had happened but Casey, craning his neck out the window, reported to Murray that one of the cars had overturned and the other was smashed up pretty badly. Casey pulled his head back inside the car and rolled up the window, shutting out the cold and violent wind.

"This really isn't our night," he remarked as the traffic continued backing up.

Murray nearly laughed out loud at his friend's insensitive comment, but instead remained silent, only just then realizing how close he was getting to home.

It was nearly midnight when Casey dropped Murray off at his house. He fished his key out of his backpack and opened the front door, laying his bags down carefully in the hall. The house was dark and so silent he felt even his breathing was too loud.

He loaded the washing machine with his laundry but didn't run it, then rummaged around in the kitchen for something to eat. Even though he was exhausted, he wasn't ready to go to bed. He needed time to think. On the car ride home, he had made a decision: he would tell his father he remembered everything about his past and, depending on how that part went, would try to do what Menashe suggested and ask him to go to counseling. Murray made himself a peanut butter and jelly sandwich, which he ate quickly, then brought his things up to his bedroom, hoping to work out a plan for the next day.

It was two-fifteen a.m. and he lay in bed, flat on his back, turning Menashe's business card over and over in his hands. He didn't have a plan. *I've just got to do it—it'll be fine. If Mr. Everett thinks it's best . . .*

He rolled over and picked up the other business card that lay next to the telephone on his nightstand. It was the psychologist's card. Dr. Timothy Vaughn. He didn't want to go to another counselor. Murray wished he could stay with Menashe, but he'd made it clear that it was time to move on. He sat up and drew his wallet out of his back pocket, carefully placing both business cards between his gym pass and his student ID. He turned off the light and lay back down, though he knew sleep would be impossible.

* * *

"So how did finals go?" his mother, Deana, asked the next morning over breakfast.

"Not so good, I think," he said. He had somehow managed to forget about his grades until that moment. "Probably really bad, actually," he added, attempting to lower their expectations so when his grades did arrive, they would most likely be relieved.

"Oh, I'm sure it wasn't all that bad," his father reassured him, reaching across the table for a napkin. "You always think you did worse than you really did."

Murray nodded.

"Anyway, you're on break now," his mom said, "so don't worry about it."

She smiled at him and this made Murray feel a bit better.

"What are you guys doing today?" he asked them after a moment.

"I've got to work on that damn water heater," Adam grumbled. "The piece of shit broke again this morning."

"Adam—" Deana gave him a sharp look. "Easy, all right?"

"Dee, Murray's a grown man now. I think he can handle a little language." Murray smiled to himself. "I could use a hand, if you don't mind," he said, turning to Murray.

"Sure."

"Well, that sounds like a lot of fun," Deana began, standing up and clearing her dishes, "but I'm meeting your Aunt Linda to do a little Christmas shopping. You guys need anything while we're out?"

"Maybe a water heater," Murray smiled, looking toward his dad.

Adam laughed loudly. "What a smartass you've turned into. But you may be right."

The Hendersons' basement was cold and damp, unfinished. Exposed two-by-fours and leaky pipes were abundant, and large tufts of pink fiberglass insulation were poking out of the walls. Murray jumped suddenly, hearing his dad's heavy footsteps behind him, coming down the stairs. Adam emerged with the old red toolbox he kept in the garage.

"Something in here ought to do it," he muttered as Murray followed him to the water heater.

Not knowing much about home repairs, Murray watched as his father pried and twisted different parts of the heater, occasionally handing him a tool he asked for. An hour passed and still no progress had been made.

"Can you get me some water?" Adam asked, sweat beading up on his forehead despite the cold.

Murray nodded and immediately got up. He climbed the stairs back to the kitchen, but soon he heard his father calling him again. He jogged back into the room a moment later with the water glass.

"Dad?"

His father was struggling with a wrench, attempting to fix a leak in the pipe right above his head.

Adam looked down at him and held the tool still. "Glass? Really, Murray? We've got plastic cups, you know."

"Oh, I . . . I—"

"Forget it. I need you to get a different wrench out of the garage. The bigger one. It should be in the brown toolbox."

"Okay." Murray turned to leave.

"Hey." Adam wiped his hands on his jeans and took a few steps toward his son. "Can I have the water?" he laughed, pointing to the glass in his hand.

"Oh, yeah," Murray said embarrassedly, handing it to his dad and sloshing a bit of water over the edge in the process.

He returned with the correct wrench and went back to standing next to the toolbox, handing his father tools intermittently. After another half hour or so, Adam dropped everything back into the box and laughed triumphantly.

"I think it's fixed," he said. "Good thing, too. I was afraid we'd have to call the plumber pretty soon."

"Dad?"

"Oh, don't think I've forgotten your part in this," his dad assured him. "You can't do a good job without a good assistant."

"No, it's not that."

"Yeah?" Adam replied, still bent over the toolbox. "Then what is it?"

"I want to—well . . . I think I should tell you something."

His heartbeat quickened with the knowledge that he was really going through with it.

"Okay." His dad got to his feet and looked at Murray expectantly. "Is this about school?"

"No." *I'd give anything for this to be about school.* "I wanted to let you know that—that I remember . . ." He had intended to say more, but the words never came.

Adam frowned. "What?"

Murray took a deep breath. "I remember what it was like before—what you were like. You know, when we were growing up."

He stared at the ground intensely, his face flushing. He was hoping he could get the point across to Adam using very vague, safe language. He wasn't comfortable talking about the details and he didn't feel his father would be either. Adam hadn't stopped frowning.

"Okay," he said, still looking confused. "What's the problem?"

This caught Murray off-guard. "You know what I'm talking about, right?" he asked carefully.

"Oh, yeah," Adam said. "You're talking about how I acted before I went to anger management."

Murray nodded, relieved it was clear.

"So what do you mean, you remember? We all remember. The point is, it's over, and I hope you're not trying to make me feel guilty for shit that happened years ago."

"Dad," he began again, his voice trembling, "I didn't know what happened until a few weeks ago. I didn't remember."

"What the hell are you talking about?" His dad was looking at him like he was crazy.

"I was having a lot of trouble a few months ago. I just kept huh-having these problems and I didn't know why, and then last month, my therapist—"

"Therapist!" Adam broke in. "You got a therapist without telling anyone?"

"Dad!" Murray shouted back, getting angry himself. "I'm telling you I remember what happened and I want us to go to counseling."

He pulled Dr. Vaughn's card out of his wallet and held it out. The card danced spastically in his shaky hand. Adam took Vaughn's card and read it, then began laughing.

"Murray, this is ridiculous," he said jovially. "You're making way too much of the whole thing. So I had a temper back then," he dismissed. "You and your brothers turned out all right, so what's the problem?"

Murray didn't know where to begin, so he kept quiet.

"If there's one thing I wanted to teach you boys it was how be strong. And I always wanted the best for you. Your mother was the one who didn't understand that." A cold tone had crept into his dad's voice and Murray suddenly felt trapped and helpless, like a child. "Can you believe she actually threatened to take you boys away from me for good?" he laughed. "Although I can't imagine how she would have supported you. I'm the one who's always taken care of this family."

Murray couldn't believe what he was hearing. He wanted to run but he also wanted to see what would happen. He was finally at the end.

"You know," Adam said, turning his attention back to Murray, "if you want to see a shrink so bad, you should go with your mom. What a piece of work," he muttered, tearing the up the card.

"Dad," he murmured, holding his hand out as if to stop his father from doing what he had already done. Tears glistened in his eyes. "I wanted to go with you," he managed to say weakly in spite of the large knot pressing against his throat.

"Mur, the sooner you stop being such a baby and learn that you've just got to get over things, the better life's going to be for you."

Murray could see he believed this was a sound piece of fatherly advice. His stomach began to burn and he could feel his whole body grow hot. He summoned all his strength to keep himself from throwing up; he needed to see this through.

"Now," Adam said with finality, looking into his son's eyes, "I expect you not to bring this up again." He picked up the toolbox and headed for the stairs.

Murray sensed a terrible feeling welling up inside of him. Before his father reached the stairs, he ran after him and grabbed his arm angrily, causing him to drop the box and spill tools all over the basement floor. Adam instantly spun around and hit Murray in the face with the back of his hand, knocking him to the floor. It was clearly an unconscious reaction, but Murray could see his dad immediately felt better. In that instant, the part of him that had been hidden so well over the past six years had suddenly been unlocked.

Murray got to his feet before his father could tell him to and stood steadily, waiting for whatever would happen next.

"What the hell is wrong with you?" Adam yelled, panting with shock.

"We didn't turn out all right!" Murray yelled back at him, wiping away the thin line of blood trickling out the corner of his mouth. He couldn't believe how far he was going, but his mind was made up. He pushed up his sleeves and showed his dad the white scars on his arms. "I started doing this in seventh grade!" he shouted. "I almost quit college because of what you did. And I used to—" Murray faltered for just a second. "I used to hit Emma."

He paused but Adam said nothing.

Murray laughed bitterly. "And the worst thing is, I never wanted to hurt her at all. But now I know it was because of all the things you did. Every time I lost control, you were there."

Blood pounded in his temples, hurting his head and distorting his vision.

"And look at Jake," he continued. "He won't even talk to you. I never knew why until now," he added, in a lower tone. "And what about Matthew? He turned into an asshole cop, just like you."

At this remark, his father, who had been silently fuming while Murray spoke, grabbed his shirt with his left hand and punched him brutally under the eye with his right, like he would a grown man.

"You don't ever say a thing like that to me," he said severely, letting go of his son's collar.

Murray was unable to move. His rage was fading and that last hit had robbed him of the fleeting confidence he had used to stand up for himself.

"I'm sorry," Murray said.

Adam smiled. "Well, I really can't believe this, Murray," he began calmly. "I can't believe I'm going to have to punish my nineteen-year-old son, but you've been acting like such a child I don't really have a choice."

Murray suddenly yelled out and lunged at Adam, giving him no time to react, and they fell hard onto the concrete.

Murray couldn't let things go back to the way they were, and he knew it as soon as he whimpered another meaningless, self-defense apology to his dad. Murray jumped up and grabbed a hammer off the floor, trying to make Adam believe he would use it. But his father just laughed and got to his feet, a sinister glow radiating from his eyes.

"I'd think about what you're doing, Mur," he warned, taking a few steps toward him. "You've gone way too far."

Adam suddenly lurched forward and grabbed him, pulling him down and causing the hammer to fly out of his hand. Murray knew he wasn't willing to lose control again. He mercilessly pummeled Murray with his fist, causing blood to spurt from his nose. Murray kicked at him blindly and eventually connected with Adam's stomach, knocking the wind out of him. He lost his grip and Murray ran to the tools again, grabbing one after another and throwing them frantically at his father, who was only a few feet away. He threw four or five tools, missing, before the wrench finally hit Adam on the right temple with a terrible *thunk*, leaving a gash in his head that immediately began bleeding. He fell to the ground, cursing fiercely, but was only stunned by the blow. When he tried to get up, his legs buckled, forcing him to sit back down on the basement floor, but Murray understood this daze was only temporary.

He ran up the basement stairs and kept running up to the second floor. He rushed into the first room he came to, locking the door behind him. Only once he was inside did he realize he had fled to his parents' bedroom. Rummaging through his wallet, Murray found Menashe's card and knelt down by the telephone that rested on his mother's sewing table. With quivering fingers, he dialed Menashe's number, praying he would be home. Blood gruesomely stained the front of his shirt and his left eye was already beginning to swell shut.

As he listened to the rings, Murray suddenly wished he'd had the foresight to run out the front door rather than up to the second floor. But he was still thinking as a child would, causing him to follow his muscle memory over his reason. But he couldn't ignore reason any longer. His heart pounded fiercely as he waited for Menashe to answer his phone, each ring on the other end confirming his fate.

When Menashe's message kicked on, Murray slammed his fist against the nightstand, tears of defeat springing out of his eyes. He reset the dial tone and hurriedly punched in 9-1-1. He told the dispatcher his emergency and begged them to come quickly. He dropped the receiver back into its cradle, thinking suddenly of Casey, and how much he'd give to be with him in Lakewood at that moment.

Chapter 45
Can't Take It Back Now
December 1988

Menashe dressed slowly on the cold morning a few days after Chase's visit, when he was finally allowed to see Austin. He'd met with Officer Douglass the day before and still admonished himself for worrying so much about it. He had given the officer details in the context of his friendship with Austin, letting him know about Austin's troubles and his background, but was never pressed about the information. Menashe stood blankly in front of his closet. He wanted to look nice, carefully choosing khaki work pants and a new shirt he'd just bought. Glancing into the mirror, he thought he looked faintly like his father, which served to lift his spirits for a moment.

He arrived at St. Vincent Hospital at ten-thirty. The temperature was in the single digits but the sun shone brightly—it was the type of weather that often caused fierce migraines to erupt inside his head, sometimes so severe as to cause him to be confined to a dark and silent room for hours at a time. But he wore sunglasses that day and carried with him five tablets of ibuprofen in his jacket pocket, which he would most likely need either way.

He checked the room number and made his way to the elevator, riding alone to the ninth floor. He wondered if anyone else would come to visit Austin. He supposed his family was in town, but maybe they hadn't been contacted. He walked down the hallway, looking around. No one. He made it to Austin's room, 914, but everything was quiet. The door was open and he looked in to see an older man, perhaps sixty-five, standing up to leave. Menashe cleared his throat and he looked up suddenly. The man smiled and came out into the hall.

"Hi," he said. "Are you here to see Austin?"

"That's right," Menashe replied, peering around him into the room. He saw Austin, ashen and unshaven, asleep in his hospital bed. His heart sank.

"He drifted off a few minutes ago," the man told him. "But I did get to speak with him for a little while. He sounded good. They say he'll make a full recovery."

"That's great."

"I'm sorry," he continued, extending his hand. "My name's Mark. I'm the minister at All Saints Lutheran, where Austin attends."

"Ash Everett," he returned, shaking his hand.

"Are you close with Austin?" he asked, leaning against the wall.

"We're friends," he replied abstractly. "I haven't known him for very long, though."

Mark smiled distantly. "He's such a good man," he began. "Served in Vietnam, you know?" Menashe nodded. "I've known him for nearly eight years. He came to All Saints very troubled, and now, in light of what happened, I'm afraid we haven't been able to help him much."

He looked up sadly and Menashe looked away.

"I just never knew Austin was in such bad shape that he'd even consider doing what he did," he continued in a low voice, as if he were alone. "I wish I could have been with him that night."

"Mark," Menashe said quickly, "did he say anything about why he did it? I mean, did he tell you what was going on before it happened?"

Mark shook his head. "No, he didn't want to talk about it. He just told me that he didn't know what to do about his past anymore. We talked about him coming back to church regularly, which is encouraging. And I hope he'll be willing to start counseling—I have some experience with it, but I know there are specialists who deal with soldiers' trauma. He definitely needs to see somebody, though."

Menashe's face grew hot.

"I think I'll wait with him," Menashe said, moving toward the door. "Until he wakes up."

"I'm sure he'll be so happy to see you," Mark said warmly. "I'm glad he's got a friend looking out for him."

Menashe sat in a plastic hospital chair opposite Austin's bed, watching him closely, trying to decide what he should say. *I just can't believe this, Austin,* he thought, a wave of sorrow washing over him. *I'm sorry I was so wrong.*

After about thirty minutes, Austin began to stir. He shifted in his bed, making slight groaning sounds. Menashe stood and moved closer, his heartbeat quickening.

"Austin?" he murmured. Austin opened his eyes slowly. "Austin, it's me. It's Ash."

"Ash?" He coughed several times, then sat up in his bed. Menashe handed him a cup of water that was on the table and took a step back. "Where did . . . ?" he trailed off in a hoarse whisper, taking a gulp of water and waving his hand toward the door.

"Oh, Mark? The minister?" Austin nodded. "He left about half an hour ago. I talked to him a little. Seems like a nice guy."

"Yeah."

Menashe moved his chair to Austin's bedside and sat down.

"How do you feel?"

"Ugh," Austin groaned, putting a hand to his forehead. "Like I wish those campers never found me."

Menashe frowned. "Listen, I'm really sorry. About everything."

"Ash," Austin began, wincing as he sat up straighter, "it's not you. I just can't talk about it. I can't even really think about it yet. Okay?"

He nodded. "Will you be coming back?"

"To the museum?"

"Yeah."

Austin shook his head. "No, man. No way I can risk it. I mean, the way we do it there, it's too brutal, you know? It's like it triggers this shit for me, and then I can't let it go." He laughed. "But look who I'm telling—the guy I beat to hell during one of those sessions."

Menashe's stomach sank. He felt the impulse to leave, as he always did, but forced himself to hear Austin out.

"So what are you going to do?"

"Well," he said, gesturing toward some books on the table, "Mark gave me these—said they could really help. Put things in perspective." Menashe glanced over. The top one was called *The Road Less Traveled* and looked like some kind of self-help bullshit. He took a deep breath.

"You going to start seeing him?"

"Maybe," Austin shrugged, coughing deeply, then taking another drink. "He offered and, I don't know, I feel like maybe I should go in a more religious direction. People seem to get a lot of peace that way."

"If you think it might work, I guess it's worth a try."

Austin smiled. "You think it's bullshit."

"It's just not for me," Menashe answered carefully. "But if it helps you, that's all that matters."

"Okay, man, okay."

Austin winced as he shifted again, massaging his shoulder and stretching his legs out stiffly. He pushed a small button on the side of his bed.

"Are you in a lot of pain? Can I get you something?" Menashe asked, rising.

"No, no. The meds are just wearing off, that's all. The nurse told me to call if I started feeling bad before she was due back."

The nurse walked in a moment later with some painkillers and medical equipment.

"I'm gonna get going, Austin. Let you get some rest."

"Okay," he replied, holding out his arm for the nurse to take his blood pressure. "See you around."

Menashe walked across the lawn to the parking lot, his shoes crunching on the ice-covered grass that sparkled brilliantly in the sunlight. He drove his orange Datsun to the nearest liquor store, weaving in and out of traffic. He hastily picked out a bottle of cheap whiskey, paid the extremely tattooed and overweight girl at the cash register, and got back inside his truck. He drove away with the intent of going home, but somehow ended up back in the largely deserted eastern parking lot of the hospital.

He looked around to make sure no one was there before uncapping his bottle and swallowing three shots' worth of whiskey in a single breath. He coughed and gasped fiercely as he drew the bottle away from his lips, using the back of his hand to cover his mouth. Menashe's truck was parked facing a small courtyard, a cutesy area perhaps designed for meditation with a few stone benches and statues, a fountain, a few trees, and several flowering plants. After a few more swigs, he couldn't help thinking back to Austin. He had nothing left to give him.

Over an hour later, Menashe lay back in the reclined seat of his pickup with only about a third of the whiskey left in the bottle. He had gradually drifted into a hazy state of semi-consciousness.

"Shit," he mumbled to himself, reaching again for the bottle that lay on the floor by the passenger seat. He hit his head on the steering wheel as he bent down, sending flashes of brilliant light across his eyes and causing him to forget why he had been bending down at all. He straightened himself and looked over at the empty courtyard. It seemed inviting to him now. He glanced at his watch but couldn't make his brain read the time. Fumbling for the handle, Menashe was eventually able to swing the door of his car open, though it required much more effort than he remembered needing in the past.

He didn't make it out of the parking lot before he tripped and fell over his own feet. His sunglasses flew off and one of the lenses cracked. He landed on the hard asphalt, ripping through the left knee of his pants and tearing a large hole through his jacket and down the arm of his new shirt.

"Shit," Menashe muttered again, turning the sleeve to get a better look. "Can't take it back now."

He slowly managed to get to his feet and stumble into the courtyard. The horizon wavered maddeningly in front of his eyes and the ground itself seemed to pitch and roll like waves on the ocean.

He staggered around, squinting at the plaques on the benches. He had no experience with meditation, but seemed to remember seeing people sit on the ground when they did it. He fell to his knees, exhausted, and felt the melting ice through his pants and against his bare skin. Menashe didn't know what to do next, so he just knelt silently for a moment, thinking.

It seemed like every day now held a new failure. He'd lost Austin, even if those campers did save him. And their conversation only punctuated the uselessness he felt. But it was worse than that. He wasn't just ineffective as a therapist; he was harmful. When he reluctantly thought back to the phone call during which Austin had begged Menashe for help, crying from the fear and shock of having seen Veneman, the enormity of his situation hit him and he slumped down, burying his face in his hands.

"I'm sorry," he whispered in a ragged voice. "I—"

Menashe stopped cold as he felt a strong hand grip down on his shoulder. The feeling sent a tremor through his veins and caused a searing pain to shoot through his already aching head. With his heart hammering, he turned to face the man who had so silently approached him.

"Dad?" he breathed, squinting into the sun.

Lewis Everett looked exactly as he had when Menashe was growing up: his dark hair was still growing thin, he wore the same respectable wardrobe and confident expression, and his eyes remained deep and thoughtful. He helped Menashe to his feet and adjusted the thick Buddy Holly glasses he still wore.

"It's cold," Lewis remarked, drawing his black overcoat tightly around him. "Don't you have a better coat?"

Menashe looked down at his tattered and thin jacket. He shook his head. "No."

Though embarrassed, he suddenly felt clear-headed, as if his father's presence erased the previous hour and a half he'd spent drinking. Menashe avoided his eyes, ashamed at having been caught crying to Austin, a man who wasn't even there.

"Are you going home?" Lewis asked, nodding his head toward the parking lot.

"I don't know," he laughed, wiping his nose on his sleeve.

His father turned and took a few steps away from him, thrusting his gloved hands into the pockets of his coat.

"You know, I really only wore these glasses for reading," Lewis said. Menashe could tell from his voice that he was smiling. "Having them on out here, walking around, it kind of feels like I'm underwater. I guess you just imagined me wearing them all the time."

Menashe nodded. "I thought you did."

"Nope, just for reading."

"Well, you did read a lot."

Lewis laughed and turned back around. "I did read a lot," he agreed.

"I've missed you," Menashe said suddenly. He felt the stinging return to his eyes as soon as he spoke.

"I know," he replied. "I've missed you, too." He walked back over to his son. "Do you know why I'm here?" Menashe shook his head. Lewis sighed. "I think you need help, Menashe."

"What do you mean? Why?" *What did I do?*

"You know what I mean," his father answered. "I'm talking about what's happened to you. It's like you're not even trying anymore."

Menashe felt his palms grow sticky and he rubbed them on his ripped pants. "Trying to do what?"

"To be happy. You keep torturing yourself with these memories and it's killing you. It's time to move on."

"But I've been doing okay."

"No. You haven't."

"I've been helping people," he said weakly.

It felt as though the sun was burning into his brain. He fumbled in his pocket until he produced his cigarettes. He separated one with his teeth and held it in his mouth while he dug out a lighter.

"Is it okay if I smoke?" he mumbled, already clicking the lighter.

"What about Austin?" Lewis asked, ignoring him and motioning to the hospital. "Why didn't you help your friend?"

Menashe's heartbeat increased.

"What do you mean?"

"Menashe, stop pretending," his father snapped. "You know what I mean. The glass just wasn't going to work for him. And you knew it."

Menashe couldn't speak. He felt trapped.

"Come on," his father pressed. "You could have leveled with him. Helped him find something else. Why didn't you?"

"I . . . I," he stammered, his legs feeling as though they would buckle any second. "I don't know. I thought he was getting better."

"No, you didn't," Lewis answered. "You were just ignoring all the signs that told you he was getting worse. A lot worse. Face it, Menashe, you ran out of ways to help him so you gave up."

"No, no. I tried to help him," he cried.

"All right, just forget about Austin for a second," his father replied, ignoring Menashe's protest. "What about Murray? Or Wesley for that matter?" *You'll be careful, won't you?*

The trees and stones of the courtyard began to spin and Menashe was afraid he would faint, but Lewis seemed to recognize this and put a strong arm around him, holding him steady until he could regain his balance.

"What about them?" he repeated.

"What do you mean?"

"Damn it, Menashe!" his father exclaimed. "You know what I mean! Now tell me what happened with Murray."

"I told him to reconcile with his father," Menashe whispered.

"Why?"

"I don't know."

Lewis took off his glasses and threw them down in frustration. "You do know."

"I wanted him to be happy. I wanted them to work things out."

"Menashe, Murray told you about his father. A man like that . . ." He shook his head. "You really thought they would just 'work things out'?"

"I'm sorry."

"Don't apologize to me."

Menashe turned away from his father and took a long drag on his cigarette. He closed his eyes, wishing the glass museum had merely dissolved, unrealized, like every other idea he'd had.

"You shouldn't have done that, Menashe," his father continued. "You shouldn't have put Murray in that position. I know you were thinking about Wesley."

Now that he had turned away from his father, Menashe wiped his eyes and allowed the expression on his face to reflect the unhappiness he felt.

"Please," he said, turning back around, "I don't want to talk about Wesley."

"You admitted it was your fault. You said it, remember?"

"Please—"

"But you've never addressed your problem with alcohol."

"Dad, please stop. I can't do this."

"Menashe," Lewis replied, unmoved, "you need help."

"I'm sorry," he murmured, ash falling from his shaky hand. "I'm sorry I let you down."

Lewis bent down and picked up his glasses, folding them and letting them drop into the breast pocket of his black overcoat. His eyes were tired and stern.

"It's not me you let down, son."

Chapter 46
Menashe's Last Session
December 1988

The next day, Menashe awoke at nine a.m. to the sun shining through his uncovered window. He had forgotten to close the shade when Chase pulled it up the other day. He felt steady upon standing up, so he decided to have a cup of coffee and a shower. Walking back into his office, he knew he needed a project to get through the day—a way to make him believe there was still some degree of worth to his life. He had already decided to reopen the museum for next week, which would take a lot of work, and he wanted to begin immediately.

Menashe began by cleaning his office, which had always been a natural starting point for him. He threw away empty bottles, emptied the trash, and made sure his paperwork was all filed. He didn't trust himself to think about the file that was now conspicuous by its absence. Feeling compelled to continue, he moved into the bathroom, scrubbing the tile and even unclogging the horrific shower drain. The kitchen was fairly clean already, but he inspected it anyway, making sure everything was in its place. After washing the few dishes stacked in the sink, he finally sat down to have another cup of coffee. He sighed unconsciously. His brain just worked better when his apartment was clean, he noticed. He finished the coffee and then washed out the mug as soon as he was through.

Menashe then decided to do some work in the museum and prepare for the appointments he would have next week. He swept the floors and cleaned all the tables and pedestals. He changed the light bulbs that had either burnt out or been broken. He'd picked up new pieces from his storage unit the day before, and now set to work carefully placing them throughout the four rooms.

Then he stopped. He heard a familiar sound, like a child laughing. He dismissed it. But there it was again. He could hear it more clearly now: it was the voice of a small boy talking excitedly to his parents about what he wanted to see at the zoo. The Cleveland Zoo was fairly close to where he lived, so they must have decided to walk over despite the cold. He heard the boy say he wanted to go see the lions first, and his mother asked cheerfully, "They won't be too scary?" Menashe smiled unconsciously. Wesley had been terrified of the lions.

It's not me you let down, son.

His dad. He'd been there—at the hospital. Menashe's vision began jumping nauseatingly, like it did when he had a migraine, but he felt no pain in his head. His stomach burned fiercely and his heart thumped with such power that he suddenly needed to gasp for breath. He looked around frantically, instinctively searching for an object to focus on. But he couldn't make his mind register anything but panic. Something inside of him had been unlocked.

His mind began to fill with horrible details from the night of his son's death. He remembered the warm air and the smell of chlorine. The lights and chaos of the ambulance, the pitying eyes of the doctor. He pushed them away and viciously cursed his father and ex-wife for bringing the memories to the forefront of his mind.

He thought of Austin, sick with the knowledge that he had spent that terrible night alone and confused, believing no one cared whether he lived or died. And it pained him to think of how he'd handled their conversation in the hospital. *Dad was right. I failed him from the beginning.* His mind jumped all over, drawing his attention to the other stupid decisions and missed opportunities peppered throughout his entire life. He thought of his useless art degree, his wasted years at the bank, his pathetic need for escape. His willingness to live in a drunken haze. The women, like Eva, he never pursued. The ones he did. The spider web cracks on the mirror at his father's funeral. The failures piled up maliciously, taunting him. He never realized until that moment how many of them there really were.

Menashe rubbed his face roughly with his hands, overwhelmed by the flood of emotion he was experiencing, unable to control it. Unable to control anything. He shook his head to clear the thoughts but was assaulted by another memory—another failure—before he had a chance to recover. He thought with intense regret of what he had done to Murray. He tried to shut down his imagination and resist picturing the myriad scenes that could have taken place when Murray confronted his father, but he couldn't block the image he feared was most accurate: the image of that poor kid getting the shit beaten out of him. Or worse.

But it always came back to one thing. The memory Menashe couldn't push away was the one he feared and hated most: the image of Wesley floating in Jeffrey's pool. It was now more than a memory; it was a permanent fixture in his mind. He felt his eyes and face grow hot. His fingers trembled as blood and adrenaline rushed through him violently. He looked around at the peaceful, perfect room of glass. He destroyed it all.

Chapter 47
Menashe's Flash
March 1958

In 1958, the Toronto Maple Leafs dominated hockey. Early that spring, Lewis Everett took his seven-year-old son to see his favorite team play at Maple Leaf Gardens. In the car on the way to the arena, Menashe studied his collection of hockey cards, organizing them and making sure he knew who all the best players were, while his father told him stories about growing up playing hockey with his brothers and cousins.

"Anyone who saw him knew he was a natural," Lewis reflected about his brother Noah, turning to his son and smiling.

"Were you good?" Menashe asked.

"No, but I had fun," he laughed. "We'd play every day on the ponds at school or at the park. Your uncles and I would even hide in the woods when it was time to go home for dinner."

Menashe thought about this, trying to imagine his dad as a child, or even a younger man, but he couldn't.

They arrived an hour early because, according to Lewis, it was as much fun to watch the Leafs practice as it was to see them play. Menashe found this wasn't exactly true, so as his father sat glued to the sprints and drills the teams performed, he looked around the arena and let his mind wander. Most of the seats were already full and it seemed everyone was decked out in blue and white. He noticed a few of the men were already yelling at the players and each other, letting foamy beer slosh over the brims of their cups as they waved their arms.

"What're you looking at?" Lewis asked his son.

Menashe pointed down a few rows. "Those guys. Looks like they're having fun."

"Yeah," Lewis began, frowning.

Menashe laughed at little when one of them stood up and started dancing. Lewis turned toward him.

"Now, I don't know those guys," he said, "but when you come to games like this, there will always be people who would rather drink a lot of beer rather than watch what's going on."

Menashe nodded.

"But that can be really dangerous." He paused. "Do you know what it means to get drunk?"

Menashe nodded again. "Yeah, I think so."

"Okay," Lewis said. "That's what they're doing. It makes them get out of control and it can hurt them, or make them hurt someone else. And really," he paused, "it just shows how little self-respect they have, you know?"

He could see this was important to his dad, but he didn't really understand why.

"I know."

Lewis didn't exactly look satisfied. Menashe wished he would go back to rambling off hockey statistics.

"I was just looking at them because they're loud," Menashe added.

His dad laughed at that, turning his attention back to the practice.

When the game began, Lewis rose from his chair excitedly, cheering for his team as they skated onto the freshly zambonied ice.

"Menashe, look! It's Billy Harris—see?"

Menashe stood, looking for his father's favorite player. "I don't see him."

"Right there," Lewis said, pointing to the tall center-forward. "Number fifteen."

Menashe dug through his hoard of hockey cards until he found Billy Harris. He carefully pulled it out and put it on the top of the stack.

At the end of the second period, the Leafs were beating the Rangers 1–0. Lewis leaned back in his chair.

"They're really good," Menashe observed.

"Oh yeah. The best," his father replied.

They sat in silence for a few minutes, watching the Zamboni clear the rink again. Menashe sighed inadvertently.

"You doing okay?" his dad asked.

"Yeah."

"Are things good at school?"

Menashe nodded but couldn't hide his weariness.

"What about your friends? How are they?"

"They're good."

Menashe didn't really have any friends. He rarely saw anyone outside of school and there wasn't anyone he could really talk to. Thinking about this saddened him and he sighed again. Lewis looked down.

"I'm really proud of you," he said.

Menashe turned his eyes away from his hockey cards, surprised by the remark.

"What?"

"I just want you to know I'm proud of you. I mean, you're turning into a really amazing person. I can't wait to see the things you'll do as you grow up." He shrugged. "And I just like hanging out with you."

He smiled and Menashe looked down at his cards.

"Thanks," he murmured.

Lewis put his arm around his son and they turned back to the game. It was tied now, 1–1.

The final period was intense, but Menashe could no longer focus on the game. He felt his fog of unhappiness starting to break apart. At that moment it didn't matter that he had no close friends, or that he lived with a mind full of anxious thoughts, or that he had been the first student disqualified during the school's spelling bee last Friday. He knew his father was right: nothing about his life was decided and, once he overcame the constraining force of childhood, there would be no limit to what he could accomplish.

Chapter 48
Causing to Forget
December 1988

Menashe punched and kicked and threw the pieces around the entire museum. He picked up a blown glass figure and smashed it into a large vase. He cried and whimpered as he struck glass with his bare hands. *I'm sorry! I'm sorry I let you down.* Blood flowed from deep gashes in his skin, but he couldn't feel a thing. When everything in the four rooms was destroyed, he went into his office with the old baseball bat and started smashing everything in his path. His forehead was shimmering with sweat and his eyes darted madly, searching the room for anything he could destroy. He beat his flimsy file cabinet until it fell apart and then moved on to his desk, shattering the small television set and coffee mug that sat on top. Menashe bashed his cheap wooden desk into kindling and destroyed his bedside lamp and telephone before staggering back to the museum. He wiped a thin line of drool from his lips with the back of his torn sleeve and entered the rooms already swinging the bat. He savagely pummeled and crushed the already broken glass, sending gleaming fragments shooting across the floor. He gagged on his ragged sobs and had to sit down in order to catch his breath. He looked around at the clear brilliance he had infected with his blood. He finally understood how much he hated himself.

I won't fuck this *up*, Menashe thought, sitting on the floor and moving the mounds of powdered glass around with his fingers. He felt his mind clearing and everything started to make sense. He understood he was in control: if he said stop, it would stop. And it needed to stop. Menashe needed to be stopped.

A spark came into his eyes and he picked up an intact shard of glass, not yet smashed to powder. He sat cross legged in the middle of the first room, laughing at himself for being so blind. *It's so obvious.* But it didn't matter now. All that mattered was the redemptive truth that he could still change everything.

He turned the single shard over and over in his hand. He wished he had been in Vietnam with Austin and John. He would have been the willing victim of a sniper or Claymore mine or guerrilla attack. Anything would be better than living every day with his worst nightmare.

Without hesitating, Menashe took the jagged slice of glass and slid it forcefully along the insides of his arms, feeling warmth rise up from the snow that now surrounded him. More flakes fell in slow motion, glimmering beautifully before they joined the smooth, white tundra all around. Gritty ice grazed his lips and he looked up to see a pure white sun glaring down. He blinked and turned away from the harsh light of the bare bulb. A dull, burning sensation had gripped his focus. Blood soaked his clothes and he looked away to avoid vomiting. He lay on his back and closed his eyes to return to that sudden dream, but when he opened them he was still on the floor. He shifted gently, feeling soft powder cushioning him. His eyesight was dim now and he knew his body was giving up, submitting to his decision. It was so different than he had imagined. No real pain or struggle. There was only the stillness of the empty glass museum. With a rush of relief, Menashe felt as though he'd finally done something right.

Chapter 49
This Is It
January 1989

Austin was already waiting on the bench when John pulled up to the entrance of St. Vincent Hospital. He was about twenty minutes early. Austin stood slowly, brushing off his pants. He'd told John not to bring him a suit—that he'd come up with something. He ultimately decided to wear his military uniform. He'd found it rolled up, long forgotten, in the side compartment of the suitcase John had first brought him at the hospital. The nurse had even pressed it for him. It had been jarring for Austin, putting it on again, knowing what that life had done to him, but he needed to do it. It was the only way he could really say goodbye to Menashe.

John put the car in park and came around to help Austin into the front seat, but Austin waved him off.

"I've got to do it myself," he grunted, moving gradually toward the car. He steadied his cane. "They told me I'm getting too stiff," he added as he gingerly lowered himself into the passenger seat.

John nodded as he closed the door for Austin, then made his way around to the driver's side.

"You comfortable?" John asked as he got in.

"Not really," Austin grumbled.

"Uniform looks nice," he said. "That's a really nice idea, wearing it today."

"Thanks." Austin sighed. "Your wife's not coming?"

"She'll meet us there, after her shift."

Austin looked directly at John for the first time. His suit looked good—classy, black wool with a gray shirt and striped tie—but the rest of him looked awful. His eyes were raw and watery, and his skin was pale. His hair was pulled back in a messy ponytail, and Austin could see there were mats and tangles running through it.

John's hands shook as he attempted the ignition. He tried again, but the keys fell at his feet. Austin looked at him thoughtfully.

"You want to take a sec?" he asked gently, knowing this day would be harder on John than most.

John nodded slowly. He retrieved the keys, then leaned back in his seat.

"Here," Austin said, pulling a flask out of his cargo pocket. "Have a drink."

"How did you get that in the hospital?" John laughed in surprise. "Or has it been in your pocket since the war?"

Austin took a swig. "Do you really want to know?"

John took the flask and shook his head.

They both stared off out the windshield, looking past the hospital offices and courtyards. The sky was dark gray and it looked like it might snow soon. John took another drink.

"Man," he breathed, "I just can't believe this. I can't believe this is it."

Austin nodded. "I know."

"I never thought things would go this way."

"Yeah."

"And it's weird," John began with a faint smile. "It's like, in the back of my mind, I know something big has happened, so all I can think about is calling Menashe or going by his place to tell him, you know?"

Austin frowned, lowering his head. He'd thought the same thing that morning. Over the past few months, if anything had shaken him up, a nightmare, or a terrible thought, anything, he'd gone to Menashe, or at least thought of him. Just the thought of him had been comforting. Now, the thought of him was empty and sad. *I guess the glass was too much for him, too.*

"Did he ever talk to you?" Austin asked after a moment, turning in his seat to face John. "You know, about shit in his own life? I know you guys were close."

"I wish he had," John sighed. "I mean, we would talk a bit, and I'd try to ask him personal questions sometimes, but it always seemed to make him uncomfortable." He leaned against the window tiredly. "I should have tried harder."

"No," Austin said. "You were a great person in his life." He sighed. *Not a drain on his health.*

"I don't know," John said. "Sometimes, I just don't know."

"I think with what happened," Austin murmured, "with all his work—it's guys like me who drove him there."

"What the hell are you talking about?"

"Oh, come on, John," he replied calmly. "You think I didn't test Ash's sanity every day? Trying to fix my fucked up mind . . ." He shook his head, looking out his window. "I'm sorry I put so much on him."

"You were doing what you were supposed to do," John said firmly. "That had nothing to do with it. I mean, Ash has always been a troubled guy."

Austin nodded, but something else gnawed at him.

"I still feel real bad about what happened with us, though," he said quietly. "I don't think I'll ever really forgive myself now."

"Forgive yourself?" John frowned. "For what?"

"You know, for attacking him."

"What?" John nearly shouted. "You attacked Ash?"

Austin's face reddened. "He never told you? I thought you guys were friends."

"Sure, we were friends," John exclaimed. "But he would never talk about his clients with me, Austin. You know that's all private."

Austin felt his leg starting to jitter. He shouldn't have mentioned it. He just never expected Menashe to keep his secrets like that. Not from John.

"So, what happened?" John asked in a softer tone.

Austin rubbed a hand over his head, smoothing his glistening, gray hair.

"I really don't know, man," he began, his voice wavering. "I started a session, like normal, then somewhere in the middle everything changed. I was back in the jungle, on a mission—like I had never left. I heard the noises—the birds and the gunshots and the screaming, I felt the leaves and the rain. Remember, that constant dripping on your helmet?"

John nodded.

"Then I saw one of their guys—a fighter, all in black—leaning over, setting a trap. For some reason I knew, if I just got this guy, I could start to make sense of the whole goddamn thing. So . . ." he trailed off, glancing up at John, ". . . I just went after him. I wanted to kill him. I was going to kill him."

"But you went after Ash?"

Austin nodded. "By the time I came back to myself, he was in terrible shape." He closed his eyes. "There was so much blood."

John sat silently for a moment. Austin hoped he wasn't thinking of him differently now. *No*, he thought quickly, *not John*.

"You mean he really never told you?" Austin asked again.

John shook his head. "He told me he fell down the stairs."

"Crazy," Austin breathed. His heart felt heavier somehow.

"Yeah."

John was quiet again and Austin didn't know what to say. He glanced at his watch.

"We should probably go," he said. "It's after ten."

John nodded and started the car. They rode in silence for about ten minutes, until John merged south onto the highway. Then he started laughing.

"What?" Austin asked, startled.

"I was just thinking," he began. "I don't know what made me think of it; maybe because I came down this way all the time from school when I worked in Parma. Anyway," he smiled, "when Menashe and I were both freshmen at John Carroll, there was this crazy lady who would come on campus sometimes. She said she was psychic and would read people's fortunes."

Austin nodded. He wasn't sure where this was going.

"Well, it started to be a thing around school, kind of like a dare. It was cool to go get your fortune read by 'Crazy Florence.'"

"Did you do it?"

"Not at first. I mean, I knew it was bullshit, and so did Ash, but then people really started talking. They said she was getting things right—like, incredible details from their lives no one would have known. It's funny; she had a lot of people fooled. I was starting to believe it, too.

"Anyway, a few weeks later, my lottery number came up. I was just a wreck; I mean, really sick about it. My dad had just shot down my deferment plan, so I was sure this was going to be the end of my life. Ash suggested we go see Crazy Florence. And I figured I had nothing to lose."

"Let me guess," Austin said with a smile. "She knew everything."

"She knew everything," John repeated emphatically. "She knew crazy stuff about my childhood and my family. And remember," he said, glancing at Austin, "I was eighteen years old. It was really impressive."

Austin laughed.

"So, she told me I would be fine in Vietnam, that I would come back and get a great job and have a family. And all I could do was sit there. I was just on top of the world."

"What about Ash?"

"He waited till I got back home to tell me he'd paid her off."

"You didn't figure it out before then?"

John shook his head. "I guess I never wanted to. I mean, thinking back on it now, the whole thing is ridiculous. But when you're looking at that draft card, that three-week average lifespan—you know what I mean, Austin—you just want something to believe in."

He turned back to the road. They were almost there.

"Yeah," Austin nodded, tucking the flask back into his pocket. "I'm glad you got it."

Epilogue
January 1989

Murray walked quickly down Fulton Road, glancing at his watch every few seconds. He hated to be late. It was 10:20 a.m. and Ripepi & Sons was still a few blocks away. *Maybe I shouldn't go*, he thought nervously, slowing his pace. But his desire to say goodbye to Menashe overcame the fleeting uncertainty he felt, causing him to speed up again.

"Are you Murray Henderson?" asked the kind-looking man who greeted him at the doorway to the funeral home. He had graying blond hair and handed him a folded program as he spoke.

"Yeah," Murray nodded.

He extended his hand and Murray shook it. "Chase Stephens. I'm the one who called you," he explained. "I hope you don't mind."

"No," Murray replied. "But, how did you know to call me?"

"Well——" Chase motioned for him to step aside with him so they could talk privately. "First of all, are you all right?" he asked with concern, staring at Murray's puffy black eye and scabbing lip.

"Oh, I'm fine," Murray said dismissively. "It looks worse than it is, really."

"Did you get in a fight or something?"

He thought about this. "Yeah, I did. Once is enough, though," he laughed. "I'm not too good at it."

Chase smiled and rubbed his beard thoughtfully.

"Anyway, son, I was Ash's landlord. I went to his apartment the other day to check on him, just because he'd been acting so strange lately, and that's when I found him. God, it was awful," he added, touching Murray's arm. "He was just—I'm sorry," he paused. "I won't tell you about that. It was just so . . . terribly sad. The thing is, after I called the police, I went into Ash's bedroom, just to look around and see if I could put together some idea as to why he'd do

261

something like this." Murray nodded for him to continue. "That's when I found the files."

"The files?"

"Yeah. Everything was destroyed, it looked like he'd taken a bat to the whole place, and I saw these files spread all over his room. I found yours first. And I swear I only looked long enough to find a phone number, but still, I know Ash had something going on down there nobody knew about."

Murray held his breath.

"And this is where things could get sticky, so I'd like your word that this'll stay just between us, okay?

"Okay."

"I took the files home before the police came. I know," Chase interrupted himself, "I know it sounds terrible, but after looking through them for only a second or two I could tell that, whatever this was, it was something none of those people wanted getting out."

Murray nodded.

"So when it was time to arrange the funeral, I just called everyone in the files. A few of them couldn't be reached, but I think we'll still have an okay turnout."

"You arranged the funeral?"

Chase nodded. "I mean, I talked to his mother about it, but she's been too upset to deal with any of the planning. And I really don't think he had anybody else."

"And what are you going to do with the files?"

Chase pulled a soft leather briefcase out from under the table where the funeral programs were stacked and opened it for Murray to see.

"You can pick it up on the way out."

Murray walked in the main room and glanced around. The first few rows of chairs were already filled, and most people were sitting quietly, looking down at their programs.

"Hey," a gruff voice called from behind him. "Murray, right?"

Murray turned around and saw the man he'd once met outside the museum, standing against the wall. He looked very different; clean-shaven, evidently sober, and wearing a soldier's uniform. He leaned on a thin, metal cane.

"That's right," Murray smiled, walking toward him. "I'm sorry, I never got your name."

"Austin."

"It's good to see you again."

Austin smiled, shaking his hand. "I look better now, don't I?"

Murray laughed. "You do."

"I've got to say, though," Austin continued, wincing as he shifted his weight, "you look a bit worse."

Murray shrugged. "I'm doing all right."

"Really?"

He nodded. "Yeah."

"Okay."

"How about you?" Murray asked, indicating his cane.

Austin shook his head. "Just been a bad few weeks, man."

"Was it a car wreck or something?"

"Something like that."

Murray nodded. He didn't want to press him.

"And listen," Austin said, motioning for Murray to come a little closer, "I'm sorry about what happened, with Ash. I know, especially as a young kid, things like this can be pretty shocking. And I'm sorry he can't be there for you anymore."

Murray looked down, his stomach starting to lurch. "Thanks."

Austin took a breath. "And really, if there's ever something bothering you, something you'd go to Ash with, you can always give me a call." Austin took out one of Menashe's old cards and wrote his number on the back. "Here," he said, handing it to Murray. "I mean, I'm no therapist, and there's a good possibility I'd make everything worse, but, I'll be there if you need me."

Murray took the card and tried to thank him for it, but was so touched by the gesture that he couldn't find the words. He just shook Austin's hand again, and made his way to the last row of chairs.

Murray tried to get a good look at the people who came in, even though he knew he wouldn't recognize anyone else. There was an older woman who emerged from the hallway leading to the ladies' room and sat in the front row. She looked like she'd been crying for days: her green eyes were practically hidden by swollen, puffed-up skin, and the funeral director had given her a handful of tissues to keep during the service. *She must be his mom*, he thought sadly. Murray turned back to the door. Two guys came in together and sat down with Chase, and after a few minutes an older man joined them. They all looked completely worn out, but the older guy was shaky and his eyes were bloodshot. Murray didn't think he'd last the whole time.

About ten minutes after the funeral was supposed to begin, Chase stepped up and introduced himself, explaining what would happen. Because Menashe didn't belong to any religious organization anyone knew of, the funeral director would lead the service and John Cook, Menashe's oldest friend, would give the eulogy. Murray looked around the room, trying to guess which one was John Cook. He brushed some lint off the sleeve of his suit coat and winced as his hand touched the deep bruise that covered his upper arm. His brother Jake had offered to come with him to the funeral, but he had declined the offer, explaining that it was something he needed to do alone. This wasn't exactly true. In reality, Murray was more concerned with the fact that he had no idea what kind of emotional reaction he would have to the service, and it comforted him to think no one in the place would ever see him again after it was over.

He counted the people who sat solemnly in their chairs. Eighteen. He was surprised, especially after Chase told him Menashe really didn't have anyone. *Are they all clients? Did he have any family?* Murray was struck with a pang of guilt at the realization that he had virtually no idea who Menashe really was, especially after Menashe had taken such a keen interest in the details of his own life.

Murray put his hand on his stomach, trying to calm his nerves, when suddenly a young man rushed in and sat in the empty seat next to him.

"Is this taken?" he whispered.

Murray shook his head.

"Thanks."

His hands shook as he took off his coat. He was very good-looking and wearing the sharpest suit Murray had ever seen. He opened the program, but dropped the insert, then ended up dropping the whole thing as he tried to pick it up.

"I'm sorry," he murmured, looking around self-consciously. "I didn't expect to be this late."

"It's okay. They haven't really even started yet." Murray smiled reassuringly. "I'm Murray."

"Roger." He looked down at his shaking legs. "I've just been so scattered these last couple days," he continued, running a hand through his hair. "I guess it's all still sinking in."

Murray nodded. "Did you know Mr. Everett a long time, then?"

"Five years." He took a breath and started to settle into his chair.

"Wow." Murray raised his eyebrows. "You must have been really close."

"Well, we didn't really talk much until recently."

"Oh, yeah?"

"Yeah, it was kind of weird." Roger paused. "Were you . . . well, were you a client?" he asked cautiously.

"Yes."

"Okay. Well, anyway, I was a jerk to him for a long time. I really thought the whole thing was bullshit, but he never gave up on me." Roger smiled faintly as he tucked his black hair behind his ears. "He knew there was something wrong before I did."

Murray nodded.

"And I don't know," Roger sighed. "It had been such a bright spot for me, coming in every week . . . I'm not really sure what I'll do now."

Murray's throat tightened. "Right."

"I've just never had anyone listen like that before."

The funeral director got up behind the podium before Murray could reply. He said Menashe would be greatly missed by everyone who knew him, even though they'd never met before.

Murray shifted uncomfortably in his chair. He didn't do well with funerals. And he could see why Jake had so zealously offered to accompany him that day. He could sense his whole family watching him carefully, waiting for him to lose it. After a few more minutes of vague, prescribed comments, the director asked John Cook to step forward and deliver his eulogy.

A man of about thirty-five stood up, whispered something to the woman sitting next to him and made his way to the front. When John turned to face everyone, Murray could see his eyes were bright red and he held a tissue clenched in his hand. He looked as though he hadn't slept in a long time. He drew from his pocket a folded-up piece of yellow paper torn from a legal pad and smoothed it out on the podium.

"Good morning," he began, flashing a miserable smile. "You don't know me. I don't know many of you either, but, as I'm sure you understand, we share something very special." He looked around. "We all had the pleasure of knowing Menashe Everett."

"He was unlike any man I've ever known. He gave everything he had to those around him, often neglecting his own wants and even needs. Yes, this is a description of a deeply confused and troubled man, wrestling with issues most of us were blind to. But it is also a description of a great man: a man of character, selflessness, and understanding. I just wish it didn't describe Menashe. I wish he had been more selfish. I wish he would have interrupted his passionate concern for others to think about his own health and happiness." John's eyes flashed and his voice shook. "I wish that, as Menashe helped the people in his life see their own strength and goodness and worth, he could have seen the same potential in himself. But what I wish most is that Menashe could have had a friend as caring and dedicated to him as he was to all of us. If that had been the case, I think his life would have gone in a much different direction."

John paused to collect himself and when he began again, the faint trace of bitterness that had crept into his voice was gone. He looked back at his paper, but ultimately turned it over and focused back on the room.

"Menashe would have hated this," he smiled. "What are we doing? We're sitting around focusing on him, and that's something he was never comfortable with. But he's not here. And I don't have to tell you all that this funeral is more for us than for him. Whether he likes it or not, we won't let him go without the chance to honor his life and his accomplishments.

"If he heard me now, Menashe would probably laugh and say he had no great accomplishments in his life. But all he'd have to do is look around at all of you to see that he was wrong. Menashe, in all aspects of his life, was extremely hard on himself. He had his share of faults and weaknesses for which he never allowed himself forgiveness. In spite of all that's happened, I truly believe his work was momentous, even if he could never see it. I'll never forget what he did for me," he added in a lower voice.

Murray could see John only through a watery haze of tears that coated his eyes. Even though he had only known Menashe for a fraction of the time John had, Murray knew he was right about everything. And he fervently wished he could have been that person in Menashe's life John spoke of—the person who could have changed his mind the morning he killed himself. The thought hit Murray more intensely than he expected. He began to cry. Roger put his hand on Murray's shoulder for a moment, and Murray could feel him shaking as well. When he looked up again, Murray saw John was watching him. Murray drummed his fingers together uneasily, but John was looking at him with such sympathy and tenderness that he stopped.

"Everyone," he continued, taking his eyes away from Murray and gazing around the room, "if there is one thing we can take away from this tragedy, it is the understanding that we have a great responsibility toward one another. Menashe Everett had no idea how much he meant to the people in his life, myself included. He saw himself as a failure and obviously felt no one truly cared about him. There's nothing we can do to take back his death, but I beg you to help me keep this from happening again. Menashe gave me hope at a time when I thought living was impossible, and I can see no better way to honor his memory than to provide the same compassion and comfort for others."

John looked like he wanted to say more, but seemed to have reached his limit. John moved quickly back to his seat and his wife rubbed his back as he sat down and then kissed him on the cheek. Murray could see she had been crying. He hadn't quite stopped crying himself and looked around the room for a box of tissues. He didn't see one so he made his way quietly out of the room to find a bathroom.

Murray trudged into the men's room at the end of the hall, feeling drained. He blew his nose into the abrasive toilet paper and washed his face in the sink. He looked up to see not only his tired, battered face staring at him in the mirror, but also the weary figure of John Cook standing behind him. He jumped at the sight.

"You scared me," he laughed nervously. Water was dripping from his face onto his shirt and coat. He dried himself off and turned around.

"I'm sorry," John replied. "I didn't think anyone was in here. I just needed to get out of that room." He sighed and looked back at the door. "I told my wife I was going home."

Murray wasn't sure what to say. "Are you going home?"

"Not yet." John leaned his back against the bathroom wall and looked blankly at himself in the mirror.

"I liked your speech."

"Thanks." John smiled, but didn't move his eyes. "I'm glad so many people came."

"Yeah." Murray looked down at his shoes, wondering if John wanted to be alone.

"What happened to your face?"

"Oh, I got in a fight."

"Are you okay?"

"Yeah, it looks a lot worse than it feels."

John nodded and Murray wondered how many more times he would have to lie.

"You want to have a drink with me?" John asked suddenly. "Get a cup of coffee or something?"

Murray was surprised but didn't hesitate in answering. "Sure."

John and Murray walked the short distance down Fulton Road to Faustino's Café. It was beginning to snow and Murray didn't have a hat or gloves, so he pushed his hands deep into his coat pockets and lowered his head to avoid the brutal wind. There was hardly anyone in the place, and they were seated immediately at a table in the back. The coffee shop was decorated in a vibrant southwest motif and, for some reason, Celtic music was playing softly from its embedded speaker system. John shook the melted snow off his gloves and coat, and laid them on the empty seat next to him. The waitress came over and John ordered black coffee. Murray kept his coat on for the time being and ordered hot chocolate.

"So you're in college?" John asked after the waitress left with their orders.

"Yeah, I'm a sophomore at Case Western."

"What're you studying?" John unwrapped his silverware and arranged it neatly at his place.

"Political science," Murray answered, watching him closely. "Pre-Law."

"That's great. You want to go to law school out here?"

"I'm not really sure. I'd like to go somewhere on the East Coast, but I think I'll just apply everywhere I can."

"That's really great," John repeated.

"Thanks. What do you do?"

"I'm a writer."

Murray was about to ask him more about this when the waitress brought their drinks over. She told them about the pies and cakes of the day and asked them if they wanted anything else, but they didn't. She walked away and John gazed into his green, ceramic cup of coffee.

"Murray, I want to tell you something," he said without making eye contact. "I was Menashe's friend for nearly eighteen years, but that wasn't the extent of our relationship. For the last few months I was seeing him as a client." Murray was silent. "Is that how you knew him?" John asked carefully.

He nodded. "Yes."

"Okay," John breathed. "Do you want to talk about it?"

Murray paused but ultimately nodded again. "Yeah."

"Me, too."

Both men were silent for a minute or so, taking occasional sips of their drinks. It was unclear to Murray who was supposed to go first, but then John spoke up.

"So, how did Menashe help you?"

He ran a hand through his hair and breathed in deeply. *It's okay, I should do this. I want to do this.*

"Well, he helped me do something I needed to do," he began vaguely. "It made me scared to think about, but he showed me I didn't have to be scared anymore."

"What was it?"

"I confronted my dad about . . . about things he did, when I was younger. He had some anger problems," Murray added, hoping John would put the pieces together and not make him say it.

John nodded. "How did it go?"

"Not very well," Murray laughed, his voice quivering. "I told him everything, and when I did, it was like I couldn't stop. It just kept coming." He paused. "Remember when I told you I got in a fight?"

"Yeah."

"That's not really what happened. I said some things maybe I shouldn't have and he came after me."

John leaned forward and frowned. The concern in his eyes reminded Murray of Menashe.

"He hit you?"

Murray nodded. "He wanted to kill me this time."

"Why?"

"Because I fought back. I hit him in the head with a wrench." He laughed again anxiously.

John smiled. "Good for you."

Murray shook his head, his eyes wide. "No, no. That's what really set him off. I ran up the stairs into the first room I came to, which was my parents', and tried to call Mr. Everett. Except he wasn't there. I know I should have called the police first, but it didn't feel right—I mean, my dad was an officer and I can't help seeing him and the police as sort of the same thing."

He was starting to feel frightened all over again, and his heart raced from the memory.

"When Mr. Everett didn't pick up, I had to call them. But I knew they wouldn't come fast enough."

"Jesus," John murmured, clearly getting caught up in Murray's story. "What did you do?"

"I got my dad's gun," he said. "I knew where he kept it. When I turned eighteen he actually showed me how to use it. He said every man should know how to fire a gun. So when he got upstairs, I was ready. He broke open the door and I had it pointed at him."

He was having trouble breathing, so he paused for a moment. John reached across the table and put a hand on his arm.

"It's okay," he assured him. "Take your time."

Murray looked up gratefully and took a few more seconds before he continued, but was close to breaking down.

"I shot him," he whispered. "I didn't want to, but he wouldn't stop."

John's eyes widened but he said nothing.

"I told him to stay back," he continued, looking around to make sure no one was watching. "I said if he ever beat me again, I would kill him. He didn't believe me. He just laughed and said I was making things worse for myself."

John shook his head.

"Then he said if I gave him the gun he'd forget about everything, but he was lying. I knew he'd kill me, so I said I wouldn't give it to him and that's when he ran at me. He wasn't moving too fast because I'd gotten him with the wrench, so I saw him coming. Then I fired the gun."

"I'm so sorry, Murray," John said after a pause. "I can't believe that happened to you."

"Yeah, sometimes I can't believe it either."

"Listen, I know a really good lawyer if you need someone."

"Oh, thanks, Mr. Cook, but all that's over now."

"Yeah?"

Murray nodded. "I didn't have any trouble. I mean, there was an investigation, but it didn't take long for them to decide against filing charges. I just looked so bad when the police came. I don't think anyone would have doubted it was self-defense." He managed a weak smile.

"Right," John muttered in a strained, hardened voice. He rubbed his forehead.

"I'm sorry about this," Murray said, wiping his eyes with his napkin. "I didn't mean to get so upset."

"No, you should be upset."

"And I know it sounds terrible," he continued, "but I feel better than I have in . . . well, longer than I can remember. I feel safe."

John nodded. "I can imagine."

They sat silently for a minute or so, drinking and staring off past one another until John looked pointedly at Murray.

"Did you close your eyes?" he asked.

"What?"

"When you pulled the trigger, did you close your eyes?"

Murray looked at him curiously. "Yeah."

John got up and brought Murray a few tissues from the box on the cashier's counter.

"Will you do me a favor?"

"What?"

"Don't be too hard on yourself about this. It wasn't anything you wanted to do and none of it's your fault. He did it to himself, okay?"

"Okay." Murray blew his nose. "Thanks."

"Sure."

Murray looked back up at John. "Do you want to tell me how Mr. Everett helped you?"

John looked down at his watch, smiling. "I do, but we should get our files from Chase first, before he leaves. It makes me nervous knowing they're floating around out there."

"Yeah," Murray agreed, getting up.

The two men paid their check and walked out together into the frozen city, where thick flakes of snow had begun to cover the street in a beautiful and glimmering blanket of white.

About the Author

Kate Kort

Kate Kort was born in St. Louis, Missouri, in 1985. She studied English and world literature at Truman State University. She currently lives in a suburb of Portland, Oregon, with her husband and two children. Some of her favorite authors include Salman Rushdie, G.K. Chesterton, Carl Hiaasen, Mikhail Bulgakov, Andrei Bely, and Arundhati Roy.

Glass is her first novel.

www.KateKort.com

CPSIA information can be obtained
at www.ICGtesting.com
Printed in the USA
FSOW01n2311191015
12369FS